INNERSPACE

J R BRYANT

PART I

BEFORE

ETHEL

The library is busy for a Friday. The steady flow is punctuated by the tension-induced banter of tired weekday staff who just want the weekend to come. Celeste bustles over to me – I always think of her movements in this way, probably because of the high heels and tight skirts that inhibit her movement. I'm shelving romances. She brushes lint from my shoulder. I try to hold back the instinct to recoil. My smile is a grimace.

"What are you up to this weekend?"

Usually I say something like "reading" or "cleaning the house" because that's a usual weekend thing, and Celeste responds with "aw" or "sad" or "lame" and looks pityingly at me. Her idea of fun is going into town, barely clad, and drinking until she falls over. This time I try a different approach, just to see how she reacts: "I'm getting wasted with my friends at the beach."

"Wow, Ethel." Celeste puts the back of her palm up to my forehead, a playful-mocking gesture. "You feeling okay? I've never heard you say such a thing!" She heads towards a customer at the counter, but pauses, looks back and squints, "I thought you didn't drink."

I don't. Hopefully she won't start inviting me out clubbing under the impression that I do. Drinking and I don't mix well. Alcohol makes me nauseous if I have any more than a drink or two. I continue returning the heavily thumbed romances to their shelves. These ones are getting old. They'll be out on the $1 rack soon and we'll replace them with newer pulp. Their yellowing pages and the smell of cardboard and vanilla give them away. These books with their formulaic plots and two-dimensional characters don't mean anything to me, but I hold them up and inhale anyway.

Real books have smells that eBooks can never replace. The process of the paper breaking down, slowly, releases a compound similar in structure to vanillin. So that is what I'm inhaling: the smell of books dying.

I push my empty trolley back towards the counter. A familiar foreboding figure awaits, her back straight as a ruler, grey hair pulled into a tight knot. Agatha Millen. I contemplate going into the back room where we catalogue books, just to escape her, but I see Celeste has gotten there before me. Agatha turns her head and I instinctively want to duck behind the biographies. It's too late. She's seen me.

"Excuse me." Her tone is overbearing, even when her words are polite. She beckons with her bony fingers.

"How may I help you?" I try to smile.

"Oh, it's you, the clumsy one. Well, don't dither about. I need to track down the first edition of my father's History of Paraguay. Of course, the family has several copies, but I know there's one in the library system and I want to ensure it is returned to us before you toss it out like those poor sods outside."

This is a fairly common Agatha request. She comes in every week asking for obscure volumes written by her family and acquaintances. Her unpleasantness forms a kind of parody of herself, reminding me of the judgemental elderly neighbours in my childhood who asked invasive questions about my broken shoes, my messy hair, my mother. I flinch but try not to show it. I can't find the book on the system, anyway. It must have been tossed already. "I'll look into it for you."

Agatha fixes me with one of her piercing stares, emitting a kind of psychic toxin from behind her spectacles. I feel my soul withering. Thank God it's almost the weekend.

MOANA

My words land, clumsy against the varnished studio floors. We sit side by side on matching rubber mats, waiting for class to start.

"What would you do if you found out... something... so bad that you couldn't talk about it?"

"Secrets are bad news, hun; they burn you up," Ari responds with a quick glance in my direction. Her sun-kissed arms stretch up above her head in preparation.

"But what if it's... too dark to talk about, and would hurt someone you love?"

"I don't know, Moana. It sounds like the plot of a bad movie. We should probably have learnt the Hollywood lesson by now, hey?"

"Come into child's pose everyone." Mira's voice rolls gently through the room. I've been coming here so long that I instantly obey even though I want to keep talking. That is what we come here for – to switch off our chaotic brain chatter and be told what to do. Today my mind keeps babbling *What if it's not even yours to tell?* I want to ask. *What if it belongs to the person who should never find out?* I want to talk to Ari because she is lovely and because she has nothing to do with my life outside of these walls, so it's safe. I want to talk about it now, so I don't bring it up later today when we finally go back to Atamarie Bay.

"Gentle breathing." Mira's voice drifts over as I sink deeper into a forward fold. I have been in this loop since the autumn. Isaac and I have talked about it over and over, "ad infinitum", in his words. The conclusion is always the same: telling is worse. But by not telling I am trapped in this cycle of thought.

"Engage your core and lunge back to downward dog." I tighten, pull back, pushing my bum high in the air, and walk my legs to loosen my calves. The secret is still buried and struggles, trying to claw its way out of a shallow grave.

"Don't be dramatic." Isaac says. He has never approved of emotion – or of me – but here we are, co-conspirators in the same boat, sitting far apart on the same park bench across the road from the hospital surrounded by autumn leaves.

I wish I brought my camera, if only to distract me from the psychic rollercoaster. "Keep it simple," he reasons, "We absolutely must not hurt her. Telling her would hurt her, therefore we absolutely must not tell her." It's a perfectly constructed logical argument. Of course. But logic isn't everything.

"Now float into your swans." Mira's voice brings me back to the studio, but as soon as I melt into my favourite pose, releasing the tension in my hips, my mind drifts back to the memory.

A leaf zig zags in the air before descending sideways into Isaac's nose. Even the word "hurt" is too simple; it's almost offensive. "It would destroy her," I correct, but I can already see his brow crinkle. Irritation. "She's been through so much already."

. . .

"TIME FOR DEEP RELAXATION. Lie out on your backs and find your eye pillows." Mira's voice transports me into the present, but a fragment of my mind is still with Isaac on that bench.

I WANT to make it clear to him that I know her better, that I know her best. I've known her longer. I know about the past. I want him to recognise it, but he won't. I don't know why I even care. I reach down and clasps a stem between my fingers. The star-shaped leaf is red but green and orange freckle its surface, its veins almost throb with the slow ebb of life's surrender, more beautiful and complex than anything human beings could ever create. My thoughts are too gushy for Isaac, so I hold them back.

"Yes," he acknowledges, finally. "We can't take that risk."

"WELCOME BACK EVERYONE." Mira smiles at each of us as we open our eyes. I look around for Ari but she is packing up already, rolling up her mat and pulling on her cardi.

"Time to get the kids," she blows me a kiss. "Take care, sweets."

It's probably better not to talk about it anyway. Secrets are volatile. They have a way of sneaking out. My Sagittarius moon wants to talk it out, but I know it's better to seal my lips and keep contained, for Ethel's sake.

Ari turns as she heads out the door, "Wait, when are you leaving?" she asks me.

"In three weeks."

"Let's have a proper catch up before then. Come over for tea or a smoothie or something."

I nod as I hug her. I know it will be a kale smoothie or nettle tea, but that's probably the kind of nourishment I need before leaving the country for the great known unknown continent of Australia, like so many Kiwis before me. It's getting so close now. I shudder. *Am I really moving to Melbourne?* I need a bigger city to try to make a living as a photographer although I know I'll probably just find retail or hospo work and earn way more per hour than I could here, like half the other people I grew up with. How did my life become a cliché? I cringe at the cliché of asking that. I roll up my yoga mat and head towards the changing rooms. Isaac will be here to pick me up soon, full of his usual pompousness, and I will see Ethel and Henry: my favourite people in the world. God, I will miss them when I go.

ISAAC

This part is decidedly awkward. The emporium sells all kinds of things, costumes, hardware, so it's not a big surprise they'd stock something remotely illicit. It's only illegal by context, I remind myself. Caterers and restaurants use them all the time. The balding man behind the counter is busy fidgeting with chains. I'm in no hurry to be judged. Several years ago, before they changed the law, there was no issue. Every corner dairy sold NOS canisters. He turns towards me.

"Hello there."

"Yes, excuse me." I clear my throat, "I was wondering if you had any refills for my cream whipping machine." It sounds innocent enough, but he lowers his eyebrows.

"How many do you want?"

"A couple of boxes should last me a while."

He retreats to the back room and after a moment, returns with two innocent-looking white boxes.

"That will be 42 dollars." Jesus, the price has gone up. I remember when they were ten dollars a box. I hand over the cash. Cash is always better for questionable transactions, even those which are technically legal. For all he knows I may have the cream whipping machine at home – I may indeed require large quantities of cream for a pancake party. This is all starting to sound absurd.

He places the boxes in a paper bag and I receive them, grateful that the excruciating part is almost over. On my way out I can't stifle my internal rant: *ludicrous Government! Why did they have to make taking a harmless substance illegal?* Or in Henry's words, *they are just trying to ban fun!*

TEN MINUTES later I'm outside the yoga studio to collect Moana. I sound the horn. When Moana says she'll be ready in ten minutes, it means at least half an hour. I told her to be here at 1pm, in the hope that she's ready when I arrive at 1:30. Henry is much the same. I have given him 1:30 as an estimated time of arrival. I loosely follow Seneca's philosophy – that we should adjust expectations in accordance with reality or do without them. My hypothesis has turned out to be accurate. Moana's already out the door loaded with a number of suspicious bundles: bags, blankets, and a yoga mat. I bite my tongue in anticipation of her words.

"Hi."

I nod to her.

"Did you get the supplies?" she asks, mildly anxious.

"Yes, and I'm still raging that they made it illegal. NOS is probably the least harmful recreational drug in existence – they give it to birthing mothers for Christ's sake!"

"Yeah, they were annoyed that people kept leaving empty canisters in car parks."

"That's right, and there was that bullshit about mouth burns from the cold gas." I add, "but that doesn't stop them selling disgusting McDonalds coffee which is also known to cause mouth burns."

"Caffeine is probably more dangerous as a drug."

"No – caffeine is certainly more dangerous!"

"Why do you have to disagree with me even when you're agreeing with me?" Moana is only slightly frustrated.

"It's a way of life."

"I read that if they'd discovered caffeine now instead of a long time ago it would be prescription only."

"That sounds probable."

"Alcohol too."

"Obviously – evidence shows it's the most dangerous drug."

We turn the corner onto Henry's street. Tall oak trees line the footpaths. Moana and I simultaneously realise time is running out in which to privately converse.

"Isaac, I have been thinking about Ethel." She has this irritating habit of stating the obvious.

"Of course you have. Look, can we not talk about it? I mean, can we just agree that we won't say anything?"

"I don't know." She is picking at her chipped fingernail polish. "I can't stop thinking about it."

"That's your problem. Don't make it hers." I pull up outside Henry's flat and toot the horn. Someone pulls back the curtains, clearly it's Henry with his recognisable messy red hair. At least he's up. Now all we have to do is pick Ethel up from the library and we can head out.

HENRY

I have a million things to do before we leave. Isaac is tooting his horn again. "Yeah, yeah," I call out, despite the fact that he won't hear me from outside. "Settle down." Now what was it I needed to do? Feed the goldfish, water the plants, pack the snacks, shorts, a warm thing, a very warm thing, towel, sunglasses...

"Can you not, for once in your life, be ready on time?" Isaac has barged in to berate me in order to hurry me up. It will only slow me down. It bothers me that he is a whole head taller than I am.

"Calm your britches," I instruct. "I'm almost ready."

"You expect me to believe that." Isaac gestures around at the chaos that is my flat - clothes strewn everywhere, most of them clean. I gather a pile of freshly dried washing from the couch and dump it on my bed.

"No," I respond through gritted teeth, "I don't expect anything from you. I have learnt over the many years of our friendship to lower my expectations to zero in order to avoid disappointment and frustration. You would do well to do the same!"

"Touché!" Isaac has dropped the pretence of being in a hurry.

"There's really no reason to be in a hurry anyway. It's not like the beach is going anywhere."

"It's my job to round up all you stragglers. If it were up to you we'd never get there. Anyway, Moana is waiting in the car – even *she* was ready on time – and Ethel's expecting us at the library in five minutes." Isaac helps himself to a beer from the fridge. It's a random lager, left over from some party. I don't tell him this – he has always been iffy about left-overs. "What more do you have to do, anyway?" he asks as I scurry around the flat, remembering and forgetting things simultaneously.

"Oh you know…" I mutter breathlessly "Water the goldfish and feed the plants."

"Hah!"

"Do you think I'll need anything with sequins?"

"What kind of weekend are you expecting?"

"Well, you never know." I throw a sequinned waistcoat into my old uni backpack with the broken zip.

Moana sounds the horn from the car and Isaac looks around in irritation. "That girl," he grumbles.

I'm just about to head out the door when I remember: "Torch! Sunhat! Sunscreen!"

I'm expecting Isaac to complain about me again, instead he follows me into my bedroom with an unusual expression on his face.

"What's up? You've seen a ghost or something?"

"No – well – not exactly. Has… has she…" He gestures towards the car and Moana. "Has she said anything strange to you lately?"

"What are you on, man? It's Moana you're talking about here. She's always saying strange things." The kinds of strange things that I like and that Isaac abhors, but he doesn't need to be reminded of this.

"Oh, never mind." He is being dismissive now. Isaac who is perennially dismissive of Moana. Isaac who detests the otherworldly, the unstable, but never quite seems stable himself. Why should I be surprised? But something seems wrong. What has Moana said?

"What's going on?" My heart is racing. Moana. Everything Moana. "Is there something wrong with Moana? Is she sick?"

"No. Nothing like that. It's not to do with her. She's fine. Look, it's best we don't talk about it." Isaac is being so unlike his usual cocky self. It makes me wonder... maybe something significant has shifted. A glimmer of hope shines.

"She's changed her mind about me." I speak my thoughts, before I have the chance to hold them back.

"God! You're so full of yourself!"

"It's okay, you can tell me" I try to be nonchalant, but Isaac is silent.

I give up all semblance of togetherness, "Please tell me."

I'm down on one knee, my hands clasped as if in prayer. Isaac is used to my flamboyance by now, which irritated him so much in our high school years. Obviously, it would be just my luck that Moana would change her mind the minute she decides to leave the country and move to Melbourne. Either way I *have* to know.

"I beg of you," I raise my hands. The front door opens.

"What are you – oh – sorry to spoil the moment." Moana obviously has to come in at exactly the worst moment.

"It's alright." Isaac seems delighted. "Henry was just proposing – again – and obviously, I'll have to tell him no."

"Hah!" I try to laugh it off, but my cheeks are bright red. "I was just pleading with Isaac to be able to take my sequinned waistcoat. He's worried I will upstage him."

"Well, I hate to get in the way of whatever this is, but Ethel will be waiting. Let's get a move on!"

Just like every other glimmer of hope with Moana, I feel it slipping away. I've ruined it. Fuck.

PART II

ARRIVAL

ETHEL

A tamarie Bay, that first time, is still so clear for in my memory. The whole journey out was inflamed with anxiety. Looking back makes me realise what a nervous wreck I used to be.

BREATHE. I close my eyes for just a moment, wary of the road in front, hands steady on the wheel. Picture the dandelion clock. The white tufts drifting in the air. Just breathe. Accept. Allow. Breathe in. Release. The anxiety fades a little. It's the technique the mental health nurse taught me. Everything's fine. Breathe in: Accept. Breathe out: Allow. My battered VW Bug and I rolling and bumping slowly over the hills, getting further away from town and closer and closer to the beach. I hate driving on the open road alone. An arrogant red Ford is tail-gating me. Asshole. I pull over to the side and let him pass. Stupid Henry and his stupid organising. Why did he have to arrange this for a work day? Why am I doing this alone while my two best friends are already at the bach having fun with some guy I don't even know, drinking beer in the sun, no doubt, while I'm stuck in a hot stuffy car freaking the fuck out. Never mind that I have to arrive alone and awkward, never mind that we are supposed to be doing something I've never wanted to do before in my life.

"It will be good for you," Henry kept assuring me. "You need to unwind, get over your anxiety disorder, let go."

Right now I need a quiet, empty room. I wish I'd never left work. The studious peace of the library always calms me. This is the last place in the world I want to be – on the open road, by myself, on my way to meet someone I don't even know.

Six years later and I'm on the same dusty gravel road sitting next to that stranger. This time I'm in the passenger seat of Isaac's '90s hatch. He's driving, taking the sharp corners in his stride. I'm safe and, more than that, I'm on my way to another adventure.

Henry and Moana are in the back seat. They look so placid that for a moment it's as if none of the conflicts of the past few years ever occurred. I'm probably the only one who knows about them anyway, the only one not involved, the only one everyone talks to about all their problems, even if no one ever understands mine. In any sense, I'm glad we're all together again.

"It's been too long." Isaac's voice is gentle and soothing to my ears.

"Since we were all together?" I always want to make sure I understand exactly what's being discussed. "Maybe a year or two? Moana's 25th maybe?" I remember that night so vividly – Chelsea flying into one of her crazy moods and kicking things over. I'm relieved Moana broke it off with her. Unstable people unnerve me. I'm relieved it's just the four of us. Just the people I love and trust most in the world.

"It's been an eternity since we last came to Atamarie Bay." Moana cuts into my thoughts.

"Mmm hmm," Henry agrees. "It's always nice to come home."

"Home." I repeat. It's a warm, welcoming feeling. It's not the correct word, but it fits somehow. I close my eyes in the gentle breeze rushing in from the open inch of my window. The warmth, the musty smell of the car, and the cool damp air rushing in transport me to my happiest memories: picking mushrooms with my grandfather in the valley behind the house, flipping them over to check the gills and make sure they were the right kinds, cooking them in butter to be served on crunchy toast, sitting on his knee by the fire. It's not often I indulge in memories, always wary of some sharp painful object intruding – always watching out for Gretta.

"Are we there yet?" Moana asks in a parody of a small child, and for a moment Isaac and I are the parents taking our kids on a beach holiday, despite the fact that I'm the youngest here by a few months.

"Hush your mouth." Henry scolds. "Good things take time."

"Tiiiime..." Moana sings in her rich, deep voice "...is on our side."

We roll up over the last big hill and the horizon spreads its beautiful blue majesty. My eyes open wide to drink it in. Yes.

"Home." I say under my breath.

"Let me come *home*. Home is wherever I'm with you," Moana croons.

I let myself rest into her voice – that warmth which will always feel a bit like home to me. Moana is the closest friend I've ever known. She's been there for me since I was six and everything else in my life imploded. It's hard to believe she's moving away. I can't imagine my life without her.

Moana turns around, as if in answer to my thoughts "Hey, you'll always be family, Eth." She has a knack for reading my mind. Isaac would dismiss this as nonsense, but he's the first to admit he lacks empathy. He just won't admit it has much value.

THE ROLLING FARMLAND hills give way to wide open spaces, and glimpses of the deep blue expanse that is the ocean amid patches of dense dark green forest. Isaac pulls down a narrow gravel driveway which seems unfamiliar now, it's been so long.

We have arrived. The car doors are thrust open and our cramped legs welcome the space of the outdoors. I've kicked my jandals off in the car so I could sit cross legged and I don't bother putting them back on, letting the springy beach grass caress my soles as we clamber up to the bach.

Six years ago I made my way up these wooden steps alone. They look just the same, perhaps they've faded a bit or perhaps my memories are brighter. Moana probably has the before and after shots as evidence. She has her camera out already.

"I see zou're not vithout zour appendage" I call to her in a terrible parody of an Eastern European accent, maybe Russian.

"Von, ah ah ah" She clicks away as she imitates the *Sesame Street* Count as she clicks. "Two ah ah ah ah ah"

These are the pop culture fairy tales that bind us together. Our modern mythology, Henry would call it. He is already at the door, his aunt's spare keys in hand, fiddling for the right one.

"Aha!" He cries "Victory!"

The first time I came here the door was ajar and I could hear voices.

THE MID-AFTERNOON LIGHT IS DIFFERENT, *brighter, the dust particles float exposed through the air. In that moment I feel so alone, so afraid.*

I SUPPOSE I was afraid a lot of the time back then. I would hold myself in tightly, scared to take up space, scared to interfere in other people's worlds.

. . .

I CAN HEAR *their voices as I walk down the hall: Henry laughing and Moana scolding him for something. I can't hear the third voice, but Isaac is the first person I see, his profile set against the ocean view. This stranger is the reason I'm panicking, the reason I'm half tempted to jump back into my car and escape. I'm not good with strangers. It sounds silly, I know. I interact with strangers every day, at uni and in the library, but they quietly follow the rules and keep their distance. The conversations are always the same. This is different. It's irrational, yes, as anxiety tends to be. He's a friend of a friend not some axe-wielding psychopath, as far as any of us can tell. I have no reason to fear him.*

Henry sees me first and there is no escape.

"You made it! Finally!" He always speaks in exclamation marks. I see Isaac's head turn towards me as Henry rushes over for a hug. Hugging is so awkward for me. Being so close to another person makes me cringe, but Henry's plan is to desensitise me at any and every opportunity. Moana comes next, knowing the appropriate distance to take, brushing her lips against my cheek, one hand rested on my shoulder as she passes me a cold beer with the other.

"This will sort you out."

Can she tell I was flustered? Probably, she has a knack for things like that. I'm avoiding Isaac's gaze when he walks right up to me, not too close, and holds out his hand. I switch my beer across to the other side and reach out my cold, damp palm to touch his dry one.

"Isaac," he says. His voice is confident but not overbearing. A little shiver runs through me and I nod.

"I know." I say.

"Of course you do." He seems a bit embarrassed. Situations like this, where I say the wrong thing, normally make me feel even more uncomfortable, but the change in his demeanour is amusing. I can't help but smile.

THAT DAY SITS SO VIVIDLY surreal in my memory. I suppose it was when everything started to change; then again, things are always changing. Now the shadows of early evening have been firmly cast. My dearest friends have fired up the barbeque and the smell of burning animal carcasses floats into the house. I cook my soy sausages separately in a frying pan so as not to taint them with unnecessary death. If the day Isaac and I first met was the start of a great adventure, I wonder what this reunion with Atamarie Bay will mean for us.

MOANA

The fresh air and the smell of the forest hit me as soon as I'm out of that hot, musty car. There are two things I think of: camera and swim. I don't remember what photos I took last time we were here. They are stored on a hard drive somewhere, buried in the archives of the zillions of images I have captured over the years. Still, I feel a subtle déjà vu as I shoot the sky, the horizon line, my friends as they stretch and talk and try in vain to be organised. I change to macro so I can focus on the coarse grass beneath my feet, the wrinkles in my toes, the cracked concrete slabs of path. I'm close to the house. But my mind is already in the sand, in the sea. After spending hours in a confined space with three other people I just need room to breathe.

The others won't miss me. I slip off without a word – down the track, through the bush. I need this. I need to be alone. I need to let go, to clear my mind before engaging in this kind of sacred journey. I need to let go of guilt, over family, over Henry, over Chelsea. I need to let go of the need to be everything to everyone. I hear tui overhead. A cheeky fantail darts from tree to tree, teasing me. My eyes soak up all the different shades of green. My bare feet carve up the cool damp dirt around tree roots and kick up rotting leaves releasing that earthy smell, the fresh decay of the forest floor. There's something divine in this simple pleasure. I'm lucky to be alive, to be here. There were plenty of times in the past when I wasn't so grateful. Sometimes the past seems so dark, so distant. I shudder and focus on my footsteps.

In a few moments I'm clear of the trees and the sky opens up. My feet find the sand, my face finds the breeze and I inhale the fresh salty air. Black sand spreads out all around me. Glorious, but hot on the soles of my feet.

I'm just in time to catch the afternoon sun. The best part is I'm completely alone. There are no houses in sight, no strangers or friends. Even still I hesitate before I strip off, not used to being exposed in such a wide open space. I leave my clothes on a rock: pants first, then top and bra. There is a thrill in being naked outside, even when no one is looking. The water is cooler than my body temperature and I hold myself, around the chest, as I wade out. There is a moment of clinging to security, of holding back, then the dive.

Water always feels like a lover's embrace. I swim out, breast-stroke, then fall back and float. The bay is calm enough right now that there is no risk of waves interrupting me. My breasts rise above the water, my belly, my feet. My ears are submerged in the music of the ocean. Sometimes it's just as hard being the one in love as it is being the one who isn't. My mind floats back to Chelsea and me on a hilltop at Arawhata.

PSY-TRANCE BEATS and lights cushion the distance. We have never felt so close, so connected, so real. In this simple moment after dancing ourselves into a frenzy and escaping Chelsea's ex-girlfriend, running across the beach to the island surrounded by sand; ecstatic wet release and dissolving into each other. Everything is perfect, still, but this is the moment I realise: it's all downhill from here.

· · ·

HENRY HAD to watch it all fall apart with Chelsea, piece by piece. We both knew it was coming, but I had to hold on to the hope. He was always there for me, but he was always hoping that after I let go of Chels he would be the next in line. I sometimes wish that I could return his feelings; I've told him as much.

"That's easy," Henry replies. "Just put them in the bag they came in with the receipt and take them back to the feeling store to exchange for something more suitable." His tone is cutting and dark. "What do you think would suit me better?" I shrug my shoulders, masking the inevitable pain of hurting someone you love. "Come on, Moana. Maybe a full-blown crush on the next leggy blonde I walk past in the street. That would be convenient for you. Maybe I should settle for something more subdued, a subtle appreciation of the head librarian at Ethel's work." He is being more light-hearted now, comical. "Oh, I know, I'll buy the feelings that will put me head over heels in love with the muscliest guy at the gym so I will have to get fit while checking him out." I laugh but Henry's eyes are dark. I wish I could hold him, rock him, mother him, but being close suggests a promise that I won't be able to keep. I'm not the one who can help him. He's the only one who can do that.

I look out towards the far side of the bay. Somewhere there, hidden behind big boulders, is the cave we found last time we were here. Henry told me that back before colonisation, the local tangata whenua hid here when an enemy tribe invaded. The sounds of the sea god Tangaroa kept them safe. I relax into the sound now.

Maybe it's also the sea god Tangaroa, or Neptune as the Romans called him, conjunct my moon in Sagittarius when I was born, attracting endless dramas and delusions into my life – endless impossible love stories, endless exhausting adventures. I am so easily overwhelmed. Emotion seems to pool in me over time and I need to pour it all out again. The ocean is always the best place to do it. I dolphin dive and kick out behind, propelling myself as far as possible with each breath. I reach the other side of the lagoon and breast-stroke back in the direction of my clothing. I float on my back for a while in the warmer, shallow water, waves lapping gently. I close my eyes and drift, weightless, timeless, alone, tranquil.

I emerge with a clear head and make my way back up the hill with damp clingy clothes and sandy feet. Just in time for dinner.

ISAAC

No one thanks me for driving us all out here. I suppose they have just come to expect me to do the driving. It's my contribution to friendship: driving and logic. Moana has already buggered off, probably to go worship nature or something. Henry is on one of his ranting rampages as we make our way into the house. No one should ever let that man get excited.

"Tonight, I'm Peter Popper!" he exclaims.

Ethel is as self-contained and quiet as usual. She opens the doors between the living area and the deck with an air of purpose, as if this has all been scripted. I observe her defined features, her tiny delicate hands. She's as much of an enigma now as that day we first met, in this very room.

I load my beers into the fridge.

"Craft IPA this time."

"Legend." Henry pats my back.

"Point of interest: I don't think I'd even heard of craft beer six years ago. I probably bought some kind of lager here."

"Yeah, that was all we had back in those dark days – mass produced and bland, not batch-brewed with carefully selected hops in a street-art covered downtown warehouse by a group of mates with beards."

"Things change quickly. Everyone I know now drinks craft beer as a kind of identity prop."

"It's all part of celebrating our creative gentrification." Henry raises his fist triumphantly.

"The whole notion of identity seems marginally flaky." Sometimes I don't know who I am. Experientially, life is comprised of a collection of memories: the great times I've had with friends, the appallingly dull periods of isolation, the first day of school, the worst rugby game, falling off my bike, graduation day, meeting Ethel. The peak experiences collect into my identity: I am Isaac, I am 6 foot 1, natural blonde, blue eyes, white collar analytical prick, interested in chemistry, rational thinking, and contradictions. I imagine this is what other people think of me as well – more or less. Henry will tell you the participants in psilocybin research rate their trip experiences in the top five most meaningful of their lives, but how can we really judge meaning?

"Perhaps we are just asking the wrong question, old chap." Henry puts on his terrible British gentleman's accent.

"There is very little in life we can be certain of. Descartes pointed out the only obvious truth. *Cogito, ergo sum.* Everything else in life may well be an illusion but the very experience of thinking *this* proves that there is *something* doing the thinking. I must exist in some form, and my experience of the world – the consistent nature of my reality – has shown me that following certain rules and behaving as if other things and people indeed do exist is in my best interests."

"We all exist in *your* best interests," Moana has popped her head around the door to misquote me.

"Naturally."

I didn't even raise an eyebrow when Moana mentioned her solar plexus chakra the first time we met. I flinched internally but said nothing. I was on my best behaviour. It's not that I don't like her, I just can't tolerate all the hippy bullshit she spouts. It's like playing along with the wild imaginings of a child and not being able to correct them.

"You don't know that chakras *don't* exist for sure." Ethel occasionally reminds me. "Just because you can't prove they exist it doesn't mean they don't."

"She's not even Indian. It's the new-age twaddle that I don't understand."

"It's her way of interpreting the world, Isaac. Don't be so intolerant."

This isn't an actual conversation, rather a summary of almost every conversation we've had about Ethel's best friend. Perhaps I am an intolerant bastard, but I can't help it. My father poisoned me against religions and other fanciful notions as a young child and my automatic reflex is to cringe every time I see a Hare Krishna monk.

HENRY

We're ready to take flight on our next big adventure, supplies packed, minds clear... we've even got appropriate footwear. Set. The world is our freshly cracked Bluff oyster. The air is charged with sherbet-zing anticipation. We're in formation. Ecstatic motion. Screaming down the hill towards the beach. I'm reaching my arms out to brush against my friends' shoulders as I pass them. Laughter echoes through the lush native jungle in the paradise we call home. I'm not thinking about Moana leaving, or even about how I could convince her I'm worth sticking around for, or how she might feel if I leave the country for her. I'm thinking about everything else.

"I'm going to Never-Never Land with my chosen family, man."

"Hah!" Isaac recognises the movie reference immediately.

"We must have watched Human Traffic a hundred times back in the day," I say, reaching up to put my hand on Isaac's shoulder as we walk down the hill, *why did nature give him such height and not bless me with the same manly stature?* Sticks and stones crunch underfoot.

"The man does not exaggerate." After more than a decade of

friendship I'm used to Isaac and the aristocratic way he articulates his every thought.

"Man, those were the days, stoned as fuck in Delia's garage. It never got old."

"Undeniably, and neither did Chuck Palahniuk's schizophrenic fantasy made real by clever cinematography, Edward Norton, and Brad Pitt."

"Dude, you could just say 'Fight Club'," I say. He punches me in the arm. Not softly either. It's the kind of private school behaviour that originally put me off Isaac. He looks like the type too, tall with Romanesque facial features and blonde hair. It took me ages to realise he was just as much of a freak as I am.

"There was something particularly exceptional about those films." This is Isaac being nostalgic. I look towards Moana, but she is engrossed in her inner world, her arm linked with Ethel's, but her heart and soul soaring through the forest with the birdsong. I don't want to interrupt, so I return to the conversation with Isaac.

"They were so real to me," I add, reaching up towards the forest canopy for dramatic effect "to our generation – not like all the other corporate Hollywood bollocks We might work shit jobs, but we have good times." I want to expand to the same level as Moana's majesty. I want her to recognise me, but I don't glance back in case she isn't looking. I keep my arms raised high "We might be wasting our lives, but at least we're making peace with nihilism and trying to figure things out. We're not the puppets of society like the generations before us; we have way too much choice about our lives, and yet no idea how to achieve our dreams."

"Damn right," Moana's voice affirms my speech, egging me on. I still don't glance back, I keep going "Sometimes all the meaning in the world is in the moment, sometimes you just want to destroy something beautiful and create total chaos. That's something my parents will never understand."

This is part of the mythology of our generation: while the authorities are telling us drugs are bad, evil and dangerous, that they mess you up and destroy your life – most of us can see through all the crap. They lied to us. Not all drugs are addictive, or damage your brain. Hell, in my experience, they've done a lot of good.

"This is gonna be wicked!" I crow to no one in particular.

My nerves are zinging as we bust out from under the forest canopy. The sunset is now no more than a dusky wine stain against the horizon. We scramble over boulders then stand facing the incoming surf.

"Dregs of the day." Isaac sips mead from the bottle that Moana miraculously produced from her bag just moments before.

"Aye aye, sir."

Isaac looks at me with that glee for adventure I recognise so well, "ready to be part of another positive drug story?"

PART III

DROPPING

ISAAC

It's not an exact science, but then again, it's hard to get the dosage right with any illegal substances, let alone know for certain what it is you're taking. Ethel's hand is grasped firmly in mine as we make our way along the sand, between the rocks towards the North end of the bay, near the open ocean.

"How many do you think we should take?" Moana asks.

"Recreational doses of psilocybin mushrooms are usually between 1-5 grams, dry," I tell her.

"You're so dry. You sound like a manual," says Moana.

"It all depends on the species, of course," Henry adds.

"And individual strength of the specimens," the variation bothers me.

"These are boring facts," Moana complains, despite the fact that she was asking in the first place. Her hair is blowing everywhere in the wind. Out of control.

As soon as we get to our destination it's time to get down to business. Ethel spreads the picnic blanket and we each claim a corner. Moana is arranging her supplies, pulling them out of the bottomless pit she calls a handbag and placing them around her in no apparent order. Henry passes me the little glass coffee jar. It looks innocent enough. I remove the lid and cotton wool, added for moisture protection, then reach in for the gold.

"The problem is there's no way of accurately measuring dosage."

"Yeah, I guess," Henry says. "You just have to count."

"Hah. You take a pill from the doctor and you know what the precise chemical compound quantity is – or someone does."

Moana looks up towards us, "*I* wouldn't." The flash in her eyes. Defiance, despite all reason, and a kind of power I recognise – but from where?

"I wouldn't expect *you* to go to the doctor in the first place."

"You've got me there. I can't remember when I last went to a medical doctor." She adds, as if it's some kind of accomplishment to neglect her health.

"But at least you'd know you were taking x amount of paracetamol or antibiotics rather than mere guess-work."

Henry chimes in. "Are you going to get on with it or would you rather wait for drug laws to relax and a pill form to become available?"

"Steady on. Hold out your hands." One by one, I drop the shrivelled brown lumps into outstretched palms.

"Five?" Henry looks disappointed.

"To start with. See how you feel in half an hour and we can top up."

"Exactly what we did last time we were here," Moana recalls.

"The first time I was scared to death." Ethel is looking into her own palm. "After Grandpa..." I wince. We are all well aware Ethel's grandfather died eating the wrong kind of fungus, we know she refused to eat any kind of mushroom for years.

What she doesn't know isn't worth thinking about.

It's not.

I glance towards Moana and she looks back sternly. *Don't say anything.* I know. I won't. I look back at Ethel and she smiles at me.

She pulls at a strand of loose cotton from the hem of my jeans. I've never loved someone so much, and therefore I've never needed to conceal the truth like this. My thoughts circulate as Henry continues the conversation.

"Yeah, I can't believe you ever even tripped with us, Eth. You used to be so highly strung. I was counting on you to chicken out any moment and go and read in bed so I could get my five bucks back from Moana."

Ethel smiles. "Oh ye of little faith."

"Yeah, Ethel, you used to be such a prude," Moana adds warmly. "What happened?"

"I got over it." Ethel replies and immediately tosses the contents of her palm into her mouth. We follow suit and for a moment we are all chewing the dried mushrooms vigorously.

Moana holds out a golden foil-wrapped bar, "Chocolate?"

"Yes please."

"It does make them a lot more palatable," I concede. I always feel subtly defeated when Moana is right. I feel the urge to re-direct the conversation. "The interesting thing about mushrooms, of course, is the legality."

"Yeah, Isaac, *that's* the interesting thing about mushrooms," Henry's chides.

"Well, aside from the obvious, you imbecile."

"Who are you calling a bicycle?" Deadpan. He loves irony more than breathing and has mastered the variety that hits you in the face twice. The firstly because of its baffling idiocy, and then secondly because that kind of idiocy is an art form in itself.

"They're illegal, though," Ethel nods to the glass jar.

"They are – but only after you pick them."

"And it's not illegal to consume them," Henry adds.

"No. So you have this very strange window of legal consumption."

"You mean you can eat them straight out of the ground."

"Exactly." I imagine the four of us in a field laden with *Psilocybe* mycelium bobbing down to legally extricate the gold tops with our mouths. "Ridiculous!"

"Because it's only possession that you can be done for." Moana states the obvious.

"Possession is nine tenths of the law."

"Yes, of course, what we are doing is completely illegal - at least for whomever is holding the jar."

"Drug laws are bullshit, man," Here we go. I can tell Henry is about to launch into a rant. "It's ridiculous to tell people what they can and can't put into their own bodies."

"On the contrary," I respond in my debating voice, "you, sir, are underestimating the radical disruptive effects drug legislation change could have on society, and the dangers such substances might pose."

"No, sir," Henry responds, "as you're well aware, psychedelics are safer than most legal drugs, and furthermore, society needs radical disruption – a swift kick in the bum! We can't get real social transformation without disruption. We live in a racist, patriarchal, fossil-fuel burning society with widespread social disconnection. Suicide rates are up, violence and trauma are rampant. We need to disrupt this!"

I should remember never to let Henry go on for so long without interrupting him.

"Or perhaps," I continue, "you are overestimating the intelligence of the general population and their ability to use drugs sensibly."

"Education!" he insists, as usual. "Let's put all the money that's being squandered on failing to fight drugs into actually informing people about what they do and into supporting people with addiction issues. Everyone knows prohibition doesn't work; the conservatives are just too scared to actually admit it because it looks like they're loosening their political panties."

"He's right, Isaac," Moana sides with Henry. "People will have addictions to anything if they have issues – they'll sniff glue or drain cleaner."

"Or just be your regular garden-variety alcoholic." Henry's point falls into silence as we consider those whom we are familiar with: Chelsea with her gin fixation, Ethel's mum with her hopeless addiction.

"It's true," Ethel concedes, "addicts will be addicts. Anyway, in Portugal they changed the law years ago, and made drugs a health issue rather than a criminal one. They replaced jail time with therapy, and they have good stats. I can find you some references if you like." She winks. "Decriminalization does not result in increased drug use."

"Ethel, you and your case studies!" I reach over to brush my palm against her face, gently. I would need to actually research more counter-examples, if there are any, to continue this argument properly, but I can't help myself: "Henry, your idealism is hardly realistic. In this country you'll be lucky if they decriminalise marijuana in the next ten years. But I agree with you and Bill Hicks about using money more efficiently."

"Yep," I can tell Henry is searching his databases for another Bill Hicks quote to badly paraphrase. "Let's take all that money we spend on the military and use it to feed, clothe and educate every man woman and child and then we can explore inner and outer space, together, forever!"

"Speaking of marijuana," Moana reaches into her bag, "it's spliff o'clock."

She extracts her tin and begins to break up sticky green buds into tiny particles and sprinkles them into a pinch of tobacco sitting inside a paper. Before I know it she has presented us with a marijuana cigarette. I don't smoke cigarettes, but I sometimes partake in the odd spliff. Moana is digging around for something.

"Does anyone have a lighter?"

"Have you lost yours again?" Henry is overly dramatic in jest. It's interesting how quickly someone's repeated foibles become a running inside joke amongst friends.

"Have you ever noticed," Ethel says, "that lighters have their own informal economy?"

"Oh yes!" Henry loves informal economies, or perhaps he just loves informality in general. "Moana is one of those people who always loses a lighter before it runs out."

"I never buy lighters," Moana adds.

"I met somebody who had all the lighters that had run out," Henry speaks excitedly. "He had a big collection – hundreds of them!" He exclaims, "He was a total stoner and they all ran out while he was smoking cones… but he said he never bought lighters either."

"Who buys lighters?" Moana asks.

"I do!" Henry says "I buy lighters, all the fucking time! But I never keep them very long either. I never have them until they finish. They always disappear somehow."

"So you're the intermediary," I tell Moana. "Henry buys the lighters – he is one of *those* kinds of people. Then you steal them." Moana stares daggers at me. "Accidentally? And then that other guy, well, his people must steal them off you somehow. Or you leave them lying around, lose them, whatever."

"You make me sound like a criminal."

"A petty criminal – a haphazard and absent minded criminal."

"Just keep digging," Henry tells me.

"Lighters just seem to float around. Someone should track them to see if there's a natural migration pattern – like birds flying south." Ethel is good when she's absurd.

"They probably follow some kind of algorithm," I suggest.

We have all become parodies of ourselves before the psilocybin has even had a chance to take effect. And now we wait.

ETHEL

The taste still makes me nauseous. Mushrooms are acrid. I need the chocolate to get them down. It was so hard for me, the first time.

Moana looks at my face.

"What was it, in the end, that made you come with us last time we came here?" Moana asks me. She was an experienced tripper, even back then. I had always avoided every kind of psychoactive substance, barring caffeine and the odd beer.

"I felt so trapped inside myself. I needed more space." It was like a weight, pressing in on me, a psychological wall that I had to break through. That is really why I did it: not because my friends wanted me to, but because I needed to do something – anything – differently.

"To get out of my prison. I was terrified back then. I was scared of touch, of talking to strangers, of even being in public. Driving was hell. Walking around was hell."

"You used to seem so stoic about it all." Henry pats my shoulder.

"That's because it was difficult. There was so much tension. Something had to give. I had tried thinking my way out of it, but nothing worked. I think, at some point, I would have had a break down." I was probably right on the verge. Maybe it was even a kind of break down that made me do something so out of character.

"I'm so glad you came with us." Moana reaches for my hand. "I was so worried about you back then, and the way your world kept shrinking. I knew it would help. It always helps."

"Not always." Henry insists. "Drugs can give us all sorts of different kinds of lessons, but they only help if you treat them right."

"That's like everything though – like operating heavy machinery." Moana adds.

"You've never been good at following instructions, Henry," Isaac says.

"I've never *enjoyed* following instructions," Henry corrects. "It seems so unoriginal."

Moana laughs.

"Isn't it strange that there are fewer wars now, less violent crime, and yet always more reporting of these things?" I ask.

"People are too busy playing video games," Henry says, "Even teen drinking is down. But we still have a doom and gloom story. Every generation does. Our great wars are with climate change, neoliberalism and the corporation."

I love the way Henry speaks, like random poetry.

"Why does there always have to be a doom and gloom?" Moana asks.

"There is always struggle," Henry says, sagely, "that is how we grow."

"True," says Moana, "It's just like how butterflies need to fight their way out of the cocoon. Without that struggle, they wouldn't pump blood into their wings. They wouldn't be able to fly."

I listen to my friends talking and soak it in. This will be the last time we're together for a long time. Moana is leaving us – moving to Melbourne like everyone else. She is family and it will be different without her. A noticeable absence.

Moana was the saving grace in my childhood – her and her family. Their home was my haven. It was the only place I could run to get away from Gretta. At the thought of her my mind begins to stray down that dark corridor of memory. No. I bring myself back to the present by reaching for more chocolate. Chocolate solves everything.

MOANA

Henry and Isaac are trading Simpsons references on the picnic blanket. It seems inappropriate, somehow, like we should be more present, more focussed on what's ahead. I wander in the direction of the rocks at the edge of the bay where our sheltered, safe space meets the wild ocean. I breathe in the sea vapour from waves crashing against the rocks that form a barrier for the bay.

"I can't believe you'll be gone this time next week," Ethel's voice rings over my shoulder, merging with the waves. In her tone I can hear sadness, longing, more emotion than Eth usually expresses.

"I'm trying not to think about it," I respond.

"Sorry. It's just so – different. You've always been here, in my life. I can't imagine what it will be like with you gone." It's unlike Ethel to share vulnerability.

"You'll be fine," I tell her. "You have Isaac and Henry." We look across to the rocks where Isaac and Henry are now balancing in what could only be some kind of battle re-enactment – their limbs poised as if to attack. Ethel and I look at each other and crack up. Our laughter echoes seems to echo and merge with the sound of the sea.

"Anyway, we can Skype. It will be like I never left," I say when the calm returns. I have no idea what it will really be like. I don't even know why I'm going. It was just something I felt I had to do, and I don't want to think about it anymore in case I change my mind.

Henry and Isaac yell obscenities at each other. I flinch at what feels like disrespect. For me, mushrooms are sacred. We are going on a journey into ourselves. We are preparing to open up to a precious glimpse of the complex interconnectedness of the universe. That is why Isaac offends me more than usual at times like this. This is a spiritual practice – or it should be – otherwise, what's the point? Why not just get drunk and obnoxious instead?

I look across to him. He and Henry are back by the picnic blanket, foraging for something in Henry's bag. *Everyone has secrets,* I think. *What are you hiding, Isaac? What is it about me that makes you so angry?*

I close my eyes and take a moment to check in with myself. I know Isaac is here to challenge me – just one of the many lessons in my life, as I am in his. I know I can learn something from my frustrations, my irritation, my anger. I can learn to let go. I can practice tolerance. I can develop compassion. Underneath the tension there is joy, pure love.

"Why do you think it is that traditional cultures have taken psychedelic substances as a spiritual ritual for thousands of years?" I ask Ethel. "How did they know?"

"I guess they experimented," Ethel says.

"They are mystical," I say, "...the plants, the mushrooms. I bet they communicate with us in some way."

"Possibly," Ethel says, non-committal.

"What does psychedelic even mean?" I can't remember if I've forgotten or if I've never learned.

"Mind-manifesting," Ethel says, "It's from Greek."

"I like 'entheogen' better – doesn't it mean 'god-inducing'?"

"Yes."

"I love that," I say, lying back on the sand. 'I love how each plant teacher is different. Ayahuasca winds like a vine into another dimension, cactus is a wise mystic."

We smile at each other.

"Mushrooms are interconnectedness," Ethel says, "Their mycelia spreads out like spider webs through the earth. Intelligent, sublime connectors; a sentient brain for the surface of the planet."

"They are AMAZING" I sigh. "They show us the truth about our paths. They bring us closer to the parts of ourselves we struggle to face - the fruits of autumn, the season of letting go, of dropping leaves, they are close to death and dying."

"That sounds so morbid," Ethel pulls back.

"But that's exactly it – we are so shit at dealing with death in our culture. We are so afraid of change."

We sit in silence for a while.

It's a time for change – for me. I've never moved away before. I've never even been outside of New Zealand. This is probably what I need to process, even though I have been trying not to think about it. Actually, the fact that I have been avoiding it *means* that it is exactly what I need to face. Denial will get me nowhere.

I look across at Ethel. Her face is peaceful. I am reminded of what she doesn't know. That is the other thing I need to process. I wonder if it's something she needs to face up to as well. Are we holding her back by not saying anything... keeping the buried wound festering, invisible below the surface? Isaac would say no. He would say there is nothing to be gained here, but what does he know about spiritual development, soul journeys and deep learning? To him everything is black and white. Logical... in a way that makes no sense to me. He sees in boxes and straight lines that don't even *exist* in nature. *Everything* is curved or jagged. Everything spirals.

I look up at the sky and breathe deeply. The fresh sea air fills me with excitement that rises as a wave, up through my spine. Tingles. We are *here*. I'm going on a journey into myself. I never know where it will lead or what kind of psychic muck it will turn up, but I know I'm never given more than I can deal with. I look at Ethel. The left side of her mouth rises into a half-smile. She guides me back to join the others.

HENRY

We have been given the keys to an alternate dimension where anything is possible. I can still taste the mushrooms, and even though nothing has happened yet, I can feel the new mystical reality approaching. Fast.

Moana lies on her side across from me on the blanket. Her legs stretch out towards the sea. Her left hip curves perfectly, like a hill over the horizon. I could melt into her and everything would be perfect. If only she wanted me. If only she would let me get close enough. For a moment, I wish the others would melt away along with the rest of the world, leaving us alone.

Have you ever met anyone who you knew, instantly, was your soul mate? I've tried to tell Moana, but my words fail me every time. I stumble over myself and look pathetic and she pulls away leaving me in more pain. I know she feels our connection, she just doesn't get it. I spent so long yearning for this kind of closeness when I was younger. The first time I found it was with Terrence, but before I could tell him how I felt it was too late.

"What are you thinking about?" Moana gazes over at me. I look out towards the horizon."

"High school," I'm telling a half truth. "I felt so alienated and different from almost everyone. The whole place was like a holding cell."

"I know what you mean," Moana agrees. "It's like a farm for children until they reach adulthood. I mean – it actually is!"

"Yeah. The whole school system is a training camp for the labour market," I spout, straight out of Labour studies 101. My words feel hollow. It doesn't matter, my ego is about to dissolve anyway, setting me free to explore.

"Not a very good one, either," Moana continues "they don't even tell you about most of the careers available."

What is the point of words, anyway?

"Well, they probably don't even know," I say these things I'm sure I've said too many times before, "most teachers go from high school to uni and the back to school... and then there's the fact that so many new jobs are being created all the time that most of them didn't even exist when we were at high school." Hollow. Hollow. Directionless. Like my life. I have no higher calling, no career, no vocation. I'm just doing the same care work I did six years ago. Care. So under-valued. I might as well be cleaning toilets instead of caring for disabled people, for all society cares.

"It's hard to imagine. Everything is getting so complex."

I sigh. "Yeah. I wish it could be simple."

Moana rolls towards me. My gut leaps into my chest. I reach over and casually stroke her hair, although there's nothing casual about it. Every strand is charged with electricity, possibility and regret. Every movement is a risk. It's like this every time with Moana – hope and despair and bliss at just being near her. She is *the* everything.

So many years yearning for a soul mate. Someone I can connect with on every level, someone who can look at me and see me – really see me – and understand. All these years of longing, only to find that the one person I meet who I can connect with can't connect with me... not in the same way. Or maybe she doesn't want to. I respect that. I respect every boundary, honestly. I just can't help how I feel: not good enough.

Last time we were here I learned so much. It was one of the best and worst experiences of my life. Going through hell over Chelsea. Right at the edge of sanity. I could have gone over. I could have ended up lost, like her.

"People shouldn't trip," I say, out loud.

Everyone laughs. "Yeah, right."

"No, hear me out. People shouldn't trip unless they know what they're doing."

"Since when do you know what you're doing, old chap?" Isaac jabs me in the shoulder with his forefinger.

"Unless they're in a situation with people they trust, and feel safe, and know what they're taking, and know the dosage."

"All very sensible advice, Henry." Ethel reassures me. "We need to be prepared to deal with these things." Her words are followed by an ominous silence that seems deeper and more foreboding than the conversation really should have made it.

"I think I've lost my glasses." Ethel is checking through the bags.

"You silly goose, you didn't leave them on a rock or something?" Isaac follows Ethel over to the boulders, and suddenly we are alone.

Moana stretches out like a cat on the picnic blanket. She reaches up to the darkening sky spreading her fingers like she's sprinkling fairy dust. She turns to me. "I'll miss you, Henry."

Those eyes, so deep and blue. They look right through me leaving nothing untouched. When I found out Moana was leaving the country part of me broke. I went through the five stages of grief. It was all so irrational. The anger burned me up and yet, really, who am I to her? I'm just a friend. It's so good to be her friend, and yet – and this isn't about sex – I can't be more. I used to think disconnection was the hardest thing to deal with, in my jaded youth. Little did I know that connection was even harder.

PART IV

COMING UP

HENRY

"It is now officially dusk." I make the pronouncement in my most pompous voice, but I've got nothing on Isaac's drone.

We loll around the picnic blanket, feet in the sand. Moana offers us sour dried cherries that tear a new level of awareness from my taste buds, complimented by Moana's dark chocolate. I'm grateful that my friends have excellent taste in snack foods. I can feel a tingling in my temples and tightness in my forehead.

"I'm starting to feel something." I reach up and rub at the odd sensation.

"Me too." Ethel is doing the same. We are usually the first to feel it: chemically sensitive.

"Clearly psychosomatic." Isaac insists. "It's too early to feel anything." He always has to assert his superiority: Isaac who never quite finished his law degree, or his science degree, and opted instead for economics; who spends his days as a bank teller, always pondering the shape of the post-grad thesis he can never quite get off the ground for lack of passion, commitment or determination.

As a child I used to press my hands over my eyelids until I saw shapes emerge like computerised visualisations of music. When I close my eyes now I can start to see it again – my brain expanding to the blissfully open state of a child's; hold on – a wave is coming.

"Thanks for dictating our experience." Moana responds to Isaac's comment that seems like a lifetime ago. Her voice has an edge, intended to put his lordship in his place. She is now flat on her back, spread gorgeous and horizontal, gazing at the sky. I feel some of the past swelling up, but I hold it back.

I look around, out towards the open sky, sea, horizon, I breathe the cool fresh air. Things are good here, now. I'm so relieved it's just the four of us. Four of my favourite people in the world. "Thank fuck Chelsea isn't here," my thoughts escape audibly.

Ethel and Isaac both sound agreement. Moana is silent on the topic of her ex but it's just as well she isn't here, invading our quality time; catching Moana off-guard with her long golden locks and her fairy-tale eyelashes; catching the rest of us with her tantrums, fits, and dramas.

"Remember her screaming blue murder at the Wrench concert because she couldn't take her bag in?" Ethel is still in disbelief. "Poor Moana. You had to comfort her in the bathroom all night instead of enjoying the show with us."

"There are so many crazy Chelsea stories, like when she accused me and Ethel of plotting against her that night at my flat-warming, throwing the furniture at us; all that attention-seeking bulimia bull-shit," I recall.

"Not to mention the times she tried to overdose on Panadol or her own anti-depressants and had to get her stomach pumped," Isaac adds.

I nod to find tightness in my cheeks, my temples. A warm cosy feeling: coming home. Tingles run down my arms and I reach up into the night, fingers spread wide but the talk about Chelsea gives me a sick feeling in my stomach. I'm sorry I brought it up. *I've brought her here and now I can't get rid of her.*

"That woman should be famous," Ethel insists. "The media would love it. They could follow her around taking streaked mascara photos every fucking day."

Moana breathes out deeply.

"Sorry, sweetness," Ethel reaches over and rubs Moana's shoulder.

"I'm sorry you guys had to put up with her too."

"What's done is done." Isaac is full of tautologies.

"I'm just glad to be over that phase of my life." There is still some sadness lingering in Moana's voice.

"Ethel is the one who grew up with the crazy mother," I tell Moana, trying desperately to change the topic of conversation to something probably even worse. "By rights, she should be attracted to unstable nutcases." Perhaps my judgement is impaired.

"She is." Moana throws a pebble at Isaac.

"Excuse me?" Isaac protests. "I'm sure you could come up with worse and more fitting labels to describe my character."

"I'll try harder next time." Moana rolls onto her back again and covers her eyes with her hands. I know she's still thinking about Chelsea. "I'm going for a walk." She says, pushing herself up. It's like magic. She's here one minute and then there is just cold empty space. I can see her, already in the distance as she floats towards the sea.

I should never have brought the topic up. I wish I could have saved her from all that crap: the emotional roller-coaster, the chronic mind-fuck. But really, it didn't matter what I said at the time. Moana was in love – the zombie kind. Everything Chelsea did was excusable – even when she, drunk and hysterical, tried to push Moana through a window, ran after her with a baseball bat, threatened to call the police on *her*.

I breathe a sigh of relief and breathe in the sea air and calm. It's just us. No Chelsea, no drama. I look over to Moana, hitching up her pants as she walks, toes in the gentle wash of incoming waves. I have tried so many times to let her go, but I just can't seem to shake the feelings. Story of my life: desperate unrequited love. At least she's worth it.

MOANA

I am.
    Walking towards the bay.
    I just am...
Walking in the small lapping waves on the safe side of the water while dangerous waves crash against the rocks on the other side

A bigger wave rolls in sweeping up to my knees, accompanied by a wave of magic inside my mind.

Coming up
Swelling ocean
High tide
I'm filling up
Pouring over
Overflowing.
I'm expanding
Connecting with everything, everyone I love, every feeling, even pain.

. . .

IT HURTS to be the one being pushed away, to always be pulling on the rope that goes slack. I felt like that with Chelsea. I always wanted more from her and every time she cut me off it hurt. I've shed too many tears over that girl. But it hurts to be the one holding back too, at least it does for me. I don't want to hurt Henry, but he keeps prodding. He doesn't understand. The night that Chelsea and I finally broke up Ethel was away with Isaac. I called Henry, crying into the phone.

"I'M COMING OVER," he insists.

"No, I don't want to be here. Too many memories." I look around my bedroom and see the clothes we shared scattered about. The scarf she gave me a week late for my birthday is draped over my headboard. The photo of us on our first and only snowboarding trip is on the bedside table and her running shoes poke out of my wardrobe. This space that I carefully decorated to make mine, that used to be my peaceful shrine, now gloomy, painful.

"Come over then, I'll pick you up."

"I'd rather walk."

"Moana, it's pissing down!"

"I'll take an umbrella. See you soon." I hang up before he can argue. I don't own an umbrella, but I put my raincoat on.

Sometimes the weather reflects my mood, especially times like this. Walking in the rain is medicine, even if it's not enough. I traverse the four blocks in silence, listening to the drops all around me, to the passing cars swoosh through the puddles, to the invisible birds calling out. I'm drenched by the time I get to Henry's.

"You silly girl," he patronises.

"Are you trying to make me feel better?" My black mood seeps into everything in the room.

"Come here." He holds up a towel.

We huddle by the heater on dusty couch cushions. I'm relieved his flat-

mates have gone out. He tries to feed me two-minute noodles, but I can't eat. It takes a while for me to talk but when it comes it all pours out: everything about Chelsea. Every now and then Henry agrees with me that she was disturbed, unstable, hurtful, unpredictable, destructive. He re-states his long-held conviction that I'm better off without her, that I deserve better, that I'm worth more than that. Mostly Henry just listens. I love him for that. I know he's biting his tongue. He loves to rant and rave but this time he lets me do it. He never says 'I told you so'. He cares. But I've always known that.

When everything has poured out of me I collapse into a disintegrating arm-chair.

"You can sleep in my bed." I'm wary of this kind of invitation. I hesitate.

"I'll sleep on the couch if you're more comfortable."

"No. I can sleep on the couch." I don't really want to. I crave human warmth and closeness.

"Can I sleep in your bed with you?" I wouldn't feel safe with any other man, but Henry is one of my two best friends in the world. I trust him, but I know how he feels, and I want to make things clear. "Just sleep."

"Of course, Moana." He looks offended. "I wouldn't dream of crossing your boundaries. Not ever. Never."

"It's just better to make it clear."

"Yes. Come." He ushers me into his chaotic bedroom, scattering things from his bed to the floor. "Come, cuddle, be safe, be warm."

MY TOES SINK into the sand
    I lift myself gently back to the present
    The warm summer breeze drifts over me
    Through me
    I am spirit
    I am goddess
    Consciousness
    I am the stunning core of everything

My DNA reflect the structure of the universe

The atoms of my being flash in and out of existence

Microcosm solar systems

My feet are rooted in the earth mother. Papatūānuku

The grains of sand beneath my feet are connected

I reach my arms up towards Ranginui, sky father.

The universe sends us sacred messages: be aware, be conscious, be here now.

My soul rolls like the waves towards Tangaroa, god of the sea, like Neptune, dissolving my dream consciousness, dissolving my delusions.

I am home.

ETHEL

For the first time this evening I'm alone, deserted by the others who have spun off into their own worlds. I sort the contents of my bag to make sure I know where everything is. I move the objects belonging to my friends, shake the sand of the picnic blanket and place everything back in a more orderly way. As I work, the sound of the ocean merges with a tune in my mind. I'm unconsciously composing a symphony of sorts, or the sea is and I'm just joining in.

When I've finished organising I sit, I straighten my back. I look out to the bay on the right, and then towards the rocky waves on the left. I see a familiar shape approach, it seems an eternity since she's been gone.

"I'm definitely feeling something." Moana says. Her return from the lagoon feels like a cycle of some sort has been completed. She is rubbing her forehead. Mine is starting to feel the familiar tightness as well, like going through a tunnel too fast. Time seems to fold in upon itself bringing me perilously close to the jagged edges of the past. I pull myself back, sinking my fingers into the sand.

"My fingers are tingling." I reflect. Moana reaches out as if she ought to be able to feel the sensations I feel. Maybe she can.

"Where are the boys?" she asks.

"They went running off down the beach."

"Typical," Moana smiles and I smile back. "I love you, Eth. So much." She pulls me into a hug. I collapse into her arms as I have learned to do over these years of getting used to being human. "You are my sister."

"It feels like you're my only real family." Otherwise I suppose I have no family. I haven't thought about this in a while, and it's never seemed quite so... cavernous, like my life would be a desperate void without these friends. "When you leave, I'll be an orphan."

"You'll have Mum – she loves you, you know... and Isaac – hah – for what it's worth!"

"I'm grateful to your mum," I only gush like this when I'm tripping, opening up, "– so grateful, and to Isaac as well." The feelings are becoming more vivid. Everything feels like it's starting to flow... like a water colour painting, blurring at the edges, bleeding through into the next thing. The boundaries are starting to dissolve.

"I don't think I'll ever understand Isaac." Moana sounds exasperated.

"It's just that your brains are different." I have spent a lot of time thinking about this. "Isaac's brain is a well-organised reference library. Everything acceptable to him has a place."

"Hah – I bet it's indexed alphabetically!" Moana laughs.

"...or Dewey-decimally," I suggest.

"Knowing Isaac, it will be organised in an even more superior system – in a system forged by his machine of a mind to be ever more logical," Moana imitates Isaac's way of speaking.

"Yes, information is filed away efficiently, ready to access at any moment." My words start to merge into Moana's.

"I bet everything he deems illogical is binned straight away," Moana says, although our story flows together.

"He has no fiction section. He doesn't even read novels. His structure is simple: just files of facts and shelves of logical argument forms," *and a small balcony at the back filled with nothing but air and possibilities*. Not many people see this room, he rarely lets his guard down, but it's there all the same. We sit in silence for a while, Moana and I, our stories diverging.

"But shouldn't your mind be the library?" Moana asks.

"My mind is a different kind of library altogether, with a large fiction section."

"And art all over the walls! And a children's corner with cushions and toys!"

"Yes! And a tunnel deep into the earth, and a vegetarian café, and a slide from one level to the next..." All this Moana understands because she knows so many parts of me, but what I don't say is that there's a secret room at the back, Pandora's box, that no one may ever enter. Everything else in my library makes sense. Everything else is safe, if a little whimsical: safe and organised and pleasant.

"So what kind of library do I have?"

"I don't think you or Henry have library minds at all."

"No? Henry's is more like a theme park."

"Yes. It's filled with wild rides with bizarre themes."

"And mine?"

"Yours is natural – organic – a forest..."

"...or an ocean."

"Yes: full of wildlife, with no boxes or straight lines."

"Just a deep bull-dozer wound." Moana looks down. I can see the wound clearly in my mind, scarring the terrain, that has long begun to heal over but will never be erased.

"I suppose your mind and Isaac's look similar, but they're not really." Moana changes the subject.

"Yeah. My mind couldn't be any other way. It is fixed like this whereas Isaac's could be anything – a mountain top, from which to gaze at the world: a shopping mall of ambition and competition."

"I can't imagine it any other way. It's a reference library because he wants everything to be certain – because he's terrified of uncertainty." Moana insists, but I still see the possibilities that she doesn't.

"Isaac's religion is Science," says Moana.

"So maybe his mind is more like a natural history museum, a science lab?"

"No. He doesn't experiment," Moana says, as if she is the expert on my boyfriend.

"Even with ideas?" I probe into her misconceptions.

"Maybe."

ISAAC

"If anyone would like a chewing gum experience, I highly recommend it." Henry says, holding out the packet.

I reach forward and extract two white pellets. I bite through the candy shell, unleashing icy fury. It is almost too much.

"Oh wow. This is making my mouth explode."

"It's fucking intense man."

Moana passes me the spliff and I inhale through the peppermint blizzard of my mouth. It's remarkably refreshing. For a few moments we all chew and inhale and exhale in seeming synchronicity with the sound of the waves crashing, it's strangely relaxing.

It is as if the sounds around us have been turned up several notches. The crickets are deafening.

"I feel like moving." Ethel says, jiggling her legs in an incoherent yet adorable way.

"Shall we walk?" I suggest.

"Where to?" She gets up and scatters sand all over me. "Oh sorry." She brushes it off my face.

"To the other end of the bay?"

"Oh... to the karaka tree?"

"Yes – let us go!" The two of us begin to move along the beach, although I'm sure we are walking in quite the usual way, it seems more like gliding somehow. Peculiar things, these substances. Perhaps it is just that my perception is enhanced, my medulla oblongata is functioning more smoothly than normal. It's nothing spiritual, nothing mystical at all. Everything is physical.

"I just don't understand what it is," I say to Ethel, grasping her hand as we walk across the beach at Atamarie, "that draws people to ludicrous beliefs."

"Maybe they need it, Isaac." Ethel is withdrawn as usual. I can never tell what she's thinking, only that she is thinking a lot.

"Why would you need to believe in the bizarre notion that the stars and planets so very far away are in some way dictating your everyday life?"

"Astrology isn't deterministic, not anymore. It's about synchronicity and patterns reflecting. But you don't really want to know about it, you just want to discriminate." She is petulant but she has a point.

"You're right. I want to pick it apart and demonstrate that it's full of shit."

"So why do you believe the things you believe?"

"Because they make logical sense. Because they're rational."

"Why are your beliefs more rational that anyone else's?"

"Simply because I choose what to believe based on whether it is rational and logical or not."

"Is that because you need to?" Usually these discussions are more light-hearted banter with Ethel, but something seems to have struck a chord. She lets go my hand and continues to walk.

"It's because I choose to, because it makes sense."

"And do you do that out of some deep need you have for the world to be an ordered sensical place?" She looks me in the eye. "Are you afraid that it isn't?"

I'm taken aback. "Why would you think that?"

"Because a belief is an attachment, Isaac, no matter what it's in, it comes from the need to hold on to something. Believing in tarot and crystal healing is just as much in that category as believing in safer things like physics, which, by the way, is changing all the time."

"There's something bothering you, isn't there?" I try to take her hand again, but she slips my grasp.

"There are lots of ways of seeing the world, Isaac. I know you desperately want to be right but please be sensitive to other people." Of course this whole conversation is about Moana. Ethel guards her like a wolf mother guards her cubs. I get it. Moana is sensitive. Moana is important to Ethel, but Eth was the one with the hideous childhood of abuse. Moana came from a wonderful home. Maybe Ethel is trying to protect Moana in the way that no one protected her.

PART V

ATAMARIE. TAKE X1

ETHEL

"Y"ou were the biggest surprise," Henry tells me.

Isaac reaches for me, looks at me, "You were," he confirms.

"What are you two talking about," I ask, feeling decidedly unsurprising as I brush the sand off the picnic blanket.

"I just find everything about you surprising," Isaac says.

"I never thought you would come with us," says Henry, "the first time."

"Neither did I," I admit.

"No," I tell Henry, firmly. "Not me." We walk to uni side-by-side, typical twenty-year-olds. It's the winter before our first trip to Atamarie Bay.

"Oh, you're so closed minded, darling."

Control was so important to me when I was younger. I wasn't interested in controlling other people, just my own life. Every decision I made came down to what felt safest. I didn't wear anything with bright colours, lest they draw attention. I kept my hair plain, tied back. I didn't speak too loudly, if I spoke at all. I crossed at the pedestrian crossings. I did my homework. I followed all the rules. I learnt as much as I could about science and maths and grammar because the certainty was so comforting. It wasn't until later, when I learnt about particle physics, anthropology, and sociology that I realised how ambiguous everything is. The concrete walls of my reality came crumbling down at university, where my views were challenged over and over by clever lecturers trying to inspire critical analysis. It was overwhelming; and combined with the immense pressure of the weight of my childhood, it was too much to bear.

"I'M SENSIBLE. You can do whatever you want to your brain, but please be careful." We walk down the path into the campus, through the trees, past the lake. It's the nicest way to get to class.

"Psychedelics aren't addictive Ethel. That's more the realm of cocaine, meth, and heroin — which I never touch, personally. Honestly, a geek like you — you should have done your research."

"What about psychological addiction?" We walk under the big old redwoods planted decades ago, possibly in an attempt to imitate a Californian college.

"Sure people might want to trip again. It can be a wonderful experience, after all. But if you do it too much it stops working and if you're trying to escape things you really shouldn't touch psychedelics."

BACK THEN, I filled all my time with study and sleep. No time to think about anything else, except in the sometimes-bleak walks to campus where I could feel my feet treading the jagged fault-lines of memory, guarding closely for quakes and geysers, for the childhood anguish that bubbled up, reminding me of how broken I was. It helped when someone else walked with me, distracting me.

I used to believe there were good drugs and bad drugs, he says, but now that I've done more research I can see the problem is all in how they are used, or supressed.

I SCUFF my shoes against the footpath, the way I did as a young child. I feel tired, my bag is heavy, full of text books and notes.

"My mum was into bad drugs, Henry," I say. "I don't want to make her life any easier – she's had a blessed life."

"That doesn't make any sense, Eth, you can't make her life any easier now, anyway. But I get it, it's complicated. It's not meant to make sense."

The conversation rouses a web of complicated emotions and I'm looking for my panic button, my escape switch. Navigating through the broken glass towards my protected inner spaces.

"Well then, I'll keep escaping things, and save my brain the damage."

"That's just the thing, Eth. The only reason I'm even suggesting it is that substances like this can open neural pathways – re-wire your brain. You know all that senseless anxiety you carry around with you? Imagine not having to live with that every day."

"What if it just makes things worse, Henry?" A life without constant debilitating anxiety sounds like an improbable miracle. What does it even feel like?

"In the inexplicably unlikely event that you were to join us in this adventure, you would be with your nearest and dearest. It would be just like hanging out with us normally, in a beautiful place, but a lot more awesome. If you started to flip out we would bring you back, hun."

"People go into psychosis, Henry. Can you bring me back from that?"

"You're one of the most solid people I know, Eth, anxiety aside. But sure, it's possible. I flipped out one time and thought I was God, but I was tripping alone which isn't a great idea, especially not your first time."

"Do you think you could handle me with a God-complex?"

"Perish the thought."

. . .

I suppose I knew it at the time that I was depressed – that I was winding myself so tightly into a ball that there was no room in my life for me, that I felt trapped, that I was living in hell. But even still, I held my ground when Henry tried to persuade me to take mind-altering substances.

"You know I don't even drink, Henry. If such a common substance as alcohol doesn't agree with me I hate to think what something harder would do."

"Pfft. Alcohol is a much more dangerous substance. It causes more deaths than all other drugs put together times a million."

"Stop quoting Bill Hicks at me. I know."

"Do you?" Henry pauses and looks at me as we round the corner to campus.

"I don't know."

"Exactly. All I'm offering you is the one tool that has helped me break free of years and years of depression in a safe, friendly environment. I don't want to pressure you because that would be stupid. I just don't want you to have all this unnecessary fear that comes from not questioning your social programming."

"I guess I just assume there is a reason for the social programming against drugs."

"Everything is skewed when it comes to drugs. The kinds prescribed by doctors often have massive adverse reactions, but aren't generally feared. You know, psychedelics were outlawed in the '60s and '70s because conservative governments hated all these fucking hippies hanging out in the parks on acid rather than cutting their hair and contributing to the economy."

"Social functionalism."

"That's right. Which we both know is the most boring social theory."

"I can't argue with that. But, look, Henry. What if it's not worth the risk? I had a scary childhood and I don't know what kind of damage is lurking under the surface. I'd rather stay sober and get on with my life."

"Your call. I'm just planting some seeds. You never know what's going to grow."

I smile at Henry and his second Bill Hicks reference of the morning. I recognised it from the many hours of screenings I have sat through at Henry's flat – Bill Hicks, the prophet, playing in the background as Henry goes about his daily life.

I love Henry even though we couldn't be more opposite. He befriended me without even trying – he just paid attention, the way others never did. He asked me questions, written in the margins of notepads in the back of lecture theatres, he caught up with me after and before classes and listened to my quiet reflections, he invited me over to eat pizza and watch movies – and insisted I come. He made me feel welcomed, and validated, and important.

He is a pushy sort, but he does care. I wonder whether it's worth a try. Fear has long been used as social control after all – against gay people, Jews, other ethnic minorities, against 'the enemy', against teenagers and their music, even.

"Drugs are powerful, they should be used with caution."

"Maybe they should be feared." We still have ten minutes before class. I sit down on a bench behind the redwoods, overlooking the lake. Henry Joins me.

"That depends on how they're used. Even heroine is used in medicine as powerful pain relief, you know. Morphine is just a pure form of it. Psyche-delics won't relieve your pain, but they will expand your mind."

"It's not for me," I say, crossing my arms.

"It might be more for you than you could ever imagine, Eth. I know you get stuck on things. This kind of thing... it can open you up, make it easier to connect, break old patterns, make you... happier."

"You make it sound like a miracle cure for all my ills."

"It is, well, it can be a panacea. Totally."

"I don't need it. I'm fine."

"You always hold back, Ethel. What are you really afraid of?"

Yes

I always hold back.

We look out at the lake, watching the ducks swim between lily pads.

Henry thinks it's out of fear of going over the edge – of the unknown. Actually it's the opposite. The unknown is fine with me, it's the known I'm afraid of. I'm scared it will somehow come back – that the old reality will merge with the present and I will be trapped again. Sometimes I catch a glimpse of her – Gretta – stumbling down the hallway in the corner of every memory of my childhood – that black look in her bloodshot eyes. I shudder.

"Don't be afraid that you'll get lost," *Henry's voice is soothing.*

"Henry, I would love to get lost." *To lose myself. To lose the past.*

"Then honey, you're talking about the wrong drugs. Psychedelics won't get you lost, not really. They're only illuminating. They only make reality more heightened. They won't help you escape."

"If you want to escape, let me get you some opiates," *he suggests, even though he knows my response will always be 'no'. Firmly.*

"You know we don't want to go down that road." *The one that leads to chemical dependency. Institutionalisation. Losing control.*

He knows, but he doesn't understand.

To Henry, escape is a one-night thing, or maybe a weekend. For me, I have been working out clever corners of my mind to hide from my childhood all my life and I'm not about to make it even harder.

"Anything can be addictive." *I think about the exercise junkies, people addicted to eating, or to not eating, sex addicts.*

"Sure, but, like I said, psychedelics will stop working it you take them too often."

"Haven't you heard of a 'gateway drug'?"

"That old slippery slope fallacy," *Henry nudged me, gently in the arm.* "Hey. Look, it's all about the cage you're in. You know, they did those experiments on rats – feeding heroin to rats in small cages and they behaved just like addicts, but put them in a big, fun cage, with lots of things to play with and with other rat friends, and they stopped drinking the drugged water."

"But we aren't in a cage, Henry, it doesn't apply."

"Our cage is our surroundings, our freedom to do stuff, our society, our minds."

THAT WAS THE MOMENT. Something flared inside me. *My mind is a prison.* I thought. *Carefully constructed to keep my fears at bay... but I am the one who is trapped.*

Something started to open up, to unravel inside me, and my resistance crumbled. *Maybe this can help.* But even still, after all these years of occasional psychedelic experiences, I've never really lost control.

Psychedelics aren't escape, but they are controllable, or maybe 'focusable' is a better term, especially at low dose. If I don't want to think about something, I know very well how to shut it out. That's how it works in a library. I close a book and shelve it and don't need to think about it anymore.

ISAAC

Nothing is really happening. I might just as well be sober. I came out here seeking something but now I don't remember what. The others are enthralled. Moana and Henry writhe on the picnic blanket, absorbed in sensations, so full. Ethel is practically glowing, expanding well beyond her usual introverted self. I am just empty, pointless. I want what they have. I'm afraid of being left behind but I'd never admit it, my jealousy, my disconnection, something darker pushing its way up out of the depths of nothingness inside me.

Oh. These aren't my normal thoughts at all. I'm not sober but I'm not where they are.

"How did we get here?" I wonder out loud.

"You drove us," Henry reminds me.

Moana laughs. "I think Isaac is asking something deeper and more profound for once."

"Don't speculate, Moana. I was actually thinking about the first time we came out here. I was trying to remember".

"I invited your snobby arse, remember?" Henry says, and the memory returns as clear as day.

. . .

I HAVEN'T SEEN Henry for a year — not since the last time I came back from Otago for the summer. He has been planning this expedition for months and is irrationally excited when I pick him up. Babbling incoherently. Quoting Human Traffic and Bill Hicks. I've known Henry since high school, but I haven't met the others yet. The women. Henry tells me Moana is stunning, amazing, intelligent. I can tell he's infatuated already.

"She's a photographer."

"Professionally?"

"Semi-professionally. She's still studying, but she picks up some part time gigs — graduation photos, weddings, the usual paid stuff."

"And how do you know her?"

"Through Ethel. They grew up together."

"She's the one you've told me about before. Your uni friend?"

"Ethel is... oh... How can I describe her?" Henry scratches his auburn goatee as if digging for an answer. "Ethel is unique. She's self-contained. She's solid — you know? Sharp as a knife. She's... different. She has a different way of looking at things."

"What does she look like?"

"She's got brown hair. Oh, I don't know. I'm not good at describing people. You'll meet her soon enough."

"Where are we picking Mona up?"

"Moana — It's a long 'o' sound — Almost like Mor-ana, but without the rrr."

"Right."

"From the meditation centre."

"Riiiight."

"Oh yeah. Moana is spiritual. Don't judge. Behave yourself."

"I'll do my best." I placate automatically, although I have no intention of restraining my judgement.

. . .

HENRY DIRECTS me to a gentrified warehouse on the east side of town. A curvy Māori girl with long dark hair stands outside in teal yoga pants and a navy poncho. She sees Henry and waves. Once inside and settled in the back seat of the car she groans as if in pain.

"What is it?" Henry inquires.

"I think it's my solar plexus chakra."

I restrain myself. The drive out is going to be a long one. We briefly stop for supplies at the supermarket. Moana buys all kinds of strange things — supposedly "super foods". Henry buys chewing gum and lollipops. I buy beer and crisps.

Back in the car Moana begins to ask questions.

"So how do you and Henry know each other?"

"High school."

I didn't have many friends early on in childhood. I was teased for my intellect and ostracised by my peers. I didn't mind terribly. I wouldn't have gained much from the company of imbeciles.

"We were part of the same group of intelligent outcasts." Our social marginality brought us together in an easy way, but even in that group, as a much taller and classically good-looking chap, I was an outsider.

"Are you still friends with the others?"

"Not really — not since Terrence."

Terrence and Henry became my good friends. We would knuckle down in the library pouring over classics in our lunch breaks, get stoned in the park across the road after school, and watch movies with Terrence's girl-friend and her friends in weekends. Both of them seemed to bridge various social boundaries effortlessly, Henry with his cocky self-certainty, Terrence with his natural charisma — one of those rare ones who everybody likes.

"What happened?"

"We knew he wasn't 'right'." Henry and I have gone over this a thousand times. The surreal period leading up to the tragedy has become something of an intimate personal mythology. He started saying things that didn't make sense.

"He was paranoid." I clarify.

"Not depressed." Henry adds.

"No."

His disappearance and the discovery of his body, three days later, were subjects of infinite speculation.

"They found his body in the river." The words I speak seem so weak, so typical, like so many other stories. He could have been anyone, but he wasn't.

"He told me he was abducted by aliens." Henry says.

"Certainly psychosis." I'm sure of it.

"Why didn't we do anything?" Henry repeats the same line every time we talk about Terrence. The living always find a way to feel guilty.

"His family did – they got him institutionalised." I add, to make clear that we didn't just abandon our friend. It wasn't our fault.

These familiar circles of blame and doubt. Anger. Shame. Terrence had been in the local psychiatric unit. They had let him go. He had disappeared, leaving a gaping void. Henry and I became closer. The others in our group drifted further apart. We blamed the psychiatric services for different reasons. Henry said the public health system was under-funded and deserved more government spending. I argued the public system was inefficient and had the free market had the opportunity to work, a private system would have better looked after Terrence.

"His family were wealthy enough."

"But what if they hadn't been? Would he not have deserved care?"

"Charities would probably do a better job with all the tax deductible donations they could receive."

"Bullshit, Isaac. The US health system is appalling, and you know it."

"Everything comes back to economics."

I'm surprised his family had relied on the precarious public system at all. Some share of the blame belonged to them, and to us for not doing anything about it.

"How can you even be friends with him, with views like that?" Moana says, clearly offended by me, not bothering to soften her blows with politeness.

"How indeed?" Henry's comedic tone turns everything into jest.

BY THE TIME *we arrive at the batch at Atamarie Bay I'm in need of solitude – or at least some space from Moana's solar plexus chakras. She has produced a large camera and is already taking pictures of inane things: her feet, the dusty wooden steps of the bungalow style batch, the peeling paint of the weather boards.*

Henry finds the key and unlocks the front door, while I walk around the deck until I find the best vantage point for observing the view. The sea. Horizon. Stretching out.

Moana and Henry chatter away. I can't make out their words, nor do I want to. I walk down the steps on the other side thinking about Terrence, thinking about my law degree, my life direction. My father, a High Court Judge, has always pushed me down his path. Work hard. Get rich. Be a successful high-functioning alcoholic. I could finish my degree in the next year. I could get a summer internship. Work my way up. Be a "success". It just seems less and less worthwhile.

I have been thinking about changing my course of study to physics or chemistry, or maybe philosophy. I just don't know exactly why. I don't know what I'm looking for or what I want to look for. I want to do something important.

I urinate behind a tree. It's always liberating, pissing in the fresh air. The native bush stretches out. I hear the sound of birdcalls – probably tui, with that guffaw.

I feel mildly apprehensive about the weekend ahead. I enjoy psychedelics, but I don't know about taking them with someone as irritating as Moana, and her friend is probably not much better. Henry's taste in everything is unforgivably gauche. I walk around a bit under the trees to chase off my apprehension, but eventually realise that what I really need is a beer. I make my way back to the house.

"Thanks." Henry and Moana both gratefully receive their bottles on the deck, still cold, despite the long drive. We sit for a while, gazing out to sea. I

mostly manage to ignore Moana and Henry's conversations about tripping as a spiritual journey.

After a while, Henry glances at his phone. "Jesus, it's almost seven."

"Ethel will be here soon." Moana turns toward the entrance to the house, despite there obviously being walls obstructing our line of sight. Her expression is anxious. "I can't believe you convinced her to come." She smiles at Henry. "I never thought she'd take... anything. She doesn't even drink, really."

"She doesn't drink?" What kind of infernal hippie are we talking about? I imagine a dreadlocked white girl, covered in beaded rags.

"Well, she'll have the odd beer, but just one." Henry sounds defensive.

"Alcohol doesn't agree with her. It makes her feel funny," Moana explains.

"She sounds like a hypochondriac," I say.

"She doesn't invent illnesses." Moana looks perpetually offended by everything I say. I realise I'm going to enjoy winding her up.

"We should have just waited for her to finish work. She could have come out with us."

"I thought... well, never mind. It's a bit late now."

"But you know how anxious she gets about... well, everything. She would have hated the drive out."

"Really?" She sounds absurd.

We are distracted by the sound of an old engine approaching. Moana walks to the end of the deck and peers around towards the driveway.

"She's here!" We collectively move towards the kitchen. I need another beer.

"You made it! Finally!" Henry exclaims. I turn towards the door to see a demure figure in a green cardigan and plain grey skirt. I only get a quick glimpse before she is eclipsed by Henry's hug, which she receives awkwardly, tapping him on the shoulder. Henry moves away and Moana moves in, more familiar, maintaining more distance. I feel as if I'm conducting a study. Moana hands Ethel one of my beers, without asking me first. I don't mind, of course, but I would prefer to be the one to offer it.

"This will sort you out."

I step forward and hold out my hand. Ethel seems shocked. I watch her delicate features tighten then relax. She does not smile. There are no pretences. It catches me off guard. Her hand is cold and damp from the beer.

"Isaac." I introduce myself because none of the others have the courtesy to.

"I know." Ethel replies.

"Of course you do." Somehow my etiquette seems out of place. Irrelevant. We all know who we are. Then something happens. Some kind of flash. Electrical impulses through my nervous system. She smiles.

HENRY

Moana, Moana, Moana... My head is full of her. Isaac is sick of me talking endlessly about it. How is it that in the infinite possibilities of this universe, that all these factors could combine into such a wonderful human being? I barely knew her that first trip, but I already knew there was something amazing about her from a handful of casual meetings. My heart would ring with a sudden thrill when I saw her in the kitchen on my ever-more-frequent visits to Ethel's. I needed her to come to Atamarie Bay with us. I needed this chance to connect. That's why I took special care to convince Ethel. I knew that if she came, Moana would come too. It was magic when she agreed. I could hardly believe my luck. And then the bomb dropped.

"Chelsea might come out here later on." Moana says, gazing out to sea, leaning against the balcony.

"Chelsea?"

"My girlfriend."

"A girlfriend?" Oh. The penny drops, along with the bottom of my guts. Spilling metaphorically out all over the floor. No.

Moana blushes. "Yeah. She's just across at the Cloudy Bay Backpackers with her cousin who's visiting from the States. It's half an hour away. She said she might hitch."

So Moana has a Girlfriend with a capital "G". She's not as accessible as I thought... not that I assumed her being single made her accessible... it's just that she seemed so... open to me.

Moana retreats into the kitchen. Isaac and I are alone on the deck.

"You, Sir, have just been friend-zoned."

"Don't give me that bullshit."

"Denial."

"No, it's just a stupid concept... that guys like you," I push his arm, "invent to make yourself feel less rejected. Just because a girl doesn't want to sleep with you, it's not a kind of 'zone'."

"Hey, hey, I didn't invent something so vulgar. I'm just using the common vernacular. Would you prefer I say you're 'Chasing Amy'?"

"Don't be a dick." I'm still processing the news. Reconsidering my position. Five minutes ago Moana was a girl I really liked. Now, she's a girl I really like who has a girlfriend.

"I bet you think she's bisexual."

"Everyone's bisexual."

"It's only bisexual people who think that." Isaac has always teased me about my sexuality, which I'm totally open about. I have always teased him about being a dick.

"Attraction is not just about gender. Gender is an arbitrary characteristic."

"Speak for yourself! Your genitals may be arbitrary, mine certainly are not!"

"That's because you are comprised entirely of a big pile of genitals."

"Lovely imagery."

"Anyway, I'm not worried about Moana. We have a connection. We will be whatever we are. Not everything is about sex and 'relationships'."

"Coupling and copulating."

"Good alliteration." Every conversation with Isaac is a fencing duel.

"I'm glad you appreciate my many talents."

Isaac excuses himself to go to the bathroom, to exercise his many talents, no doubt. I'm left alone with my thoughts. Moana has a girlfriend. Where does that leave me? Us? Is she monogamous? Is she a lesbian?

I know the despair I'm feeling is not logical, but I can't seem to fight it off. Was this thing between us all an illusion? I felt like we had something – so strong it almost seemed tangible. My soul mate.

I was so certain a few moments ago. I was flying – high on this elating inflating love. Now I'm dashed against the rocks. Misery floods in. I start to dread the night ahead and we haven't even dropped yet. Still completely sober. The sun is setting. Soon we will be down at the beach, tripping, the four of us and maybe "Chelsea", this sugary stranger unwelcomely stealing Moana away. I don't know if my jealousy is relevant yet, there are too many unknowns. The only thing I know for sure is that I need Moana in my life.

It is dark and we are already tripping when Chelsea shows up. Moana disappeared back up to the bach to meet her. My hopes are decimated into grains of sand. Moana comes back, leading a blonde girl by the hand. Her hair is long and wavy, not in the natural way Moana's is, but as if she plaits it to get the effect.

"It's okay," Moana is telling her. "We only just dropped. You can start now."

"I can't believe you didn't wait for me." Chelsea's voice is high pitched and sulky. I dislike her already. When she meets my eyes I can tell the feeling is mutual.

"Chelsea, this is my friend Henry." My friend... my friend...

Chelsea responds with a rather short "Hi." She is swaying a bit. I can smell whiskey. My mushrooms are kicking in. This is all too much to deal with...

"Nice to meet you." I lie.

MOANA

I keep feeling the need to pull away from the others. Henry and Isaac's banter is tiring. I would be happy to be alone with Ethel, or even Henry, but the group of us seem to get locked into the same dynamics that we are now so used to. I want to connect with the sea, the forest, the sky, the stars. I want to ascend.

I wander towards the pohutukawa trees, reaching up towards their soft, rounded leaves, their coarse bark, their fluffy red blossoms. I keep needing to leave the picnic blanket, to get beyond the mundane and connect with the deeper meaning always present in nature.

The first time we were here, at Atamarie Bay, was magic. It's one of those few perfect memories that I can reach back to, just to recall how it feels to be free – in perfect alignment with my body, my curves, my hips, my heart... to connect so deeply with my closest friends... although there's the part that jolts the record: Chelsea.

THIS IS what it feels like to walk on eggshells.

"Hello darling." Chelsea is swaying too much as she comes towards me

over the sand. Her words are too slow, syllables even more drawn out than her usual American accent. I know it before I smell the spirits on her breath. My heart racing.

She's drunk again.

"Hi," I display a bright smile to mask my fear. "How are you?" I try to project warmth, but I can't help the sinking dread. She's so much more stable when she's sober. How can I explain this to the others?

With Chelsea, I am always watching what I say... what I do.

Even still, there's no stopping her, there's nothing I can do.

Chelsea has been here for less than twenty minutes and I can see it starting already. Ethel and I are musing about an old pop song we used to like as young teenagers – trying to remember its name. Chelsea's tears come out of nowhere.

"You're leaving me out." The accusations start.

"Chelsea, hun, what do you think? I'm not trying to leave you out. I'm sorry you feel that way." I'm trying to comfort her.

"You always do this, Moana."

"Do what?"

"Argue with me."

"I'm not arguing."

"You're doing it again."

"No. It's okay. Everything's fine."

"It's NOT okay. It's NOT fine."

"Please, just calm down."

Here it comes. The big, shuddering sobs.

"You're so selfish."

My insides twist at the accusation, and yet she's obviously in pain.

"You never think about me – you only care about yourself." She is shuddering.

"You don't have to do this." I don't want to upset her. I need to protect her. I love her, but sometimes I don't know how to cope. I crush shells into the sand beneath my toes, just like eggshells. Sharp and fragile. Everything

breaks, over and over. In me, in her. She is everything. I am nothing. All I can do is try to make it better.

"That's it." She throws her arms in the air. "It's over."

"What?"

"I might as well die." She glares at me. "For all you care." And storms off.

I try to follow her, but she pushes me away. She's heading in the direction of the bay where her friends are staying anyway. I know she will be alright. I turn back towards Atamarie Bay, someone is not far behind me.

"Henry?"

"I'm sorry," he says, wrapping me in a hug. I realise tears are streaming down my face. I feel so awful.

"Love is painful."

"Tell me about it." Henry's voice is heavy.

"Why... does it have to be... so hard?" We look out into the breaking waves.

"I wish I knew. Maybe it's something to do with learning lessons."

"Yeah." I sigh "Sometimes I wish I could just graduate already."

"Hey," Henry touches my arm. "It's not that bad all the time... there are good things... like friendship." We both smile sadly into the sea.

I WANDER BACK to the others, I don't like to be away from them for too long.

"So much has changed since we were first here." I look around at my friends, their faces blur with the scenery, sparks of light fly off and spiral around. "Global politics has only gotten worse, and climate change... It's just too much." The wave of grief. I'm swept up. All over me. Through me. I can't swim. So. Much. Loss.

"That's life," Isaac says.

"It's injustice. It's horrendous. This is no time for platitudes," Henry is sticking up for me, as usual.

"It is. C'est la vie."

"Shut up, Isaac!" I say.

"Hey. I don't make the rules."

"This is not about rules," I tell him, "People are suffering. Species are becoming extinct. Habitats... ecosystems... this world is dying."

"What can we do?" He shrugs.

"It's a call to action, if anything ever was," says Henry.

"Action? You overestimate yourself," Isaac says.

Ethel, who has been so quiet, speaks. "We are always acting. Everyday. We make so many choices."

"This is not going to be solved with your green-washed recycled toilet paper," Isaac is clearly alluding to some other conversation he has had with Ethel in the contained life they share.

"This is no time for alienation!" Henry pushes himself up to standing position.

"I feel powerless," Ethel says.

"Listen to the waves," I say.

"What do they say?" she asks.

"Shhhhhhh," Isaac says.

"Shut up!" We tell him.

"They say we are all connected." I decide. "They say this is part of a bigger system. Bigger cycles. But everything has a place. Every molecule of water. Every grain of sand. We are all part of this universe,"

"And do they say we can save the world like Captain Planet?" Henry asks, he is still standing, awaiting the next action.

"They say we can choose which currents to swim with, and which to swim against," I say.

"That reminds me of the book by Shankar Vedantam," Ethel says "– Privilege is swimming with the current and we have this tendency not to understand or to minimise the experience of those who are swimming against it."

Isaac laughs, "The waves speak of privilege? What bastards."

"Hidden biases," I say, to no one in particular.

"I don't have any," Isaac insists.

"Scientifically, you do," Ethel states.

"Being privileged is like swimming with the current. You have no idea how hard it is," I say, "that's the point."

"You have no idea how hard it is being a white man and having people point out how privileged you are all the time."

We collectively sigh at Isaac's words, unsure whether he's trolling or serious, as usual.

"I do," Henry says.

"Exactly, Henry is a white man. He understands that discrimination goes both ways."

Henry laughs, "It's not that hard, bro."

"Hah."

"Not compared to how hard it is being a queer man," Henry continues, "and being effeminate, having people think you're disgusting and perverted and a creep, all just because you are bisexual."

"Or being Māori," I add, "People assume I have six kids by now and live on a benefit. Shop assistants follow me around assuming I'm going to steal something. In everything I've done I've been expected to fail and fighting that expectation has been harder than doing the actual work."

"Being a white woman means I can be blind to ethnicity if I want," Ethel says. " people pointing out my privilege is an inconvenience, but it's not the same thing as, say, knowing that I will be paid less than men, and judged more harshly for being confident, and sexualised, objectified, and cat-called when I walk down the street."

"You're all ganging up on me," Isaac whines.

"Privileged distress!" Henry exclaims.

I look at Isaac. "We're trying to educate you," I say, "You want everything to be logical and rational, but things aren't, people aren't; you aren't!"

"Speak for yourself."

"We all take our privilege for granted," says Ethel, "We as animals are much more primed to focus on what we struggle with than what we find easy.

"It's evolution baby," Henry adds, sitting back down. "The problem is, it's so invisible – other people's struggle. All through school I watched the other kids grasp things I couldn't – see things I couldn't. I didn't even know I was dyslexic until I was about twelve. I just fluked and guessed my way through tests. I made up excuses. I cheated. Then it turned out I had a learning disability."

Isaac puffs himself up, "See – you all think you're better than me because you've really lived. You've suffered. It's all so unfair for you. Skewed perspectives."

"Dude, if the majority of people's perspectives are skewed – what does that say about yours?" Henry asks.

"It's not easy being right, but someone has to do it," Isaac says.

"It's not easy when things are easier..." I tease him.

"Who's illogical now?" Henry jabs Isaac with his index finger.

"I'm just saying" Isaac just will not give up "– we need to be more objective. Maybe these things do affect experience, but they shouldn't. See – I'm arguing against discrimination."

The rest of us laugh.

"You're saying we should all think and feel exactly the same thing," I say.

"Exactly."

"You're arguing for a homogenised culture?" Ethel asks.

"That would solve your problems."

"Umm... excuse me?" I don't understand how Isaac can think this way, it drives me crazy, and I don't want to waste any more of my trip having the same arguments we've been having these past six years. I look out to sea, but the others keep talking.

"All I'm saying is, people get too caught up in difference rather than being objective. We should all be treated the same."

"No one is arguing for discrimination here."

"The problem with saying things should be a certain way, as if that solves problems, is that... it doesn't solve everything. It's conflating an ideal with reality. It may never happen. There is so much work to be done to get there!"

"If it can't ever happen then what's the point in wasting your energy."

"You're so defeatist."

"Every culture has ideals beyond reach. The point is that it... it's kind of like a compass."

"A moral compass"

"Sure. It's steering the boat in a better direction."

"Even if it's a boat full of holes, being swept off a cliff."

"Yes."

"Why bother?"

"Because defeatism is even worse. It never got anyone anywhere"

"And action got us the holes in the boat."

"Action without reflection."

PART VI

TOPPING UP

ISAAC

A cacophony of laughter – that's the only way to explain it. Henry's is the most nasal and grating, although he would probably have a similarly offensive critique of my involuntary response to surprise amusement.

"Look at those shimmery trees," Moana gestures to the silver birch on nearby farmland. "Can you imagine a fish made out of those trees?"

The absurdity has begun.

"The Pohutukawa is the best thing to look at," Ethel states, "in my limited opinion." I respectfully appraise its scarlet summer bottle brush blooms. They appear brighter and more surreal than usual, although it strikes me that usually I don't pay so much attention.

"That's really what these substances do to me," I vocalise my internal monologue. "Increase my concentration."

Moana is aghast. Her mouth is open for too long to be appropriate. "All the amazingness of psychedelics – the sacredness – the connectedness! And you reduce it down to 'increased concentration?!" Her consternation is infuriating but enjoyable all the same.

"And you inflate it into some kind of mystical experience."

"Now, now, children." Henry adopts his Mary Poppins tone. "Behave yourselves! This is a polite occasion."

Moana is back to being transfixed on the silver birch. "In a way it's sort of breathing."

Henry interjects. "Can you see the fat man's face?"

"Oh yeah," Ethel affirms.

"It's like a Buddha," Moana insists. "Buddha tree... actually I'm struggling to tell which parts of it are a face, but I know there's definitely a face there... some kind of tree spirit."

"Pfft. Human beings are programmed to recognise faces. It's biological." I feel this knowledge is important, although I'm not sure 'programmed' is the best word... it was just the first word my influenced mind happened upon. As soon as I've spoken it I can tell Moana is going to give me hell.

"Programmed?" She laughs. "Who programmes us? Are you getting religious now?"

"It's the wrong word." It doesn't matter. Moana is distracted.

"Does anyone know when we took them?" she asks, "because... I have no concept of time."

"Probably about half an hour ago," Henry estimates.

"Half an hour?" I interject. "Are you serious? It was more like two hours ago."

"We should take more then." Henry is right. We are only getting disappointingly mild effects. It was the intention, initially, to start out on a low dose. I wanted to see how strong these specimens were.

"Moar! Mushrooms!" Henry roars.

"Yes. It's time for a top up," I declare.

"Are you sure?" Ethel asks, "I can feel them kicking in."

I too can feel the effects of the substance from the last dose. Increased concentration. Vivid sensory input. Waves of internal exhilaration.

"But it's fairly subtle," I decide, "If we take more now, we will increase the duration of the trip and extend and elevate the peak experience."

We retreat from the rocks and wind to the huddle of bags and blankets. Henry summons the women-folk and I produce the jar of *Psilocybe* fungus again.

Henry and I foraged for these in the gully behind our old high school. We got up at 4am – well, we didn't really sleep – in order to pick the newly blooming mitochondrial fruits. It was a chilly June morning and we were still drunk from whiskey sours. This variety emerge after the early frosts. Here they don't become abundant until mid-year. Further south, mushroom season is much earlier.

"How many?" I ask.

"Five?" Ethel suggests. She was so timid last time we were here. Now her eyes are shining. Her stance confident. She reaches out her open palm to collect the dried offerings as I count them out.

Moana and Henry ask for ten more each. After distributing these the remaining contents of the jar are mangled stalks and stray mushroom heads, probably about 12 more. I take them all, as there's no point in wasting the crumbs, no point in leaving a few incriminating pieces behind, either. I throw the handful of dry, chewy, acrid fungus into my mouth and reach for the mead to wash it down.

I want to maximise my potential experience, after all.

"You just took the rest!?" Henry is incredulous.

"Yes."

"That was way too much! There must have been 20 or 30 left there, and these are strong – I'm bounding off the walls already."

"You're always bouncing off the walls."

"Man – you crazy!"

"Isaac is going for a heroic dose," Ethel comments.

"Maybe this will make you into a shaman," Moana adds.

"I daresay it will not!"

"If this won't, nothing will." Moana is so certain. There's a flash of righteousness in her face. That's it. I know who she has been reminding me of all this time. There's something about her so reminiscent of Gina. I can't believe I didn't make the connection until now, but they do say mushrooms are the great connectors of the planet – spreading out, electrifying the connections between the dendrites in my brain like mycelium through the earth – fuck. I must be tripping.

"Seriously, dude – you've gone too far, you're going to fall down a rabbit hole and get stuck for hours, but it will feel like years," Henry says.

"I'm just following in your footsteps," I chide. "Initiating a god experience."

"It's not as fun as it sounds," he warns.

"Look – we established a long time ago that the biochemical effects of psilocybin are not harmful to the human brain in these kinds of doses."

Henry is not convinced. "Maybe your brain won't suffer any long-term effects, but mushrooms can be pretty freaky in high doses."

"Mmm hmm," Moana makes agreeing noises. "Lots of death imagery, like Dia de los Muertos – all those skulls."

"Incidentally the Mexican mushroom cults took psilocybin fungus for hundreds, maybe thousands of years," Henry says "until the Spanish brutally destroyed them."

"Such a tragic awful thing – why is history full of such cruelty?" Moana says, covering her face with her hands.

Moana looks so gentle now, not at all like the woman I used to know – Gina, who wore the same kind of drippy clothes and collected crystals and terrified the living shit out of me. I hadn't even thought of her for years until just a moment ago. And with that I push her out of my mind. Goodbye.

"Is a coincidence, that those kinds of visuals are so common?" Moana asks, "At least that's what I got the time I took them when I was already tired," Moana continues, "Hours and hours of closed-eye visuals of fluro coloured death, flowers, decay and dying. I thought it might have been related to the season, you know, how mushrooms appear in the autumn – the season of dying and letting go."

"I'm sure Isaac wouldn't believe in anything as frivolous as autumn." Henry elbows me in the ribs.

"Too right," I say, shoving him away. "Down with your make-believe seasons. I support more accurate science-based observations of the actual climate, weather and temperature – especially considering climate change has mixed everything up."

Moana shrugs. "At least he believes in climate change."

"In this vast world, Moana, there are bound to be at least a handful of things that you and I can both agree on." I give her a pointed look. She turns away.

"Isaac," Moana responds cheerfully, "A handful is such an imprecise measurement! What has got into you?"

"Well look at you two – actually agreeing on something and being nice to each other." Ethel chimes in. "Will wonders ever cease?"

My heart is racing faster. I'm not sure if it is the situation with Ethel, or the mushrooms – but surely they won't have kicked in quite so much yet? I feel a wave of nausea, the pang of stomach cramps. This might be from the first dose still. I need to lie down. I clear a spot on the picnic blanket and recline.

"Are you okay?" Ethel asks, concern taints her voice.

"I'm fine."

"Did we tease you too much?"

"Never enough."

"Okay." Ethel's voice sounds distant now. "I'm going for a walk," she informs me, seems to melt away into the night.

ETHEL

Finally, I am alone again. It is quiet, save the waves' ceaseless crashing. The wind brings the salty smell of sea and the sweet scent of gorse flowers from the far hills. I crouch down and run my fingers through the sand, lifting up a handful and watching it sparkle. It still amazes me that sand is what glass is made from – that this opaque grit can be melted down into something clear enough to see through... to look out at the world. Each grain in my hand is a diamond in the moonlight: unpredictable, impossible. Like-life.

Moana insists that everything can be healed. She is wrong. Bruises heal, cuts usually do, if they don't fester. Sometimes they leave a scar, but some things are too deep. Too intrinsically horrible. Some kind of deformities are forever. Some things can never heal. We just learn to live with them, or learn to avoid them. Avoidance is a totally legitimate and helpful coping mechanism. Moana has spent so long learning to heal herself from her trauma that it has become a kind of religion to her.

I let the sand fall onto my thighs, my toes. Imperfect. Chaotic. Uncontrollable.

Lots of people are scared that there's something wrong with them, that deep down they are bad – just a lump of dirty coal instead of a soul. For them it is a fear they carry and run from, simultaneously, like a shadow.

For me it is just something I know: there is something so seriously wrong with me, that I should never have been born. It is not just a fear. It is unchangeably true, a physical reality. A fact.

I don't even have to fear it. There is no running. The only thing I fear is that someone will find out.

I met a psychic once at a festival, with long dark hair and a shrivelled stump for a right arm. He saw it. He saw right through me – right through to the back room of my mind and he understood.

"There's something wrong," he said.

"I know,"

"You know," he said, "they are always going on about invisible pathos these days, invisible illness blah blah – and how hard it is when no one believes you, but fuck, when it's visible, you can't hide it. It's right there." He looked down at his wretched arm, "every moment, every wayward glance." He caught me looking.

"So I'm telling you," he said, "you're lucky. You have the choice to hide."

I left his camp shaken - exposed – because of all the people in the world, he *knew*. I brace myself as another memory from that festival emerges.

I MEANDER *through the people and tents along what might be described as a pathway if only it had more distinction. The tents open out into a kind of marketplace. I don't see her until she grabs my arm. Bloodshot eyes. My mother's eyes.*

"Please?"

I freeze. Her rainbow shawl slips over her face.

"Can you help me?"

No. I can't even breathe. My insides scream out. I look down. Her feet are scratched and bleeding. So are her forearms. I see the needle tracks. The itches. No. A flashback of my mother in the bathroom, screaming. Scratching herself into any other possible reality but here. I want to disappear.

"My muffin's gone. Muffy muffy..." She gazes at the sky then back to me. Agony.

"Are you alright?"

I want to ask the sensible question in a calm voice, but it's not my voice. It's the security guard's. They lead the woman away towards the care tent.

"Not in the tail feathers. You don' understand. Nada! nada!" her voice trails off.

I find my breath. Maybe it's been here all along. I need to lie down.

I go back to the tent, close my eyes and listen as my friends speak around me. My mind is so full of movement that I can barely recognise whose voice is whose. The acid must be kicking in.

I could draw you the diagram

Fuck off with your diagrams.

It's interesting like you said, when you finally lost interest in Chelsea, after the break up, and it had the opposite effect on her — it's like a pushing-pulling dynamic- if somebody lets go of the rope, it goes the other way — it's like Buckminster fuller

It's like everything in life comes back to

Buckminster Fuller

Cycles and stuff

With architecture you have tensions — if you have a piece of rope, you're pulling the whole thing towards you but if you're pushing it just coils up. If you're pushing a pile of bricks, you're pushing the whole thing, but if you're pulling, you're just pulling one brick.

I wish I had my note book.

One of my favourite philosophies is like — I finish a chapter of the book of my life — like the high school chapter.

The nectarines are amazing. Have some fruit

Fruit? Don't be ridiculous

It's the most amazing fruit I've ever eaten. Try some

It's so good – like the perfect woman – squirting on you as you bite into her flesh

That's beautiful Isaac

But how better to describe a peach – it was a metaphor

These are so good

That's the thing with fruit – it seems like such a commitment but then it's really good

Do you want an apricot?

I don't think you could commit to an apricot

But you just said..

Yes but apricots – they're either great or they get all mushy.

I agree a bad apricot is awful and a good apricot is...

Good grief – you're actually pulling a science out of epitomising out of the art of the enjoying an apricot.

No – this is the perfect apricot.

Cherries are the most erotic fruit.

I don't know – oh yeah, I suppose you're right.

Eating cherries is kind of like an orgasm.

Can I have some blueberries? So I can be happy?

Yeah, I don't think you need them though, you look pretty perky.

Your pants match the blueberries and the shade of the mountain.

That's so perfect – and your top is the colour of the forest.

The colour scheme is amazing...

MOANA

Ethel has left, creating an absence like the dark void between the sea and the sky. I lie back on the blanket and look at the stars. In this heightened state of connection with the universe I see constellation lines mapping out the night sky, I breathe in awe wishing Ethel was here to share this moment.

You know how there are some people that you just click with? Maybe it's a past life thing or maybe you're just on the same wavelength. Who knows? I have always felt a special connection with Ethel, and with Henry, right from the start. We could really understand each other in the way that other people don't. Everything just gelled. They are like family, especially Ethel who practically grew up at my house. We were neighbours first, then buddies who walked to school together, then sisters. I never realised things were so bad for her. Hell, even knowing her as well as I do, it was only last Autumn that Isaac and I found the final piece of the puzzle that made everything else make sense. Despite that, we can't tell her in case we ruin the only good childhood memories she has.

I used to hear the shouting at night, but I didn't think much of it.

It was somewhere else, like the sounds of teenagers walking down the street. It blended into the night. I remember the first time she told me about it. We had just reached our twin letterboxes that always reminded me of white doves, the way they were set into the hedge.

"I DON'T WANNA GO HOME." Ethel looks at the ground.

"Why not?" I'm used to Ethel being the good girl at school. I'm not used to her being like this.

"Mum." A one-word explanation. I don't understand. 'Mum' to me is warm and cuddly and loving. The way Ethel says it is cold, sending shivers up my spine.

"Is she mean to you?" Ethel doesn't say anything. She just stares at the ground. Her dark hair falls over her pale face like she's hiding. Maybe she feels bad about saying anything.

"Come to my house. We can watch The Snorks and eat cookies." Ethel doesn't move so I take her arm and lead her down our driveway.

"Who's this then?" Mum is always cheerful. "Our neighbour! Lovely to finally meet you, dear. Take your shoes off, will you?" Ethel follows instructions obediently. I put my bag away and go to the toilet and by the time I'm back Ethel is happily eating cookies at the kitchen counter, chatting away to Mum.

MUM HAS ALWAYS BEEN magic like that. Part of me was afraid to share her, but I knew that Ethel needed her, needed us. After that day Ethel was often at our house after school. I could tell she dreaded going home. A couple of times her mum would show up, dishevelled on our doorstep; she would drag Ethel away by the arm. At night I listened more carefully for the shouting next door. I crossed my fingers and prayed that she was alright. I would wait until it was quiet. I would wait until I heard the creak of the window opening and the sound of feet on the garden path. I would put my second pillow at the end of my bed, ready for Ethel to top and tail. The first time, she hesitated at my bedroom door. "Come in," my whisper hissed across the room. She obeyed. *Are you okay? Did she hurt you?* Silence. I stopped asking questions.

HENRY

Night has well and truly fallen, as has the thin veil of reality that keeps up illusions of things being separate. I am alone, but I am also part of everything.

I am crouched on a rock overlooking the breaking waves. I press my palms to my eyes and watch the stars. This is one of those moments where time stops.

The air on my skin is perfect. Nothing else exists. Like the first time I met Moana - it's incredibly vivid in my memory. I'm on this rock now but somewhere in the folds of time I'm also studying at Ethel's that night seven years ago. Cramming for a sociology test on the medicalisation of health and illness, kneeling around Eth's coffee table because it's the only table in her flat. She ploughed through the course text while I tried to keep up, typing notes on my laptop.

"BALDNESS IS RE-CONSTRUCTED AS A MEDICAL PROBLEM," Ethel reads.

I hear the latch on the back door through my typing and turn my head toward the kitchen.

"Just Moana," Ethel explains, not lifting her head. I've heard all about

her best friend slash foster sister slash flatmate and I'm curious to match a face to a name.

"I'm home." A wave of emotion seems to wash over me from the direction of the kitchen. I shiver. This just got real. I can't explain why — or the feeling — like I've just snorted a gram of cocaine. Not that I ever touch the stuff. This is the moment I've been waiting for all my life.

I watch her, back turned, in the kitchen as she loads groceries into the cupboards, reaching up on tiptoes to the top shelf. Her dark hair falls in waves down her back over her aqua dress. I haven't seen her face, but I know already... she's the one I've been waiting for.

"I just had the strangest supermarket conversation." She turns and we lock eyes. Hers are lighter than her brown skin suggests, pale greeny blue and sparkling with amusement.

"Oh." She's surprised to see me. "Hi." I wonder if she can feel it too.

I reach out my hand. "Henry." I say, making eye contact as she comes over.

"I'm Moana." There's a moment in which we are both lost in something. Drifting open like foam on the ocean. I know she's there with me. What are these tingles? Then time rears its ugly methodical head again.

"Impotence, Henry," Ethel interrupts. "Did you make a note of that?" I blush. Surely Ethel remembers the lecture notes by heart by now. We don't need to continue going over these issues that have only become medical problems when a suitable drug was invented. I'm clinging to a moment that has already passed.

"Sorry. I don't mean to interrupt your study session." Moana retreats to the kitchen. "Nice to meet you, Henry."

I want to know more. I want to find out about the supermarket conversation and every moment before or since. I want to keep staring into those blue-green eyes, but it's too late. I need to keep pretending that everything is normal. My heart is racing and nothing Ethel says registers, but I type it down anyway, diligently pretending that everything is normal.

It's not until later when Moana comes back out from her bedroom and we are packing up, that I get another chance to be in her presence.

"How are you, Eth?" She puts her hand lovingly on Ethel's arm, not hugging her, which we all know Ethel hates, but showing affection all the same.

"You know," Ethel replies, "you know, busy, the usual."

I love Ethel but I wish she would disappear because the small talk is too much to bear. Moana's voice is musical, deep, and luscious. I close my eyes and listen to her beautiful, soothing voice; to the story of the shop assistant who tried to get her to join a conspiracy theory group.

"Chemtrails?" Ethel blinks in disbelief. "No!"

I stare, transfixed.

"It's all for a giant LCD screen in the sky so that the most powerful people in the world can engineer social control." They both break out in hysterical laughter, Ethel's giggle easily distinguishable from Moana's low chuckle that ascends in a scale to a joyful shriek. My laughter is there too, but I barely hear it.

"They're going to project fake alien space-ships into the sky." She continues. "I can't wait, Eth, it will be just like on Doctor Who."

The laughter subsides and Moana reaches into her bag and digs out a crumpled yellow packet of rollies.

"I'm going out for a smoke."

I have to act!

"I'll join you." I pull a matching packet and filters out of my jacket pocket. My hands are shaking almost too much to roll. The anticipation of a moment alone with this goddess is killing me.

Moana. I roll her name silently around my mouth. It feels good. Moana. The Māori word for ocean.

It happens so fast that I barely register the movement, her head turns towards mine and our eyes lock just as my mouth begins to roll around her name again. I freeze with my mouth in a lopsided O. Her eyes are quizzical. "Out the back?" I try to cover for my awkwardness.

"Yeah." She must think I'm an idiot. Stupid. Stupid. I want to hit myself in the head with my palm but that would just make it worse. So I follow her

silently and sit next to her on the step, answering her questions with one-word answers.

You're at uni with Ethel?

Yes.

How is it?

Okay.

God I hate small talk. The problem is I can't trust myself so speak my mind because all that is going through it is, "you're my soul-mate". I've just met my soulmate. And I'm sitting on the back porch having a cigarette with her.

"You're quiet." Moana judges me. "Ethel said you were a genuine chatterbox." I'm both flattered that Ethel has talked about me and angry that she said anything that could be less than flattering to someone so very important.

"Sorry." I feel terribly apologetic. "I feel a bit strange, actually."

"Rough day." It's not really a question, Moana is just explaining away anything that might be too awkward to talk about. I loosen my tongue and tell her, in great detail about the experimental sci-fi book I'm reading. "The insects live inside the corneas of their eyes."

"Eww!" Moana shields her own eyes from the imaginary threat.

"But they're helpful," I insist. "They let you see in the dark."

"I'd rather bump into things, thanks." She gently taps my knee and laughs, and for a moment, in the wave of intimacy, I feel complete.

My eyes are still buried in my palms, watching the universe. I'm still on this rock. My legs are losing sensation. Where is Moana? The distance between us always aches. Where is everyone? I feel so alone, and I realise I've always been this alone and, simultaneously, that it's an illusion. My body is atoms. I'm high above my life looking down on its insignificance. Everything is everything. Breathe. Where are my cigarettes?

ISAAC

The waves are coming thick and fast now. The nausea and cramps have subsided. I look over to Moana, on the other side of the picnic blanket.

"The substance seems to be having quite an effect on my brain," I inform her, for no apparent reason.

"You always look at everything in such a sterile way. Can't you just admit that mushrooms are mystical?" Moana's tone is accusatory. "South American shamans have been using them for thousands of years."

"If there's anything mystical about mushrooms it's in the mycelium," I assure Moana.

"Mycelium!" Henry's gleeful shriek. "Oh mycelium! The fairy godmother of the planet earth! Without you none of this would be possible!" He hops from rock to rock gesturing wildly at the hillside. "Mycelium! The planet's natural internet, sending messages across vast distances, enriching the earth, making this world liveable for plants who make it liveable for us!"

"Truth from the mouth of a madman," I tell him

"Excuse me, sir." He approaches me. "You're the one who

mentioned the sacred mycelium." He salutes and is off again, satyr-like, skipping down the beach.

Ethel returns, joining the conversation as if she never left. "I love that TED Talk by Paul Stamets."

"It's inspiring," Moana says in the same breath that releases toxic fumes from her cigarette.

"That is the magic of mushrooms – of fungus," I insist. "That a few spores have the capacity to transform petroleum waste into fertile soil."

"If Isaac has a religion it would be micro-organism worship," Ethel chides.

"It would be science," Moana argues. "Scientism: the unreasonable belief that nothing exists beyond what is known and knowable."

"Unreasonable? That's rich coming from you."

"At least I know my beliefs are beliefs – kooky and spiritual as they may seem. I don't need to get fixated on logic or facts."

"Nor do you have the sense to."

"Don't be a snob, Isaac."

"Insults are poor arguments, hippie." A pebble is propelled towards my torso but misses.

"Isaac wouldn't know a mystical experience if it hit him in the face." Somehow Moana thinks this is an insult.

"There's no point is arguing over cosmology, you two. No one is right," Ethel says.

"I beg to differ, Ethel," I assert.

"Of course you do." Ethel and Moana chime simultaneously, forcing us all into fits of laughter.

"Grandpa used to always say 'there's no point changing a pot to a kettle.' Things are as they are." Ethel's voice softens as she speaks of him. Moana and I both stiffen and silence descends. "That's better." Ethel thinks it's her Grandfather's wise words causing us to cease our quarrelling.

"Ethel." Moana's voice is taking on a tone that makes me uncomfortable. "What was he like - your granddad?" Shut up Moana, I'm thinking. Don't go down this road. But her words sound innocent enough. She is working hard to keep suspicion out of her voice.

"He was so kind." Ethel sits down next to Moana and leans back against a rock. We are both trying hard not to ask the question racing through our minds: *did he touch you?* But how could we tarnish those few sweet memories in her otherwise horrendous childhood. "He was so gentle. I don't know how such a nice man had a daughter like my mother." We are silent again, in our unwanted power. We could grant her this knowledge, but not without taking something infinitely more precious. I need to change the subject.

"Henry," I look at him, "tell me, what the point is in taking these substances at all, when we could all be in the comfort of our homes, watching films?"

I know this will get him riled up.

"I can't believe you've even asked me that man, were you not there on all our other profound experiences together?"

"Sure, we've had some good times, but isn't one form of entertainment a substitute for any other?"

"Entertainment?" Moana and Henry both gape at me. Ethel shrugs, she is always on to me. She knows I'm pushing their buttons.

"Dude, if you want entertainment, GFTO – I mean it. This is not casual recreation, this is actual re-creation. Psychedelics are not a cheap evening out. They are not escapist, they are the most powerful transformational tool humanity has ever discovered. Research shows they are massively more effective than the other tools we have in psychiatry – for treating anxiety and depression, coming to terms with dying, obsessive compulsive disorder, eating disorders, addictions to tobacco, and other drugs – hell – they can cure alcoholism."

"Why have you never quit smoking then?" I prod.

"It's a different application," Henry says, "and anyway, I've never tried. In the clinical trials they come in with the intention to quit. They lie down on a couch in a comfy room with an eye mask and someone trained to tell them to relax and let go if they get stressed, and then they just lie there. Whatever is standing in the way of them quitting will come up."

"You're saying it's basically a placebo," I laugh.

"Isaac, these are placebo-controlled trials, with an active placebo which proves to be much less effective. But yes... in a way it is a placebo because it all depends on the mind. It all depends on how people engage with it, on how they use it, on how brave they are to go on the journey. And in some ways, it's the mystical experience."

I laugh.

"It's fascinating really," Ethel says. "I would love to do a session like that – I bet it's like ten years of therapy in five hours."

"Yes!" Henry crows, he is loving this, "That is exactly what it's like!"

"It's fascinating how people have been using psychedelics for thousands of years..."

"Some people," I interject.

"Well, we may never know how many, or which psychedelics, or when in history, Isaac, because they keep getting supressed by the state or the church or the colonisers like the Aztecs were with mush-rooms." Moana gives me a look that shows she clearly thinks of me as a coloniser.

"Sometimes it was the elite in society taking psychedelics, like the Ancient Greeks with their Eleusinian Mysteries," I'm not sure what I'm arguing here.

"But that was supressed too."

"There's a theory," Henry starts, with a gleam in his eye, "that all our extraordinary evolution as human beings is owed to psychedelics, their mind-manifesting effects..."

"Bullshit!" I call.

"No, listen, hear me out! Even language – like the way we have these symbols, these sounds that are abstract and represent other things – there's a theory it's from the synaesthesia that psychedelics can bring on."

"Do you mean like seeing sounds as colours?" Ethel asks.

"Exactly – that sort of thing," Henry continues, "It's possible the mushrooms did this to us, for us, or maybe other psychedelics – that they advanced our evolution of consciousness."

"Be off with you," I wave henry away, "Terrence McKenna and his stoned ape theory again – really?"

"It's a distinct possibility, Isaac," Henry says, "but not the only possibility. Psychedelics are not the only way we can have peak experiences. We can climb mountains or have amazing tantric sex or heaps of other things. The brains of experienced meditators look much like those on mushrooms" Henry says.

"What the hell are you talking about?" I ask.

"You know, the ego part of the brain – the posterior-something-cortex – right in the middle? The executive functioning – narrative self – push-pull-addiction-suffering personal identity."

"You mean me?" I wonder.

"It gets temporarily diffused, turned off or deactivated or something when people are tripping."

I ponder this for a while, "So you're saying we are shutting off the main part of the brain"

"Yes," Henry replies.

"Impossible – my brain has never felt finer" I decide.

Henry looks at me, "Exactly, tuning out the part that is your default self opens you up to so much more."

I stare blankly back at him. He has obviously misinterpreted the science again. I'm still very much myself.

PART VII

THE FIRE

HENRY

"It feels like there's a storm coming... that cyclone they were talking about."

"Yeah look at the front that's coming over – it's brooding"

"You guys are tripping – it's a fine night!"

"We're all tripping here."

"I feel like we're in a movie"

"Building suspense... that's one fucking good storm front"

"There is no storm – it's all in your mind."

"A fire?"

"The fire!"

Isaac is obviously tripping. Wasn't this the plan all along? How can we be at a beach in the middle of nowhere without lighting a fire? It's getting to the point in the trip where things are beginning to blur together and I am not sure exact which role is mine to play.

"It's a bit late, isn't it?" Moana asks.

"What do you mean – late?" It sounds absurd.

"Shouldn't we have started this before all the patterns?" She's right, the patterns are everywhere, overlaid on the sand... subtle kaleidoscopic flowers... or were they always there? It doesn't matter for now. The fire is imperative.

"You just go and gather some wood. I'll figure out the logistics." I reassure her.

"Ethel!" Isaac's summons ring down the beach. "We have a MISSION!"

"What?" The distant reply.

"Fetch this man some WOOD!"

The flurry of activity stirs the air. Chaos. I rummage for a lighter in Moana's bag.

"All I can find is sour cherries!" I announce to no one in particular. Everything is absurd already.

"What?"

"Cherries and chocolate!"

"Yes please."

"But where is the lighter?"

"The lighter what?" Ethel asks; she is back carrying a few spindly looking pieces of driftwood.

"The lighter part of the sky is over there?" Moana gestures. They are being silly on purpose. They don't understand the sudden seriousness of my mission.

"Fire! I need fire! Get me a fire device!"

"Here you go." Moana, chewing gum guickly, passes me a small white fire-making cylinder. "Would you like a cigarette as well?" she asks.

I pause, momentarily, to consider this important question. The smacking of my lips informs me something is to be gained. I'm acutely aware of an emotional void that can be filled, however temporarily, with meaningless and destructive consumption. "Yes please."

She rolls me a cigarette. Deftly.

"I'm surprised I can still do this." Moana echoes my thoughts. "I can only roll when I do it automatically – without thinking." ...deeply profound as a metaphor, but I can't explain how.

Isaac and Ethel return with offerings of small bundles of driftwood, which I receive gratefully. Ethel sits on the picnic blanket and drinks mead, which she passes to me, also. I am holding too many things!

"Too many things."

Ethel looks up at me, confused. "Oh", she takes the driftwood and begins arranging it artfully into a pile in the sand.

"Too close!" Isaac tells her. "The blanket will catch fire."

"Blankets are not permanent fixtures, Isaac," Ethel informs him, "they can be moved."

"But they are looking so orderly as they are! Such a wonderful accent to the landscape."

I take a swig of the mead. It's warm and golden down my throat. Mmm. I wipe the drips from the side of my mouth. Moana passes me a cigarette. I pass her the mead. Now I just have a lighter and a smoke. Perfect. I light it and inhale. This gives me a moment of pause to consider further logistics. Isaac and Ethel are balancing sticks of driftwood up against other pieces of driftwood.

"Paper – we need paper!"

"Oh." Everyone is confused and concentrating hard.

"There's the chocolate wrapper," I recall.

"It won't be enough." Moana's voice shows concern. She understands the seriousness.

"Oh, fuck it! We don't *need* a fire!" Isaac crows.

"We don't," Ethel acknowledges, "but it would be nice."

"Nice?" I'm indignant. "It's ESSENTIAL."

"What about that dry grass, up there?" Ethel is the practical one.

"Yes." I scratch my goatee. "Dried grass and chocolate packaging might well work."

"The wood is damp." Ethel reports.

"All of it?"

"No, just some of it."

"Well, let's just use the dry stuff to get it started."

Ethel returns with dry grass, which she stuffs in between the wonky tripod of dry driftwood. I struggle with the lighter. Moana holds up her sarong as a windbreak.

Ignition.

We stuff more dry grass in, along with the twigs and leaves from an old fallen branch of pohutukawa. This is working.

Warmth.

Perfection.

Our faces reflect the flames around out primal centrepiece.

Everything is wonderful.

I'm sitting around the fire with some of the most amazing people I know.

"You're my best friends in the world. Well, you and Tanya and Elena, but Tanya is back in Iceland and Elena, not that she was ever into psychedelics anyway, is busy being a parent."

"I don't ever want to be a parent," Ethel says

"Doesn't everyone say that and then change their mind? I ask.

"I won't"

"What if Isaac wants kids one day – not that that's a good idea," I tease.

"He can find some other way to have them. I'm not his baby-making factory." Ethel folds her arms.

Isaac and Moana both look uncomfortable.

"What's up with you two?" I ask.

"I need to take a piss" Isaac says and takes off. Moana remains silent.

I look back at the fire. Ahh...

A sense of accomplishment.

I have achieved my goals.

And yet...

Undercurrents...

interrupt the red hot victory.

I close my eyes against the flames, but their light remains

I look around at my friends. Isaac has returned from relieving his tiny bladder.

And then it hits me.

"Obviously we were all together before – in a tribe, in a past life."

"Obviously..." Isaac says, "you're tripping."

"That is already evident. And I wouldn't expect you to understand, anyway – you were the village clown!"

"Village idiot, more like," Moana adds.

"I think you'll find the technical term is 'village genius'," Isaac says.

"Ethel was the wise one," Moana argues, looking over at Ethel.

Ethel shrugs.

"I believe you Henry," Moana continues, reaching out to touch my face. "We've known each other over many lives."

I nod, and close my eyes again, swept up in the deepest wave of love I've ever felt in my life. It carries me, far and wide, across the landscapes, high above the land, back through space and time, and our many, many lives. So many faces. I look around at my friends their features morph and merge, moustaches appear, eye patches, stubble, so many layers, genders, ethnicities, ages. I see Isaac as an old woman who walks with a limp. Ethel as doctor, a shaman, a baby. Moana as my wife, my child, my mother, my twin flame, just as I remember her to be. It's all so bizarrely incestuous, and yet - I breathe deeply - there is nothing wrong.

ISAAC

Henry is warming his hands on the flames. I can almost see the equations jumping around him, the physics of his movement. Fascinating. He speaks: "Beaches, fires and drugs are all liminal things."

"What does liminal even mean?" Moana asks, her movements, her features, refuse to compute into symbols and numbers. She is an aberrant force.

"In between," Ethel translates.

"A beach is between the sea and the land."

"A fire is between whole and burnt."

"The act of taking drugs is transformative."

"Drugs aren't liminal," I correct. "They're material."

"But the act of taking them is," Henry insists. "The experience is."

"They are socially marginal," I concede. "Life is liminal by definition," I reflect.

I feel the least connected to myself in my entire life.

"Everything is in-between something," Moana says. "I used to feel so alone. Now I feel more connected to myself inside a very... liminal... existence."

She lolls back against the sand but keeps talking "I feel the same way about my whole life – it is an in-between."

I quite agree with her.

She's often neither here nor there. Undefined. Liquid. This is not my usual thought process. I hold my hand up toward the flames. The light and warmth seem to emanate through my nervous system. Cells. Blood. Veins. Skin. DNA. Molecules. Atoms.

"Life's not a destination." Henry seems to be continuing the thought processes of my mind out loud, but in a way that I wouldn't think. The drugs must be working.

"It's like school," Moana adds. I see her point. Yes. The drugs are definitely working. "We come here and learn these obscure lessons and grow, then we go home." Henry is babbling complete sense for once.

"We expand – " Moana adds.

"To that place of connectedness," Henry continues.

"Whereas here we are so isolated."

"So alone."

"Everyone's different."

"Everyone's the same."

"Our bodies die, but our essence goes back to the source." Moana hits peak bullshit.

"What is this rubbish?" I interject, "You die – you're dead – that's all."

"You don't really know that either," Moana argues. I feel it again. That flash. I can't put her out of my mind. *Go away Gina. You're not welcome here.* Not anymore. In the back of my mind Terrence laughs, a hollow laugh. I shiver at the memory of my dead friend, at the guilt.

The flames swirl and flicker into geometric patterns. "The visuals are kicking in."

Henry smiles with glee. "Haha. Mine too."

"It's interesting how the brain interprets light in different ways under the influence of psychedelics," I comment.

Moana scoffs at me. "Here we go again." Her face in the firelight reminds me even more of Gina. I shiver despite the warmth and turn away.

Henry laughs, "I'm having all these epiphanies in my head that are too complicated to explain – I want to talk about them but by the time I go to do it they're just gone from my head."

The first time we were here he said much the same thing. "Do you remember that argument we had last time?"

"You mean, when Isaac said things like: 'To my mind quantum physics is more important than emotions." Moana imitates me very badly. I don't have a Tory accent at all.

Henry laughs. "Dude, you do realise that you have some serious emotional problems right?" Henry is always so ripe with rhetorical questions. "I was arguing that love gives you more serotonin and dopamine than quantum physics."

"And I was arguing that the brain chemistry of happiness wasn't high on my list of priorities." I clarify in case I have been misrepresented.

"How about now?" Henry asks.

I look over at Ethel. Her eyes widen. She blushes and looks down.

I recall the conversation, as if watching a play in a theatre in my mind:

Isaac: *"But knowledge is more important. I don't give a damn about happiness."*

Henry: "You're just scared of being happy."

Isaac: "I'd prefer to be content."

Moana: "You need to understand what it means to be human."

Henry: "It's one of those things. You're one of the most intelligent people I've ever met. I've decided you need to start thinking about other humans. Can you just take rational feedback? The other people around you are the most important people in your life right now. Listen to us."

Moana: "You have to relate to other people to relate to yourself."

Isaac: "You see – it's not myself or other people that I've related to before. It's a set of figures... or... numbers."

Henry: "What a peculiar self-deception. It's an interesting place to come from, it makes you different from other people. But if you can't move beyond it, you are limited by it."

Isaac: "It's not moving beyond that, it's moving parallel to it."

Moana: "It's not – it's another dimension."

Isaac: "Who gives a fuck about dimensions?"

Ethel: "You're doing it again! You're not listening. You're just waiting for your turn to speak. You need to actually learn to take in what people say instead of having all these walls to keep you safe."

Isaac: "But say with Buckminster Fuller..."

Ethel: "He came from a different perspective because as a child he couldn't see. You come from a different perspective because as a child you externalised everything."

Isaac: "No – completely remove my childhood thing."

Ethel: "See – you didn't listen to me."

Isaac: "But I've already thought out every possible conversation in my head."

Moana: "But you can't have because you didn't listen."

Isaac: "But I don't care – it's physics."

Moana: "It's not about physics, it's about having a genuine human interaction. It's about connecting with people."

Isaac: "No – the sort of physics that my brain can understand."

Henry: "You can't possibly have computed every possibility for the outcome of the conversation."

Isaac: "No – I did not say that."

Ethel: "Yes you did."

Isaac: "Do you want a bet?"

Henry: "What we have here is a scenario where we all unanimously think that you're incorrect."

Moana: "It's boring – he just keeps saying the same thing all the time."

Ethel: "Your mind does not expand unless it is challenged – so I'm challenging you. That you become less involved in science and more involved with people around you, and say nothing about yourself. You need to think about other people because you'll get so much more fulfilment out of life."

Henry: "The thing is, darling, you actually do have emotions, and you are sensitive. That's why you cling so much to physics – to physical and measurable things – because they're safe."

THE GROUND MIGHT WELL BE GIVING way beneath my feet and the memory continues to play out as if burned into my retinas, our voices mingling, disembodied, it is impossible now to tell who is speaking at any one time. We embark on some kind of debate, just as the flames seem to flicker and rise in competition with each other.

ISAAC: I'm the one who speaks English

HENRY: What? What? That's debatable!

ISAAC: Do you want a debate?

MOANA: You speak Isaacian

ISAAC: Can we have a debate?

HENRY: Okay – our debate will be... the existence of God

. . .

ISAAC: *The complexity of the universe – of life itself – the complexity of*

MOANA: *You hate this argument*

ISAAC: *Shut up – the complexity of, for example – human society*

ETHEL: *A man on a beach happens upon a pocket watch*

ISAAC: *The complexity of a colony of ants, of animals – which are below us of course, for surely we consider ourselves as humans – as sentient beings – to be above other things – do you not find this to be a universal truth? To be able to comprehend ourselves – to be such a marvellous creation of our creator God? Because where could such level of complexity, such a remarkable degree of complexity, come from other than from a creator God?*

HENRY: *So, in response to that very well-put, eloquent example – but what I believe*

ISAAC: *See that is but belief, good sir, but I have true faith.*

HENRY: *What I propense to believe –*

ISAAC: *That is but propensity to believe –*

.   .   .

MOANA: *Shut up.*

HENRY: *Yes, did I interrupt you sir?*

ISAAC: *Continue as you will good sir.*

MOANA: *Fragile masculinity.*

ETHEL: *Fragile reality.*

HENRY: *The reason why God does not exist is because of the fact that if God did exist – who created God? There would have to be a precursor. So the reason why we are who we are – why we exist is natural selection. If a fly were to fall off a tree and had half a wing it would have more of a chance to survive – if it had 51% of a wing it might survive from a higher drop.*

MOANA: *How did it get up there?*

ISAAC: *So does not this wonderfully Darwinian idea imply that God first created the fly so that it might have the chance to replicate its own genetic material so that it might promulgate and have a wing? Do you argue that the universe was created suddenly?*

ETHEL: *I think you two just agreed that there is a God and that God invented the big bang.*

. . .

I CONTINUE, *preaching about the all-loving compassionate God who takes us into heaven most convincingly – for an atheist.*

ETHEL

The heat from the fire is too much for me. I lie back towards the sound of the waves. My head nests into the sand. I will be washing the grains out of my hair for a week but right now I don't care. I close my eyes.

I'M six years old again, looking down that dark hallway towards my bedroom. Gretta's screams pierce the air. Withdrawals, she calls it. For me it means time to hide. The kitchen lights are too bright, but the dark is even scarier. I start to run but she is too fast. I feel the tightness wrap around my waist. I can't breathe. The ground hits me. I might be dying. "You never learn!" her voice is dull now. "You never listen."

"WANT SOME DA-LICIOUS HONEY WINE?" Henry interrupts, jolting my mind back to the present.

Every now and then the flashes appear. *Needles on the bathroom floor. My mother passed out on the couch. The screaming. The violence.* I haven't necessarily forgotten. I just haven't remembered until now. *Is that how supressed memory works?* My brain has done its best to cut itself off from trauma, but it can't seem to remove it entirely, so it is the little things that disappear– the red shoes I wore as a five year old, the polka dot clip I used to wear, the particular instances of Gretta at her worst. When I try to look back to recall, all I have is a blur or tangled ends and achy pain, but then the flashes come all of their own accord.

Sometimes it happens at work when I'm cataloguing books, sometimes it happens while I'm driving. It plays like a film in my head while I struggle to keep my attention on the road. Every time I have to figure out where it fits into my past, like sliding a book back into its place on the shelf. This one would have been just after Grandpa died. That's when things got really bad. Mum didn't want me to care. She pretended nothing had happened. She screamed every time I said his name, every time I cried.

I would lie in my bed, terrified of her, terrified of the dark, and what could be under my bed. Sometimes I was paralysed in fear and pain. Sometimes I would lie there the whole night, wide awake, heart racing. Sometimes I was angry enough, hurt and frustrated enough to run away. I would open my window quietly and make my escape. It was just as terrifying as staying. Sometimes it was even scarier to leave, but once I was over the fence I always felt better. I would open the back door that was left unlocked and creep quietly to Moana's room. Sometimes her mum caught me in the hallway. I'd stand, stunned, until Aunty May cracked one of her famous smiles and ushered me into the kitchen for a hot cocoa. Moana's house was always safe. I never wanted to leave.

I'm both too hot and too cold and everything in between, here with my friends and yet not here at all.

"It's your fault." At six years old I can recognise the smell of cheap whiskey on Gretta's breath that gives away her drunken state. "I could have left. If it wasn't for you. You ruined everything. You disgusting freak." At six years old I'm guilty of everything. That crushing shame, just for being born.

"IF SHE HATED him so much, why didn't she just leave?" Moana asked me once when we were teenagers. It's the question people always ask domestic violence victims. It doesn't make sense from the outside, but nothing with Gretta ever made sense anyway. She only got worse – more and more incoherent – as she sold my grandfather's treasures to pay for her addictions. I hated her because she hated me. There was nothing else between us. She never wanted me and I never wanted her. I learnt early on to cut off everything I didn't want – everything bad. I learnt to protect myself. I suppose that is one thing I can be grateful to my mother for: she taught me to protect myself – from her.

I hear Moana's voice in my head, despite the unusual silence around the fire.

"She couldn't cope, Eth." Moana has always been more compassionate than I am. "That's why she was so awful to you. She didn't know what else to do. I know it's not an excuse, but she was so fucked up – I feel sorry for her."

Moana's heart is too big. It always gets broken. Chelsea trampled all over her generosity, her empathy, her compassion. Chelsea was fucked up just like Gretta. I thought it was the children of addicts who were supposed to form rescuer patterns. Maybe Moana learned to rescue from her mother, or from taking me in over and over, or maybe it's just her nature somehow.

I'm slipping in and out of time and space. I'm twenty-six then six then every moment in between. The fire is too far away. I move closer. Close my eyes into the past.

I'M SIX YEARS OLD. Watching my mother cut mushrooms on the kitchen bench.

"Grandpa says to use a chopping board," I say, although I should know better than to talk to Gretta.

"Well, it's not going to matter much anymore, is it?" She is in a good mood, but I know that can be scarier than a bad mood. Definitely scarier than a low mood when she just stays in bed and I am safe.

"Why won't it matter?" I ask.

Gretta laughs. "Oh. You'll see... you'll see." Her eyes bulge – not happy, but wild. Up, not down.

The mushrooms on the bench are not the usual kind. Not any of the kinds that Grandpa and I gather in the gully behind the park. White and black spots. A liquid like black ink seeps out all over the bench, stains the knife. The smell makes me sick.

I have to lie down now.

I SLIDE BACK into the present, but I'm watching, as if from behind a screen or the projector in the back of my brain. I'm not sure what's real and what's imaginary. Was that memory or a dream? A delusion? Even memories are prone to change as we reflect on them. As Bill Hicks says, we are all the imagination of ourselves. I am watching the others on the picnic blanket as if attending a play.

I am not a participant. I am audience.

Moana: "Didn't Einstein say something about not being able to solve problems from the same level that created them?"

Isaac: "Sure, use a scientist when it suits you."

Moana: "Einstein was spiritual. He believed in deeper meaning and that God does not play dice with the universe."

Isaac: "We all have our faults."

Henry: "Do you ever think about what it is that makes some people more drawn to religion or spirituality than others?"

Moana: "Some people need it more than others. Some people need to believe there is meaning and that some authority figures and scriptures hold the key, and that all our suffering is not in vain."

Henry: "and here we are, opening the door, to genuine mystical experience with the help of a few small fungus fruits... Maybe some people do need religion more than others, maybe it's because their lives have been so painful, but surely there are lots of traumatised people who are atheists."

Moana: "Atheism can be a religion. Fundamentalist beliefs based on conceptions of 'science' and 'certainty'."

Isaac: "By definition it's not a religion, but if you insist, I'd rather have a religion based on logic and reason any day."

Henry: "Is there any point in naming it 'religion' if it's something we all do?"

Moana: "It's a bit like 'culture' or 'society'. It can be useful to name the invisible water that we swim in... It can help us get some perspective."

Isaac: "I beg to differ."

Moana: "That's because you like to use the word 'religion' to discriminate against people who you disagree with."

Isaac: "I think you mean 'whom'."

Moana: "Shut your face."

MOANA

Fire is so good, but too hot. I retreat a few feet back and stretch my feet out.

This is part of my Neptune squaring my Venus in Sagittarius. Neptune dissolving everything he touches... Venus adventurous my goddess-self, my creativity, my muse. I should be making progress as the long transit is getting towards its end. The divine mystic planet, dissolving and enhancing everything relational in me, my patterns in relationships, my surrendering to the will of the other. It started a few years ago during the breakup with Chelsea and I have been tumbled against these rough waves of emotion over and over again ever since.

Can I see myself as whole or have I stopped believing that it's possible?

I need to go deeper.

Deeper

Deeper

Beneath the projections... the evil other. Woman. Black. Gay.

The counter-projections: racist. Sexist. Bigot.

Fear. Terror. Grief. Pain.

Separation and alienation.

These all lie underneath the hate.

My feet sink into the sand. Eyelids close onto darkness.

"It's not recreational," I say, to no one in particular.

"Unless you mean literally," Henry responds, "re-creating ourselves through this psychedelic transformation."

"True!" His words are magic, "RE-CREATING OURSELVES!" With my eyes open I can see it, the transformation we are all going through. Everything.

"Quiet in the cheap seats," Isaac calls out, but we ignore him.

"This is not escapism," I continue.

"No," Henry agrees, "It is hyper-reality."

"Exactly!" I love Henry and how much he understands everything.

There is so much darkness here. Inside. This is a shadow-struggle for illumination. Understanding the self is a long journey into a dark cave. A deep ocean. Astrology is helpful... whether it is 'real' or not – the planets are guides – navigational points in the inner and outer world. I have not found a better symbolic language that so reflects – the synchronicity – my life, my journey, my learning.

Feet are grounding.

I need grounding.

I lie back and so does Henry. We look up at the ACTUAL stars. I spend so long thinking about the stars, the movement of the planets, looking at astrological charts, I forget how much I can see just from looking up.

"There's Mars!" I say.

"Where?" Henry asks.

I point out, towards the horizon, the small orange dot that is the war god.

"Mars is in Scorpio,"

"What does that mean?"

"He's fighting a battle in the underworld, for truth and life and death, for transformation."

"Woooow!" Henry says, and I can tell he can see my words in some way, see the truth of them. With my eyes closed I see ancient civilisations, with my eyes open I can see the constellations, but they all spread out and entangle like a matrix in the sky.

"Did Māori people have astrology too?" Henry asks. "Did they have the same associations for Mars?"

"It's hard to tell, because so much knowledge has been lost. I think Mars is Matawhero, because of its red face, and the god of war is Tumatauenga, so that's different."

"What about the other planets?" Henry asks, and I wish I knew more about my own cultural heritage.

"I think Mercury had lots of names, some represented darkness and evil and others represented peace and light."

"Typical Mercury for having so many names!" Henry says, "So mercurial!"

"And Venus had a different name when she appeared as the morning star compared to as the evening star."

"That makes sense."

I wish it did. I need to connect up the planets with mythology – with storytelling.

"Do you think the planets are avatars for the parts of our minds?" I love Henry's random thoughts.

"Not just your mind – your *self* I say.

"Okay – if you insist."

"I do"

"So what is the moon?"

"Your inner child – your emotional self. The mother – nurture, the vulnerable tender part of you. It reflects emotions – water – tides."

"Right – tides – that makes sense." He seems to be moving closer to me. Should I move further away?

"Yes. I told you it does."

"Okay... so the sun?" Henry reaches up into the air, towards an invisible Sun.

"They sun is your centre – your psyche. So when people say your 'star sign' – you – well, you're a Sagittarius because the Sun was in Sag when you were born."

"Wasn't everything?" Henry asks, just as I begin to shuffle away from him and the intensity of the conversation.

"Of course not. Remember, we looked it up. The moon is in Aries. Your ascendant is Gemini, just like your Sun."

"So that's my ass- end.."

"Ascendant."

"What's does that mean?"

"The ascendant is where the horizon is rising – so you were born near sunrise. It represents the outer layer of you – it's what people see when they first meet you – how you meet the world."

"My mask." He puts his hands over his face.

"If you like – but it's part of you."

"The shallow part."

"Hey – people are always so dismissive of the surface, but it's just as important as depth. Skin is an important organ too. As necessary as the liver or heart. The shallow part of the sea is just as important as the depths."

I prop myself up and look out towards the ocean. I watch the surface of the water, reflecting patterns. Nature is talking to us, showing us her magnificent beauty. The feelings well up and overwhelm me.

"But don't we always look for meaning in things." Henry is giving me that look again, like he wants to dive into me and lose himself. I pull back.

"Jupiter." I say, interrupting his daydream that I don't want to be involved in. "Jupiter is jovial – full, generous. Jupiter is the party planet. Ancient cultures associated him with good luck and bounty."

"Sounds like my kind of guy."

"Jupiter transits are pretty awesome"

"Sounds pretty magical to me."

"Oh, it is."

"And who else is there... out there?" Henry gestures to the sky.

"Saturn." Saturn makes me think of Chelsea and all the awful shit I went through with her.

"Saturn is such a pretty planet with all those rings."

"Saturn can be horrible." I insist.

"Don't be so mean."

"No – it's true – it's like... have you heard of a Saturn return?"

"Isn't that supposed to be happening... oh about now?"

"To you, yeah, you're 28. It's usually around 28 or 29 that Saturn gets back to where it was when you were born."

"What should I expect?"

"Hard learning."

"Sounds terrible."

"Only if you resist and refuse to do the work."

"RESISTANCE IS FUTILE"

"Exactly – Saturn is like a harsh school mistress – the Devil masked as an old man masked as the Devil..."

"That is giving me some trippy visuals."

"But ultimately good."

"Really?"

"I think so – Saturn is the restructuring – the pruning back of your life, the painful challenges that are ultimately rewarding."

"Hard things."

"Yes – and Saturn is symbolic of hard things – shells – bones – stones – limitations – rules."

"No pain no gain."

"Sure."

FIRST ENCOUNTERS

ISAAC

"Ethel is like a sofa." I lean against her legs, reclining, one side warmed nicely by the fire while the other cools in the breeze.

"Excuse me?" I can tell from her voice that she's using her 'not impressed' expression. She nudges me forward, but I collapse back into the same position.

"Very vell, Misteur Isaac," Henry puts on an atrocious Freud impersonation. "Tell me about zour childhood…"

"I was an only child of busy parents. Next." I don't have time for this.

"How about," Moana interjects, "…you tell us about your first ever trip."

"Hah!" My mind leaps back to the memory. "Well, of course, it was Henry's first trip as well."

"Indeed," Henry agrees.

"We must have been, what? Seventeen? Eighteen?"

"You were eighteen. I was seventeen," Henry specifies.

"Right… and the cactus was about the same age!"

"Cactus, eh?"

"Yeah. Good old Saint Pedro."

"We didn't know anyone with drugs other than weed," Henry explains.

"Henry was in his Castaneda phase," I elaborate.

"Yeah, I read all those books about peyote and vision quests and stuff."

"Of course, I didn't believe in any of that." I clarify. "I simply wanted to experiment with a relatively safe substance, to see how it might work on my magnificent brain."

"Yeah, yeah."

"How did you even find it?" Moana asked.

"Well, I had seen them before. Terrence had a little one in his bedroom, but they need to be quite big to harvest."

"Yeah."

"So we went out to my Grandfather's farm one day. Isaac drove us out. I wanted to pick up some clothes I left there. We drove the back way. I was looking out the window over the hills, and I saw it – we hit the motherlode! This cactus – it was massive, and I could just tell it was Saint Pedro. You know? The same way you recognise people. It was out the back of a farmhouse."

"So you stole it?"

"That's right – well, just some of it. We came back at night."

"Then what?"

"We cooked it up and drank the putrid slime." Henry makes a gagging gesture.

"Did you remove the spines and stuff?"

"We asked the internet what to do," Henry says.

"We peeled off the clear layer and just took the outer part," I explain.

"It was so gross." Henry is not exaggerating.

"And what was it like?" Ethel asks.

"It seemed to increase my concentration. I became more aware of physics."

"*You* would." Moana throws her jumper in my direction, as if my precise description is sacrilege – logic violating her spiritual sacrament.

HENRY

"Honestly, Isaac, you behaved more like a depraved lunatic than someone with sharper concentration."

"You assume that's not my natural state? How naïve of you, sir."

"So, what was it like, for you Henry?" Moana asks "...your first trip?"

She wants me to fill in blanks that even I don't completely understand. It's an excited blur in my young adulthood, an awakening into psychonautic exploration of the deep space of the psyche.

"We went back to the farm."

"Didn't your Grandad notice you were brewing up some weird slimy green stuff then acting crazy?"

"He wasn't there. He was... well he was here, actually. My aunty had brought him to Atamarie Bay for the weekend."

" – Hah wow," Moana says.

"It seems like a strange coincidence but it's not really. I just somehow forgot that this is my family holiday spot. Everything is too shimmery to be part of the default world right now. We might as well be floating in space."

"It is shimmery... and slidy." Moana agrees, solemnly. We crack up again and our laughter adds to the shimmer.

"So you had the farm to yourselves?" Ethel inquires, as if this is some kind of criminal investigation.

"Pretty much. Grandad had retired and his workers were running things. I think they were at home in the little farmhouse, down the driveway... but effectively, we were alone."

"Henry wanted to make it into a kind of ceremony. He tried to get me to meditate." Isaac sounds like a sulky child.

"There, there." Ethel pats his arm.

"Sure, but then we actually tried to drink the stuff and all ceremony went out the window. Yuck!" I was so torn between this sacred journey and the practicality of downing the disgusting sludge. "We tried to mix it with juice but that just increased the volume of incredibly bitter slime!"

"Seriously – it's the texture of snot, and the worst kind of bitter you can imagine."

"It felt like my body was rejecting the toxins. I mean... we put toxic stuff in our bodies all the time," I inhale on my cigarette, "but my body was like 'are you fucking kidding me?'"

"But we finally got down enough of it," I say.

"About a foot worth of cactus?" Moana asks.

"Yes – of the most disgusting slime." Isaac shudders, and I can't tell if it's in memory of the experience or if it's related to his distaste for imprecise measurement.

"And then what?"

"And then... we waited."

FINALLY IT'S DOWN. We sit around the farmhouse kitchen table, wooden and scarred from years of family life. I look at the slimy glass in front of me. That last gulp was the worst. I'm queasy as fuck and seriously questioning my life choices – but then I remember Castaneda and vision quests and everything I've been missing out on in my safe suburban life. I needed this. I need this now– to fill the void of meaninglessness caused by consumer capitalism and too much TV. A wave of nausea rises up as I stand up from the kitchen table.

"I think I need to lie down."

"Certainly," Isaac agrees with me.

We move to the lounge and relax on the couches. The cool grey leather is instant release. I close my eyes, just for a minute. I wake up to a banging door. It's blazing hot. I need to chuck. Isaac is already in the bathroom. The sound of his retching is contagious. I bust out of the back door and chunder into an old rose bush. I was expecting this, but in the moment it's horrible... and also dizzyingly satisfying. This is a cleanse. I'm releasing all the toxins – not just from the cactus, but from my body – from my mind! Ye-ah! Get it all out! When there's nothing left to spew I stand up straight and wipe my mouth. The gentle birdsong around me rises up in an orchestra of chaos and glory. The grass and clover are spiral Fibonacci fractals already. The trees are dancing in the breeze to the tune of the universe. Everything is connected in harmony and madness. This is it. I'm home!

"Isaac!"

He emerges from the back porch, letting the screen door slam behind him. "Well... that was revolting, but this is..." he pauses, "pleasant."

"Your word choice is atrocious, man. Can't you hear the music of the spheres? Thousands of luminous spheres! Can't you feel it... this buzzing... this is life..."

"Are you saying you're more aware of $E=mc^2$? It seems improbable. But I certainly feel different."

"Dude, I don't even know why I bother to share epiphanies with you."

"I say – are those ducks over there?" He gestures towards the pond.

I squint into the bright light. "They definitely are."

"Can we go and look at them?!"

"You seem to be unreasonably excited about ducks, man."

"Ducks! Ducks! What's not to be excited about ducks?"

We walk across the long grass. Every atom of my being is connecting *with every part of the universe. Rainbow hieroglyphics dance across the sky. I'm prying open my third eye and I can see EVERYTHING!*

"Ducks!"

"SO ISAAC CARED MORE about ducks than seeing the wonders of the universe?" Moana's eyes are wide in disbelief.

"Ducks *are* one of the wonders of the universe, you hippie!" Isaac laughs.

"Yeah... they were pretty spectacular ducks," I agree. "Very shiny."

"I guess ducks are often taken for granted – like pigeons – because they're so common," Ethel says. We all sigh at this potential injustice, not certain if it's worthy of our concern... but what *is*?

ETHEL

"This is where we are all supposed to tell our first trip stories, then?" I ask. "But you all know mine. It was here, six years ago – boring!"

"Why don't you tell us how you hooked up with Isaac." Henry's voice is thick with schoolyard tension. He adds an "Ooooooh" noise for effect.

"Yeah, how did that even happen?" Moana is quizzical.

"Ah, fine... I will endeavour to explain one of life's great mysteries," I smile.

"But seriously Eth – you never even looked at other guys before," Henry informs me.

"Yeah" Moana adds, "I don't think you ever had a crush in your whole childhood." These are the two experts on my life, obviously, and they are right. I was never interested in anyone before – or at least I never had the chance to be. Whenever I met someone who might have been interested in me I would be overwhelmed with anxiety and shut down. A cute dorky guy in the library asked for my number once and I nearly had a panic attack. These are things I don't talk about, just like I don't ever talk about my father.

"To be honest I thought you were asexual for a long time," Moana admits.

"I may be somewhere on the asexuality spectrum." I'm still not really that interested in sex. I'm not easily aroused. I don't orgasm unless I'm alone.

"So how does someone so... asexual – for lack of a better word, suddenly find themselves in a full-on relationship overnight?"

"It wasn't like that..." Isaac and I didn't even try to have sex until months after.

"Alright, we won't pry" Henry says, "– but what was that first trip like for you? Was it scary?"

"I was terrified."

Mushrooms. I haven't eaten any kind of mushroom for years, not after what they did to my grandfather.

Mushrooms killed my grandfather. What the fuck am I doing? We stand in a circle on the beach at Atamarie bay.

I try to push the memory back down into the room at the back of my mind, to lock the door, but it keeps surfacing, along with the pain, anger, outrage. The police left. They believed my mother; that it was an accident, that she had made a mistake, that death caps looked a lot like the edible field mushrooms our family had always foraged for. She knew damn well. But no one listens to children, so I didn't say anything. That is what I told myself. I was scared that telling the truth would make things worse. My mother had been so kind in the days following my grandfather's death. It wasn't until the police left and the funeral was over that everything fell apart.

Henry hands me some dry shrivelled brown things and some chocolate and instead of freezing, instead of running away, I stand my ground against anxiety. This has gone far enough. I need more room to breathe in my life. These are different mushrooms, I remind myself. I stand back and watch the others chew, their expressions are varied and changing, but it doesn't look too bad. I put the lumpy things into my mouth and gag. There is an acrid taste, but I am committed. I have to get them down. They are so chewy – unreasonably so. I remember the chocolate and put that in my mouth too. It seems to lubricate them and mask the flavour. Pretty soon I've got the whole thing down, but I feel sick. This was a big mistake, but I can't tell the others. I can't ruin their night by freaking out, so I resort to my usual defence mechanism. I crawl deep inside myself. I'm huddling under the counter in the library that is my mind and no one can reach me here. I sit down on a rock and wrap a blanket around my shoulders. The others are exploring the beach, smoking cigarettes, drinking mead, chatting. I'm just sitting here. Not alone but isolated. I respond to their questions automatically. Fortunately, there's nothing too complicated or demanding. I will wait this out. In a few hours I will be sober, and I can go back to my normal life.

I see something glimmering out of the corner of my eye and turn to see the moon rising on the horizon. Silver-gold water. Patterns too complex to be real. Something is tingling inside me. Something is loosening. A rising feeling... joy. I am lighter. I am here.

"Ethel?" It's an unfamiliar voice. Isaac. My heart races. Here comes the anxiety again.

"Yes?" The automatic response.

"You seem to be sitting here, alone on a rock."

"Your observation is accurate."

"Haha – yes. I mean... how is that for you?"

I reflect on this. "It's quite nice, actually." I'm surprised by how nice it is, how relaxed I feel, now that the stomach cramps that Henry warned me about have subsided.

"May I sit with you?" My automatic response is to pull away. Of course he can sit where he wants, but I am quite happy alone.

"If you want."

"But – do you mind? I don't want to disturb you if you're enjoying being alone... oh – I guess I already am. Sorry. I can go away." His fumbling words are endearing.

"No, it's fine, you can sit here." I gesture to the next rock. He sits down. "Thank you for being so considerate."

"It's nothing, really. I'm trying not to be a dick. It's apparently a problem I have, as Henry keeps pointing out."

"Haha – I appreciate Henry's bluntness."

"As do I."

We sit in silence for a moment.

"So, what are we doing here?" Isaac asks.

"I'm watching the water. It shimmers."

"So it does."

"I wonder if it's normally so... graceful..."

"It is rather aesthetically pleasing."

We continue to sit, for what feels like a peaceful eternity. Isaac shivers.

"You're cold."

"It's fine – really."

"Here – " I hand him a corner of the blanket I'm wrapped in.

"No – it's fine, you don't have to. Don't worry about me."

"It's no trouble. This blanket is massive."

"Oh, okay." He moves closer, so that we are almost touching, wrapped in the blanket.

"It's nice sitting with you."

"It is." I'm surprised. I hardly know him, but it's fine.

I reach forward for my water bottle. My arm accidentally brushes his leg. This intimacy would normally freak me out, but it feels good. We sit here, for what seems like hours that fly by in seconds. I really can't tell. We talk about life and philosophy and music and books and science. We talk as if we are old friends, as if we've known each other forever.

I enjoy the sounds of the sea, the sensations of the comforting blanket, the pleasant shiver of cool breeze.

Our shoulders occasionally touch, and every time they do electricity seems to pass over me. What is this? Maybe some kind of neurotransmitter release? I wish I could understand my own body. It is overwhelming... but good. I lean into Isaac and he puts his arm around me. We seem to melt *together into some kind of multiple personality organism... or maybe we temporarily share the same mind... everything is crumbling beautifully, and shimmering, stunning.*

Moana and Henry emerge from the shadows.

"Isaac!" They can hardly see. "Where's Ethel?"

"Here." I wave, from under the blanket.

"WHAT?!"

MOANA

"Alright, Moana – it's your turn."

"Turn?"

"Tell us your first trip story."

"Okay... I was sixteen."

"You rebel."

"No." I look down at my hands. Everything was so dark and blurred back then. I hadn't been able to function. I was so heavy. There was so much pain. "It wasn't about that."

"What then?"

"I was depressed I guess."

"And you thought dropping some mushrooms would solve all your problems."

"Yes... no. It was acid and I didn't have high expectations... only, Johanna's brother seemed to think it was the cure to everything."

"I don't think I ever met Johanna's brother."

"You were always at the library, Eth. You never hung out with us." I feel Ethel stiffen beside me, but she knows it's not the right time to talk about what happened to me. I know she has always carried that guilt – always at the library even when I needed her most. She doesn't know that I'm more worried about her than she is about me. She keeps her voice casual despite the tension.

"I had study to do. Besides, I didn't like getting stoned or wasting time."

"Fair enough."

"Johanna's brother, Kyle. He seemed to think acid was the cure for depression. He could tell there was something wrong with me. He told me about some experiments they did in the '60s or whatever."

"Oh yeah," says Henry, "in the 50s and 60s scientists thought psychedelics were miracle drugs, before the moral panic set in – I mean Hoffman discovering LSD basically led to modern neuro-science."

"Kyle was a big fan of Timothy Leary and had all these old records of him talking... Anyway," I continue "I was kind of inter-ested, but I was also scared."

"So you took it at a party?" Henry asks.

"Yeah, that was stupid," I admit.

"The music's too loud," I try to tell Johanna, but she can't hear be over the blasting punk rock. Johanna has propped herself up against the wall in the kitchen, wearing a too-tight black dress, red lipstick, dark eyeliner and fishnets. Her long, dark hair falls over her face making her look younger than she actually is. I'm not dressed up at all, in my loose grey top that hides the shape of my body. I'm wearing a hoodie even though it's not cold. Johanna tried, unsuccessfully, to get me to wear makeup. She's staring across the room at Kyle's friend, Tai. She has a major crush on him.

"Huh?"

"Never mind."

I go to her room and lie down on the bed. Her posters of Korn and Rage Against the Machine loom over me. I can't feel anything yet, or can I? Just a slight tingle in my spine, but that could be excitement, or fear. Am I going to die? What have I done? This is horrible. The music is too jarring... too angry. Everything inside me screams. I'm angry... about what happened? For the last six months I have just felt numb. I know there's pain underneath that. The numbness is a kind of mask, protection from trauma. I feel it slipping sometimes and the anguish rises up. I just want to die. I can't deal with this pain. But here it is. I bury my face in Johanna's pillow and let emotion pour out in a low moan, grateful no one can hear me above the party noise. This is all wrong. I should have stayed home, but I was hoping there was a magic pill that would take this pain away... like the little piece of paper I held between my upper lip and gum an hour ago. Nothing has changed... but my heart is beating fast. My body is vibrating. Somewhere inside me cogs are turning. A drawbridge is opening. I can't bear it. More pain. No. Blind rage. HOW COULD THIS HAVE HAPPENED TO ME? I see his face behind closed eyes. This demon. Sweating and hairy. Revolting. I want to strangle him, but it's too late. There will be no justice here.

I hear the sound of the door bringing louder music and light into the room.

"There you are!"

"I thought she would still be here."

Johanna and Kyle come in, close the door and sit by the bed.

"Sorry it's so loud." Kyle sounds a bit drunk. Maybe he is. "You okay in here?"

I don't say anything. I'm too far away, buried under the weight of all this pain and anger.

"Is she asleep?"

"No way. Just stay with her. She needs you."

"Seriously?"

"She's your friend. You've gotta be there for your friends."

"Are you okay, Moana?"

I murmur, but I don't know if I'm saying yes or no.

"Moana. You're doing great, okay?"

I turn my head to look at Kyle. Really?

"It's like cleaning a dirty oven pan, right? It's gonna seem a lot worse before it gets better."

"Since when do you ever clean?" Johanna asks him.

"I did the dishes at Christmas. It's a good analogy, okay?"

"Sure."

"You start scraping up all this black burnt stuff and grease and it looks like you're just making a mess. It looks a lot worse than when you started. But then, slowly, you get down into all the stuck-on bits and give it a good scrub and change the water – you keep going – and after a while you're sparkling clean – good as new."

"Didn't Mum have to re-wash all those dishes?"

"Yeah, well, I'm not an expert at dishes, alright. You just have to trust me on this."

I nod. What choice do I have?

"You've taken the first step. Now you have to keep going with it. There's no looking back. It's like the Labyrinth movie. Only, the baby you're saving is you – and you are the one saving him too… and you're also David Bowie as the Goblin King. You're in this epic maze inside yourself."

"Woah, that's deep, bro." Johanna punches him in the arm.

As he speaks, I can see all this inside myself. It's true. The baby I am saving is my innocence. I push myself up.

"Okay."

"We're all good?" Kyle asks, and I can smell whiskey on his breath.

"All good."

"Okay. You took it about an hour ago, right, so you should be starting to feel it, you'll be peaking in another hour. STAY TOGETHER. I cannot stress this more. Go for a walk. Hug a fucking tree or something. Be safe. Do whatever makes you feel safe. Play. Have fun. Alright. I have to get back to the party. Take care."

He blows us kisses and leaves the room, closing the door behind him.

"You don't have to stay with me," I tell Johanna

"I know. I want to. It's a dumb party anyway. Tai is hooking up with some girl from his maths class."

"That sucks for you."

"I'll get over it. Anyway, I'm starting to feel too... weird, to be here."

"What do you want to do?"

"We could go for a walk."

"Sure." We are smiling again.

We take a long time to get ready. I have my drink bottle in my backpack, and a notebook and pen, and a bag of gummy bears. Johanna has her handbag with her smokes and her keys and wallet. We decide to roll smokes before we leave the house, while we can still see what we are doing. Then we spend ages thinking about what else we might need.

"Is it cold outside?" Johanna asks me.

"It could be. Take a jacket just in case."

Johanna puts on a long black trench coat. "Too much?"

"You look fine."

"Okay... I feel good."

"Me too." I'm not lying. I swing my arms around – the air feels thick like water, soothing me. I'm floating. This is the first time I've felt good in a long time. "I don't know if it's the drugs just making me artificially happy... I don't really care either way, for now."

"Neither – but maybe it's like Kyle said – it's re-wiring your brain to feel better or think differently or something."

"Maybe."

We are as ready as we'll ever be. We open the door to navigate through lounge and out of the house. Kyle is nowhere in sight. Neither is Tai. No distractions, just a few older kids in the kitchen doing shots and spots: shots of cheap bourbon and spots of hash oil off heated knives. We go out the back door and into the night. The darkness feels so good. We are anonymous.

"Do you think it's okay to walk around at night?"

"It's a pretty safe neighbourhood." We light our smokes and look around at the identical kitset houses with identical palm trees and identical SUVs. We break into laughter.

"It's a suburban paradise."

"Sure is. Which way is the park?"

"This way."

Our footsteps are the only sound in the street. We barely seem to touch the ground. Everything is so light.

"It's like I'm floating." Johanna echoes my thoughts.

"That was so good of Kyle. I really needed that pep talk."

"Yeah, he's a pretty good big brother."

"I bet your parents don't think so."

"Hah – yeah. As if they care. They're too busy working and away on business trips."

"At least he looks out for you."

"Yeah. He tries."

"But?"

"I hate his stupid parties." She sounds so unhappy I instantly pull her into a hug.

"Are you still bummed about Tai?"

"I guess so... but those parties are stupid in general. I feel like a nobody. I feel so young and stupid and... unwelcome in my own home!" She speaks into my shoulder. For a moment I'm lost in the closeness. I wish I could tell Johanna how I feel about her, but I'm pretty sure she's straight. She wants Tai, not me. I release her and we keep walking.

"I don't know if I even like Tai." She's looking down at her platform shoes as we walk. "It's just... I want him to like me."

"You want to feel... wanted."

"Yeah. Pretty lame, eh?"

"Pretty normal, I reckon." I don't feel normal. My body is tingling, vibrating, but it's a good feeling, light, free, easy, the best I've felt in months.

We reach the entry to the path, marked by an engraved wooden sign.

"Paradise Park." She reads the sign.

"Hah – sure is!" My sarcasm echoes over the depressing square of browned grass.

"This is the only park for miles around." Johanna gestures at the surrounding houses that all look the same.

"I guess they make more money out of houses." I shrug.

"Of course. No one makes money out of parks, parks just cost money to mow and stuff."

We walk over to the brand new playground. The painted steel and plastic surfaces sparkle in the orange street light. We automatically claim the swings.

"Moana, I'm so sorry. I know you're going through some stuff. I don't know what it is. I don't need to know. I just want you to know I'm here for y... WOW!"

We both lean back on the swings. Street lights, stars, space... wow.

"Thanks," I say as we come back to earth. I put my feet on the ground, just to make sure it's still there. "It means a lot... even when I don't care about anything and feel numb... even when it doesn't feel like I have friends. I know, on some level that I do, and that you care."

"Are you depressed?"

"I guess."

"What does it feel like?"

"It feels like everything is black and grey, like nothing means anything."

"That sucks."

"I guess."

"So how do you think you can make it better... I mean... with the acid."

"I don't know, but I think I need to lie in the grass." I feel dizzy.

"You read my mind."

"The park is so well-maintained there are no prickles!"

"See, it is paradise! But look some daisies have popped up!"

"Unsightly! Off with their heads! Someone should complain to Council. This lawn needs to be mowed."

The grass around us forms itself into patterns like the ones I made with my Spirograph as a kid... we sprawl out, and roll around, giggling over the lawn and the park and suburbia, which we both secretly suspect to be Hell.

"It is Hell, but life is like Hell, isn't it?"

"Life is hell," I agree. "Not that I believe in Heaven and Hell."

"Why not?"

"Too Christian."

"Yeah." Johanna sighs. "There must be better religions... that aren't just about some dude on a cross and a whole lot of rules."

"There are – like ones with lot of powerful goddesses, and magic instead of prayer."

"Let's do that... let's join them."

"Okay... I think I can... see them."

We look up into the sky. Wisps of clouds rearrange themselves into Celtic knot-work and koru... into...

"I see Thor." Johanna sounds quite sure.

"Where... oh... maybe it's Tangaroa."

"Maybe. I don't think they are gods of the same thing."

"Maybe we are seeing different things."

"Maybe it's not even... real." We both crack up.

"But why is it... why is it I'm seeing this mythology?"

"Maybe it means something," Johanna whispers.

"Something." I roll onto my stomach and close my eyes. My breath is warm. Soothing. "Something." A pinprick of light or hope is fracturing the numbness I feel this wall of protection cracking inside me. Behind it is lava. Hot. Anger. Pain. Shame. I breathe. Breathe through this. Breathe. As next to me, oblivious, Johanna is spieling off everything she sees in the sky.

"Bunnies... just thousands of bunnies... is that mythological? Maybe it's like spring and the Easter bunny... oh... wow... now it's like the cover of a metal album...daggers... lots of daggers. Oh! It's like an epic battle in the sky, between the Norse gods on this side and the... maybe Greek? It's so intense... Oh my God... umm or should I say gods?"

I roll over into a different reality – look at the sky. Nothing at first, then a shimmer. Then I see it. I see everything. All the glorious tragic every-thing... the clouds, glowing orange in the light from the street lamps. They're on fire. The flame transforms into gods and goddesses into battles and flowers and Arabic characters that are unfamiliar and yet unmistak-

able. How is this possible? In the stars behind them I see life – I see evolution unfolding. Everything is just so... big. In this whole vast universe... this thing I have been carrying is so small. I feel it begin to melt away... and instead I'm faced with my own tiny existence against the massiveness of the universe. Am I here to learn? Am I cheating? Whatever it is, this moment feels like fate.

PART IX

THE COVEN

HENRY

Under foot, different textures, sometimes rough and sometimes soft – the grass, the sand, the rocks – myriad experiences – the universe experiencing itself subjectively – myself and my feet – slipping in between the different sensations – like liquid – melting into the grass. Marvellous! Floating – with vague sensations

The world around me is growing, breathing, shimmering with life.

Everything is still the same

everything has changed

because we don't know how to put up boundaries between ourselves

because we merge

because we're so the same

I let go of any thought of worry or loss because I know that things will just be

as they are

with Moana

and if things are meant to happen in a certain way they will and if not

they'll play out in the afterlife because we have that kind of dynamic anyway

but is it just that I'm attached to that thought?

I guess you can't go deep into innerspace without bumping into the divine presence of the universe. You can't delve into psychonautics without exploring cosmology.

I'M in the hypnotherapist's office, chasing my past lives, trying to explain away all this emotional turmoil over Moana. I'm still pursuing that meadow.

"Close your eyes.

Inhale

Release

Relax

And as you breathe

From here on in

Imagine

Relaxation spreading throughout

Your entire body"

Her voice is slow and soothing. She talks me through a relaxation of my whole body, starting with the muscles around my eyes, progressing right through to my toes.

"Deep...

Deep...

Deep...

Relaxation."

By now, I am heavy, my mind is light. I am suspended – in between wake and sleep. Fully aware but not disturbed by the usual idle chatter of my mind.

"In front of you,

You see a staircase

Descending.
You count ten steps.
Leading you deeper into your unconscious mind
Where all your memories
Your soul memories
Are stored
In a moment
I will count to ten
On each count
You will take a step
Deeper
And deeper
Into your unconscious mind
...
One...

"Wow – have you guys looked at the clouds?"

There is a collective sigh as we gaze towards the night sky, lightened by a not-yet-risen moon. I leap from rock to rock with more dexterity than a monkey. I BREATHE as if for the first time. The scene around us is heightened, mystical, glowing, morphing into patterns at the edge of my vision. I reach upwards towards those flowering prisms of cloud... I'm flying... not in a stupid way where I would jump out of a window. Like Bill Hicks says: "Ducks take off from the ground first". I'm not delusional, I'm on fire. But what can I really get out of this situation? I have to make the most of this... where is Moana?

I sail back toward the others; each step is a graceful present-moment reverie. My imprints in the sand tell the world I was here... as though it is sentient. Everything is watching, listening. Everything is meant to be. I am exactly where I need to be in my life. This is awesome.

Moana is lying on the picnic blanket with her palms over her eyes. I keep thinking that I will one day find her in the right moment, but this isn't it.

"When I close my eyes, all I see is skulls and flowers," I say.

"Maybe you're being reincarnated." Isaac jests. He and Ethel are snuggled up a few metres away, by the fire. "Henry, you know all about that."

Somehow his words leave a bitter taste in *my* mouth. I didn't talk to Isaac much about that kind of thing, about how much I needed to believe, about my past life regression experiences. Moana. She was in most of them. My mother. My child. My husband.

*"I*N FRONT OF YOU IS A DOOR.*"*

I see it in front of me in my mind's eye. A big iron door.

A special door.

White light shines through, around the edges. Behind the door is nothingness. The void. I am floating. Suspended in space. The stairs float behind me, between stars.

"It will take you into another time."

I see a clock etched into the door. The hands begin to spin.

"Into another life."

A rush of excitement.

"When you are ready... Step forward and open the door."

I reach for the round rusted iron door handle. Grasp and grapple with it. It turns. Bright light floods over me and through the void.

"Step through the doorway."

I move forward. The darkness falls away under the blaze of brightness. Nothing.

"Look down at your feet."

Feet? I look downwards. I have feet! Big hairy manly feet, clad in the leather strips...

"Describe what you see"

"Sandals." My mouth is so relaxed it's hard for me to speak clearly. I lick my lips.

"And what are you wearing?" I see light brown, coarse, draped fabric, flowing in the breeze.

"Some kind of loosely woven cloth." I clear my throat. "A toga? Something like that?"

"A toga?"

"It's pretty basic. There's a belt. A brown belt."

"What year is it?"

I can't tell.

"Where are you?"

"Somewhere around Greece... the Mediterranean."

"What is your name?"

"Sol."

"Sol."

"Something like that."

Her voice guides me to my home, a shabby stone construction, in between other similar constructions.

"Who lives here with you?"

"My wife, Uri. My baby son, Jed."

"How do you feel about them?"

"Very... warm. I love them."

"Do you recognise them, from this present life."

I take a close look. Yes. Uri is Terrence, my old high school friend. Jed is... Moana!

"What do you do, Sol?"

"I'm a messenger. I travel between the two villages to give news."

I SEE IT ALL, behind closed eyes, like a blurry film playing, vivid colours, uncertainty. She takes me back though this life, consisting mostly of drudgery. So much walking, living, dying.

. . .

"Everything dies..." Moana groans into the backs of her hands.

"It's beautiful and tragic," Says Ethel.

"On the topic of mortality... I have been thinking a lot about death lately..." Isaac begins.

"Even David Bowie died... I thought he was immortal," I say.

"Exactly – if anyone was immortal it was that spacey guy," says Moana.

"What is it you've been thinking, Henry?" Ethel gently touches my sleeve, her voice a touch concerned.

"Well, it's not just Bowie, but he's part of it... we didn't really see him waste away, but some of these people I take care of, they used to be brilliant – There's this one guy, Ted, who was an engineer, he designed electric fences and stuff; and April, she was a professor of English literature. She wrote books. Now she can barely tell her children and grandchildren apart. It is kind of tragic – this wasting away – this reverting to infancy."

"But don't you think they will come back as something else?" Moana asks from behind her palms.

"I would come back as a cat." Ethel yawns. "Cats have the best lives... oh, unless I was a stray. That could be awful."

"In some forms of Zen they don't believe in coming back as animals. Maybe animals have souls – but there is a kind of collective evolutionary process... so that souls are developing and becoming more complex," my words are flowing in a river that I'm surprised makes any sense at all.

"Ah... so we start off as plankton, with itty-bitty souls and then eventually graduate into fruit flies, and so on." Ethel muses. "I can see it all in my mind." Isaac responds with a simple "hah" of contempt.

"But are you saying you don't believe it anymore?" Moana asks. "You used to read all those books about past life regression."

"The thing is..." I lean towards her, "I don't know anymore. I used to be so certain. I guess I still do believe it in a way. It still makes sense. I used to be terrified... I clung to the idea of past lives."

"And you don't now?" she asks, leaning back.

"Now, I feel more detached. I don't really NEED the belief as much."

Isaac applauds, "Bravo! I'm glad you're finally coming to your senses, outgrowing your immature fantasies and such."

I turn away from him and look out towards the sea.

The waves could be dolphins. Unicorns. I watch the froth morph into zillions of possible creatures.

"It's not about fantasy. We are all making meaning from our lives. We don't know anything other than our subjective experiences, you ass." I lean forward and give him a playful shove.

"My experiences tell me to trust science and the physical, measurable world," Isaac says.

"Fair enough. Mine are more interesting, obviously," I assure him.

"What experiences do you have to show anything differently?"

I don't respond because I know what Isaac will say if I tell him about my regression memories. He will call it fantasy. He will say I imagined it to make sense of my life and to fulfil my spiritual wishes... and maybe he's right. I needed reincarnation and deep purpose. Moana understands this. Ethel understands. Isaac doesn't and there's no point in trying to explain.

"Don't you need meaning in your life?" I ask Isaac.

"Ah – that's easy. Ethel is the meaning!" He wraps his arms around her waist.

"So romantic." She nudges him with her elbow.

"But seriously," Isaac continues, "We choose our own meaning."

"Exactly. We create meaning. That is what we do. Human beings are meaning-making animals," I affirm.

"But to assume some kind of purpose outside of that is absurd," says Isaac.

"As is to declare that there definitely isn't," I say.

"Well, there probably isn't."

"That's a bit of a leap of faith, isn't it?" I tease him.

"The thing is," Moana speaks from deep in her flower-skull trance, "that purpose always needs more purpose behind it... so we are here because of the gods or something, but why are they here?" Her voice lilts into a child's question.

"Precisely!"

"Isaac agreeing with Moana – the world has gone mad."

He smiles gingerly at me. " 'Purpose' needs higher and higher objective until you get to..."

"Just coz," Moana suggests.

"Yes," Isaac says. "Just coz it is... Just coz God."

"Just coz learning,' I interject. "– we are the universe experiencing itself subjectively."

"Fragmenting and fragmenting into increasing complexity," Ethel says.

"But what's the point?" Isaac asks.

"The point is the sharp part of the pin," I declare.

"What? Pin?" Isaac looks around, as if expecting something to emerge from the darkness around us.

"The pin that the Angels dance on top of," I say.

"Ah, brilliant!" Isaac says, dusting the sand off his trousers. "That explains everything! Excuse me while I adjust my cosmology!"

ETHEL

"Can you hear that?" Moana asks. Her eyes gleam. She raises her arms.

"What?"

"It sounds like the ocean is chanting."

"Chanting?"

"Isis, Astarte, Diana, Hecate, Demeter, Kahli, Inana." Moana's voice blends and harmonises with the rhythmic waves. I join in, my words brittle and barren compared with Moana's deep resonating voice, are forgiven by the undulating sea. The sound washes over us, through us. We are swept up, lifted, swept away. Our voices stretch out across the horizon. We are connected with everything. We hold hands. We are little girls again. Sisters. Moana is protecting me from danger.

"Is this reminiscent of your witch days?" Henry's voice breaks the spell. I had forgotten he existed. I had forgotten everything, just for a moment, and it was bliss.

"Your what?" Isaac is looking at me in disbelief. I am grounded. Back into reality.

"Hah. In high school we started a coven," I inform him. His mouth is gaping.

"Don't look at me like that. It was fun researching all the pagan mythology."

"Of course, Eth was just in it for the geekery," Moana chides.

"There were only four of us. You, me, Haylee Estley, Johanna Murdock."

"Good witch names," Henry approves.

"Mostly we just wore black and walked around school like we were on *The Craft* or something."

"We did that ritual once – in the graveyard. Remember we had to memorise all those lines from that book?"

It comes back to me;

the dark moonless night,

the rusty chalice,

the cooking wine stolen from Johanna's mum's kitchen,

being interrupted by some guys in hoodies,

running to the neighbouring park to hide.

"How could I forget?" What I don't say is that it was all for Moana. It was all about her facing what had happened to her. It was all for her healing. I can tell she is thinking about it now. Her eyes, downcast, drift out towards the horizon.

"Kids!" Isaac dismisses. "Kids will be kids." I want to correct him. I want to explain but I can't. It's too late anyway. He's gone off to take a piss.

"Have you seen my drink bottle?" Henry has wandered away without waiting for a response, leaving Moana and I alone. Maybe he can sense the tension in the air, maybe he's oblivious. You can never tell with him. Sometimes he's almost psychic, mostly he's in Henry land – floating on clouds or buried in his unrequited romance narrative with Moana. I've wanted to explain it to him so many times in his grief over her consistent rejection.

"Have you ever thought of telling him why men make you feel unsafe?" I've never asked her before.

"It's not that, it's nothing to do with that." Moana is still watching the horizon. "I've never liked men. I've never been in love with a man in my life."

"Maybe you never had the chance."

"Eth. I've had crushes on girls since I was six years old. You're lucky you're like a sister to me – you've escaped my Sapphic obsessions."

"I'm probably not your type, anyway."

Moana shrugs. "It's not just that – it's complicated. You know I don't talk about what happened, not to anyone. You only know because you were there."

"Talking is therapy. Now might be the time to open up."

"Now might be the time to leave me alone."

"As you wish." I push myself up from the boulders, legs cramped and go in search of Isaac. Surely he couldn't still be pissing. He has only been gone minutes, but I can't see him anywhere. I am all alone in the world. Panic tightens in my chest. I take a deep breath and feel a soothing psilocybin wave rolling in. Gloriously soothing. My peace is interrupted by Isaac's familiar voice.

"I just heard a chorus of angels." He emerges from the flax bushes.

"Good piss, then?"

"Amazing."

I see Henry moving back towards the boulders, towards Moana. I guide Isaac to the other end of the beach. Our feet crush thousands of tiny shells that glint in the moonlight.

"Why is nothing ever as pretty when you take it away from the beach?" I ask, holding an iridescent fragment up.

"Because you can't play God and win."

Isaac can be exceptionally poetic in his philosophising. "Everything we touch turns to dust."

I look back towards my friends and wonder if she is telling him her story.

It was the night I was studying late at the library. I had an exam the next day and I was cramming. Moana wanted to go out to a party, and I figured the call was just her trying to convince me to come.

I'VE ALREADY PLAYED out the conversation in my head in which she interrupts my train of thought and unsuccessfully begs me to come, so as soon as I hear my cell ring and see her number I switch the damn thing off.

I CAN'T IMAGINE I will ever regret not taking a call more in my life.

By the time I get home Moana is already in bed. It's not late but I don't give it much thought.

I MUST HAVE THOUGHT something dismissive at the time. I can't remember. What I do remember is the way she looked the next day:

HER EYES,
her tears,
her anger;
her curled up in a little ball.
"Tell the police," I say.
"Things are bad enough already."
Maybe she's right.
I imagine blue uniforms and paperwork; I imagine court.
Everything is horrible.
"I didn't answer my phone." I wasn't here when she needed me most.
"It wouldn't have mattered." Her voice is flat.
Nothing matters.

. . .

NOTHING MATTERS NOW, but this time it's good. I lean in towards Isaac. "God, life is so complicated sometimes. Why can't it always be this simple?"

"It's as simple as you make it, my dear."

I grasp his hand, so warm. We stand close together. Touch is still foreign to me. I never liked to be touched as a child, never even used to let Moana hug me. It has taken me so long to learn that touch is human. Necessary. I never would have learnt that without Isaac, Henry and Moana... without Moana's mum re-parenting me.

"Onward." He pulls me towards the far end of the beach.

"Onward where?"

"Wouldn't you like to know."

"Wouldn't I?"

I shiver in the chill of the night breeze. If only we weren't outside. If only we were in bed, cosy and warm under the blankets. As if in answer to my thoughts Isaac stops and wraps his arms around me. I hold his neck and lean forward to kiss him. I'm lost for a moment in the sensation of lips. Nothing exists in the starry galaxy inside my eyelids, nothing but us. Kissing is definitely something that's grown on me.

"I just wish..."

"This way."

He leads us up, away from the sand, onto a hill. I look back but I can't see the others anymore. I feel dampness between my legs. His hands are inside my jacket and mine are pulling his shirt from his waist, just moments from touching the bare skin of his chest.

"There's no easy way to do this, is there?"

"Allow me." He carefully places his jacket on the ground. "Here." He reaches out to pull me closer. I don't usually like this position, so exposed, so vulnerable; but now it is right. My mouth is over his. My eyes are closed but I can see myself – so many layers of myself. The

183

insecure me, the anxious me, the cold, the lonely, the confident; the me that's full of love, expanding; the masculine me, the cruel me. I shudder. I'm peeling back the layers. I'm safe. This is the terrifying thing about intimacy: it strips you bare.

"You're crying." Isaac's voice says as I simultaneously notice my tears.

"It's okay." It's so much more than that. "It's... wow."

The sensations of psilocybin drift through my body, wonderful, tingly, right to my fingertips. "Wow." I'm swimming in it. My movement slows to take it all in and then I remember what felt so good moments before.

"It's convenient of time to slow down like this," I say to Isaac.

"So considerate."

"I love you." I so rarely say it.

"I know." Isaac's voice is fragile, soft. "I feel it." It's so unlike him to mention feelings. I wonder if it's possible we are feeling the same thing, no longer on our different planets. I wonder if it's possible we've travelled through space and met somewhere in the middle. Floating. Suspended in mid-air.

"Asteroids," I say aloud. It doesn't make sense, but he seems to understand or maybe he doesn't. It doesn't matter. I understand everything. Everything. Everything. I wish I could write it down. Time stops and all that exists is the waves and my breathing. Everything stands still until I feel his hands around my waist, firm, holding, rolling and suddenly we have switched places and he's the one in charge of the movement for a change – faster, faster, aiming for that place that he can never fully reach. The pressure builds and I can feel what he's feeling, or I think I can – the focus, the power, the intensity, the tension, the goal and then the explosion and he collapses onto me. Into me. Through me. We are one being, completely content, just breathing.

Everything is still and silent except the waves. Isaac and I lie together but apart. We have separated like a single cell dividing into two complete, contained objects. Peace. I close my eyes and watch the patterns whirr through my head. I breathe as a wave of bliss comes through me. It's shorter-lived than before. We must be past the peak now. I don't have any sense of time anymore. We may have been out here for hours. I'm surprised the sun hasn't risen, or perhaps it has only been a few minutes since we first started our evening over there on the picnic blankets.

The fire is still burning in the distance. I hear Henry crow from far away. Isaac stirs and I pick myself up and brush the sand off my delicate skin. Re-clothing seems impossible, although I'm not fully undressed. It seems to happen all by itself – I'm fumbling around for what feels like days and then all of a sudden I am whole and clothed again while Isaac remains dormant.

"I need a drink." Do I? I don't know, but it sounds reasonable. I watch Isaac lurch upwards, zipping up his fly. Show off. We hold hands as we walk back along the beach to the others. I feel naked, exposed, as if I've shared my whole life story with him when really hardly anything has been spoken aloud. I'm lighter for having shared, but still weighed down by the burden now burning a hole in my chest, hammering on the door of the locked back room I can't even begin to talk about.

MOANA

I need space to breathe. I need to be alone. I leave the others and the comfortable safe space of the picnic blanket. Rising feels like birthing myself into another world. I don't realise how much I needed to move until I feel the cool of standing and stretching my cramped, creased legs. Thousands of grains falls off my jeans, raining down like water mingling with the sound of the waves. My toes against the dry sand. I walk in the direction of the water, called by soothing music. I climb a boulder – my bare feet connect to its clammy surface – and raise my arms into the thick summer breeze. This is heaven, and yet it drags me into my centre, into my past pain, and bleeds into a moment six years ago. Time has folded in on itself.

"What's the matter?" Henry asks. He hardly knows me, but he can read the pain all over my face. We face the water, toes in the damp sand. The sensation is soothing enough that I let down my guard.

"I guess you could call it trauma – old wounds that never heal – or something like that." I barely know him, yet I trust him.

"You know – you don't have to tell me anything – but I've been reading

about trauma and the brain, since I've been doing this care work. It's fascinating!"

"Oh yes?" I smile at his enthusiasm. "Tell me more."

"One theory is that the brain learns trauma – you know – the neurons connect in a certain way, and every time the pathways are triggered it brings back the feelings of past pain."

"In that case I wish I could unlearn it!"

If only...

I've often wanted to turn back the clock on that night – to leave the house – to get as far away as possible.

I dream about the hallway at my parents' place. The front door. The shadow approaching. RUN. I wake up mid-scream.

"The way your brain works is entirely changeable," Henry insists, moving closer to me. "The neurolinguistic patterns... Honestly all you need to do is change the way the neurons connect – the pathways."

"Is that all?" I ask, my voice flat. If only it was that easy.

"You can do it with various technologies." I giggle at his word choice imagining cyborg computer chips. "It's all about thought patterns." Henry continues, serious despite my laughter. "It's true! You can go deep inside how your brain works and feel the difficult memories and disconnect them and then open up everything else."

I close my eyes. I can see it all. Complex neural networks. Billions of possibilities.

"It's all about how you're connecting with different neurons... you get to this point where you can stop recreating those same brain patterns because you're no longer sending signals down them."

I try to alter the patterns in my brain but all I find is a cavern opening up, a deep well of pain. "But if something's really entrenched," I ask, "with all your brain patterns – is it more difficult to break them?"

"Well, yeah."

"Do you think that doing exercises over and over to change brain patterns would help?" In my mind's eye I'm cutting the cords to the past. Cutting myself off. But still more pain...

"No. Doing the same thing over and over won't help, you need to do something big... stop thinking about them, basically..."

"People with experiences like mine have the idea that going over and over it will process it, but maybe you're actually just reactivating the same patterns?" I haven't told Henry about how the trauma occurred. I don't think I ever will. Only Ethel knows, or can ever know.

"Yes, totally. You need to go to the depth of them, and explore it thoroughly, fully, completely and then say "No, I'm never going to think about it ever again," and stop. You see, you've explored it in every dimension you can – but what happens if you look outside those dimensions and see what there is?"

"We can leave it in the past..." I'm so confused. I can't figure out the paradox – how can I go through it but also change it and also leave it?

"The only thing that matters right now is this moment in time, and whenever you let the past come into that it just interferes," Henry continues. His voice mingles with the waves. "What we need to do is burn the emotional ties to those memories – the memories and the emotion exist in two totally different part of the brain."

I see myself on the beach holding a candle, in my mind is another self on a beach, and in her mind another self – "Like fractals". I say, an image in an image in an image – but none of this makes sense.

"Exactly!" Henry seems to understand – or at least he thinks he does. "Neurological fractals – so you can stand back from it and say yeah that sucks but it's in the past – then your emotions aren't attached to it."

I hear him but it's not that simple. I still feel the pain. It's endless.

"You accept what has happened – then it's sweet."

No. He doesn't understand at all.

I zone out at Henry keeps taking. "People say everything happens for a reason. I don't buy in to that – but it's what you take from that. That's what makes you who you are."

I open my eyes and wonder who that really is.

.   .   .

THE MOMENT FOLDS BACK into now and I know who I really am – in physical form – I am atoms connected with the wind, with the ocean, with the universe. I am now – and always, when I focus on the moment there's uncertain vulnerability – why me? Why now? Why – in all the vastness of everything am I concentrated in this particular body? In this moment?

I breathe in the sea air. I need to touch the water. Once I've made the decision all I need to do is watch my body move to the lip of the bay where countless tiny ripples bloom towards me. My feet sink into the wet sand and I melt along with them. Divine. I need to touch those baby waves. I meet their cool embrace with my toes, pulling my jeans up tight against my calves. So calm. Fresh. I sigh into the dark horizon.

I've come so far since that moment six years ago. I no longer carry that endless pain everywhere I go. It used to feel like a doorway into all the sadness in the world. Now it's just a memory – as Henry said it could be. If I venture down that painful path into memory I know it all comes back as fresh as the day it happened. The smell of beer, the terror... but I have learnt to keep the past at bay so that I'm not so burdened every moment – to clear the way around.

Water washes everything away, but the scars remain – always there – in the past. It doesn't have to be me, now, in this moment. I breathe in deeply, and release... Let go...

HENRY

Moana is alone on the boulders, looking at the sea. She's always looking at the sea.

"What's up?" My voice is casual until I notice her eyes. "What's wrong?"

"I'm going to tell you about the worst night of my life. Not because it means anything, but just because I want to see if it helps."

I feel like I've been waiting for this. Moana is letting me in, she's giving me the final piece of the puzzle.

"I was sixteen. I was at home. Dad was watching rugby in the lounge with his mate, drinking beer. I was going to go to a party so I was wearing my black leather jacket, eyeliner... I don't know. It was a Friday."

Every sentence is making me more and more tense. I wish she would just get on with it.

"Dad went out for more beer. Mum was away at her sister's, the boys were in bed. I was just leaving my bedroom. I was in the hall."

Moana breaks down I can already see the whole thing: her dad's friend leering, grabbing her, dragging her. I can smell his beer breath.

Moana's tears soak through my t-shirt, as I hold her.

"Did you tell anyone? The police?"

"Just Ethel."

"Why?"

"Dad would have killed him – his best friend! I didn't want Dad to go to jail. I didn't want to make it any worse."

"So you just kept it inside."

My mind is racing through all the possibilities. I'm wondering if this is the reason she doesn't feel the same way about me as I do about her. Typical selfish Henry. It always comes back to me.

"It's not," Moana can read my thoughts. "It's not the reason I don't love men. But maybe..." She pulls away from me and looks into her open palm resting on her lap. "Maybe it's the reason why I don't want to be... close."

I understand now. Moana turns towards me and I wait for her, this time, I don't want to invade her space. I let her hug me, instead, let her cry into my shoulder. I am still for once.

This is the lesson for this life. To hold back. To hold still. My needs aren't as important as respecting her boundaries. I can't help how I feel. I can't help that longing, like the longing for Jed, repeated in so many other close configurations. Maybe if I feel it all... I can release it... I can go through it or let it go through me. I can squeeze every last drop of this longing out... or maybe it's the opposite. I can never tell.

Should I be re-wiring my brain: replacing the painful pathways with positive patterns? Moana has stopped crying but stays close. We are still standing, fused together, when Ethel comes back. We sit there, the three of us, close together, holding hands, arms. We sit there and talk without speaking. We sit and we let go and open up.

"Stars!" Moana says. I don't want to move and leave the moment behind, but my eyes follow her voice upwards.

"Oh my god."

The visuals have kicked in big time. The stars form intricate patterns. Lines of light link them like spider web. I can see constellations in the shape of lotuses. It's as if Hindi gods have been busy re-organising the night sky for our viewing pleasure.

"Do you think they're always like this?" Moana asks. "And maybe we just never notice."

"Maybe we never look."

"Maybe we're usually just too sober to notice."

"Haha! That's the real problem: sobriety."

"Are we even seeing the same thing?"

"I see paisley."

"Lotuses."

"I see the same goddamned '70s wall floral paper pattern that's all over everything else."

"Sounds like the same thing to me."

"Who cares?"

"I don't know." I say with just a touch of longing, still ebbing out. "I like to think we are in the same psychedelic bubble, that everything is consciousness, or that there is a collective consciousness between us."

"It certainly feels like it sometimes," Ethel's disembodied voice says.

"Like when you two read my mind," Moana replies.

"Or when we have an entire conversation and understand each other completely without saying a damn thing," I add.

"Or continue the same running narrative like we're doing just now."

We giggle collectively, a wobbling mass of human.

"Man, I love you guys." And suddenly I'm back in my favourite memory.

.   .   .

I'M LOOKING DOWN at my red high-topped sneakers when the pills kick in. We must have dropped an hour ago. The little grey tablets, stamped with a simple V, slipped down my throat, and the waiting began. Building anticipation. I needed to move. I left Moana sorting out Chelsea's handbag at our campsite under the trees. Ethel was having a nap. She's not into this kind of thing anyway. We practically had to drag her here. I have no idea where Isaac is. I must have been walking around for a while in this hot sun, moving gradually between the beats of different kinds of electronic music.

My shoes are so nice.

Here it comes.

The beginning.

A wave of joy and mild nausea.

I slug from the drink bottle attached by carabiner to my belt. I need more water. I walk further into the meadow. People are spread out, scattered around horizontally, with picnic blankets. A jester in red and gold is juggling on stilts a hundred meters away. It's all so fucking lovely. I have to find my friends to share this with them. I trek back to camp. It's deserted. I grab a blanket and some fresh cherries. What else? A bottle of iced tea. Perfect. Moana appears near her tent with a sun umbrella.

"You read my mind."

"The meadow?"

"Let's go!"

"Where are the others?"

"No idea."

"We don't need them."

Moana raises her arms. She twirls the umbrella with its bright blue vintage flower print.

"I feel so... good!"

"I know."

We are connected in our mutual elation. We glide along the path, between the trees and up into more open spaces and sunshine.

"Bright green."

"So, so bright."

We set up the blanket in the meadow and lounge under the sideways umbrella, hiding from the blazing sun.

"Lovely"

"So, so lovely."

"Doesn't happiness make us sound stupid?!"

"Yes... but it's so... who gives a fuck?"

Moana's smile is so wide, so wonderful... my brain can only translate the beginnings of these feelings into excessively positive superlatives... but that is all that's remotely relative to this stunning present moment.

We sit down on the perfect grass.

"Henry,"

"Yes?"

"You are such a wonderful person."

"You... are"

We lie in this bubble of bliss for what could be minutes or hours... it's impossible to tell because happiness transcends time.

"Isn't is a good thing... to know that it is possible to feel this good... even if it is a chemical thing... isn't it a good thing to have such a good memory in here?" Moana taps her head.

"I think so. All these good brain chemicals are being released. We will have to deal with the come-down later, but for now, it is... like floating on clouds."

"Candyfloss clouds."

"Exactly... and maybe the memory of candyfloss clouds is a good thing."

"It must be." Moana's voice is dead serious.

"If we try, we can take some of this back with us... into reality."

"I hope so... I hate to always feel so sad."

"I hate that you have to do that too."

"I just want to hide under the blankets."

"Yes. Blankets are good."

We continue to lie here, breathing, in bliss... processing through the juxtapositions of sad times in our lives. Our conflicts, our crises, our tensions, our pain... melts away into the picnic blanket, into the grass, into the earth, into the brilliant, warm sunshine.

"Henry,"

"Yes?"

"I've always felt so connected to you... and Ethel... and Mum. You three are the special...est people," she giggles, "in my life."

"Yes... you are so, so special... always." I notice she didn't mention Chelsea. What does that mean?

"Why do you think it is... that some people... some people you just connect with, straight away? It's like magic... like we've known each other before."

"Do you think we have?" Since I met Moana I have been thinking this exact thing, trying to explain away my mad obsession with her, my longing, my overwhelming wells of love, my desperation.

"Yeah, like past life stuff."

"Yeah... reincarnation... that would explain why..." Why I love you so damn much and have done since that moment I first saw you.

"Do you think..." she closes her eyes, then opens them in surprise. "Henry – we were sisters!"

"Sisters."

"Yes... we played together in a meadow"

"Full of wildflowers."

"By a riverbank"

"Yes." I can see it, in my mind. Two little girls in long dresses.

"And our mother, she was sick."

"Yes. They took her away."

"It was so sad."

"It's so amazing that we are both remembering the same thing!"

"Are we? Wow... maybe we are..."

"Who was our father? He had a factory."

"It was so dark."

"Yes. Creepy."

"And you grew up," I say to Moana. "You were older. You got married."

"To that horrible man. He worked with our father. Oh, Henry, I was so sad."

"You were. I couldn't do anything to help you."

"No. I was miserable, so they drugged me. Laudanum."

"I was miserable for you."

"I wish we could have been little girls forever and played in that meadow."

"Me too..."

ISAAC'S COUGHING on the smoke of a spliff jolts me back to the present, dragging me away from warmth of one of the most splendiferous, delightful, elated experiences of my life. I'd never felt such connection. I'd never been so lucid, or so sure about anything before. Lying there with Moana, peering into this distant fold of time together. We described the same reality, the same story. We were there. Later, when I tried to ask her about it, to bring it back, Moana said it was like a wall had come down and she couldn't access it anymore. She could vaguely remember what we'd said, but she couldn't access it. We couldn't go back.

Movement distracts me, it is Moana, passing me the spliff. I reach out but my hands are already full, My water bottle in my right, a lighter and half a cigarette in my left. I'm always holding on to so many things. I work to free myself of these burdens. The drink bottle goes into my backpack so that it isn't lost, the lighter into my pocket, I keep hold of the cigarette to save having to roll another one.

I had never thought much about past lives before then. This was the catalyst for my obsession. I read everything I could find. I practiced meditation and got into similar states. I even went to see the hypnotherapist who specialised in past life regressions. I uncovered at least a dozen different lives, mostly with Moana in them. This was it: the missing link that explained everything else that had never made any sense before... far too mystical for most 'rational' people even to contemplate. It explained why it was so hard to let go of Moana. She was taken away from me – repeatedly – suffering over so many lives. No wonder I felt the connection when I met her, along with all this unresolved pain.

I inhale slowly, careful not to cough, I don't really need this right now, but it's part of the process. I pass it back to Isaac because I know Ethel won't want any.

ISAAC

There's that feeling again. Irritability. The sound of Henry's nasal voice. The proximity of anyone to me. It is the feeling of sand in the bottom of my shoe – both literal and metaphoric. I remove my shoes and shake out the granules.

"Eww!" Moana exclaims as sand is blown into her face by the breeze.

I have to get away from these people. Even Ethel's silent witchy presence is grating.

"I'm off." I cast my shoes aside, and step away from the seething mass of humans into the great beyond.

"Where are you going?"

"Away," I say, simply. I don't dignify them with any other response. Why is everything so awful?

Meaninglessness.

That's what it is. Everything is futile and pointless. The sky looks beautiful. The sea is dazzling. I want it all to burn. What I'm experiencing is not real – it is just the drugs, and yet it is more real than anything else I've ever known, and all I've ever known is my perception. There is only the material, matter, science. There are no mysteries here. I will not allow it.

I walk as far and fast as my legs will take me.

I am hollow.

It hits me.

That is what bothers me about the others.

They are full and I am empty.

Full of themselves, maybe, full of illusions and lies, but full none the less.

I see her, out of the corner of my eye, the corner of my memory. Gina.

I'm running down the beach now. Running away from her, from the past. *It's all your fault.*

I'M SIXTEEN AGAIN, in Art History class.

"Isaac?"

"Yes, Miss Price?"

"I need you to stay behind after class."

IT WASHES BACK NOW. The excitement. Anticipation. Dread.

"IT WAS YOUR FAULT,"

SHE SAID AFTERWARDS.

"WHAT?"

"Terrence."

"What?"

"He trusted you. He loved you. You betrayed him."

No.

Everything about that, about her, was wrong. I know that for a fact... but still.

It's not fair.

PART X

PEAKING

ETHEL

The moon rises – a glowing bulbous egg from a nest of clouds. We gaze at her majesty, her beauty, layer upon layer of gossamer wisps, overlaid: a lady dancing in shawls. Graceful. I close my eyes and she is still there. I open them and she has been replaced by a face that morphs into a spider web, rose, a perfect glowing orb, the light at the end of the tunnel of the sky, it pulls backwards into a cone.

"Holy..." Henry gasps at presumably something different, or the same, or similar enough. I lean on him.

"Yeah," Moana holds my hand. Somehow it's more peaceful without Isaac here. Just the three of us. No conflict. No tension. We breathe in unison, as one organism.

Everything blurs into real-time – we are so close and yet so far. Wave after wave after wave crashes into us, through us, up against the rocks, lapping at the bay. Other peaks meld into this one – visuals – mythology – more paisley - spirals.

This is the part where we come near to the edge. The greatest opportunity. Challenge. Risk. Here we can confront issues, reflect on the past. There is a chance of old harmful patterns broken, of brains altered, of new beginnings.

I cover my eyes
Something nasty is welling up
Bubbling over
Inside
It's a horrible thing
In these dark places
We get tangled up with rot
Blood leaks from the library attic
We decay
Like damp books
Something
So unbearable
The stench
At the core
Of me
In that secret
Locked room
Even the thought —
My heart races
And closer
Something screams
I have to get away

I HAVE TO BREATHE.

"WHERE'S ISAAC?" Henry asks me. People always ask, assuming I have some kind of radar detector... some kind of trace on him.

"No idea."

"He'll be fine." Moana says, as if this was in question. "He's probably just off doing physics somewhere.”

“Give the man some privacy! He needs to physics in peace!” Henry begins leaping around again in a kind of contemporary improv dance. His shoulders arch back and push out.

“What are you doing?” His hands reach outward, graceful fingers, palms inward.

“Tai chi.”

“Whatever. Do you even know Tai chi?”

“Well, if it’s really so intuitive, I can just channel Tai chi.”

“Cultural appropriation!”

“Don’t you start that with me. If it’s offensive, I’ll stop.”

Moana looks around. Nothing seems to be offended. “We don’t know enough to understand anything anyway.”

“Can’t you just call it something else?”

“I name this one ‘Henry on the rocks.’” He balances on a boulder with one foot and reaches his arm backwards to grasp the other foot.

“Why is it,” Moana asks me, “That white people on the internet always get so offended about being told they are being offensive?”

“Are you asking me, as your resident white person?” I say.

“Yes.” Moana grasps her chin and narrows her eyes, “I’m all about token representations.”

“Well, in that case... I guess no one likes to be told they’re wrong, so people get defensive – like they’re somehow being violated – like they’re hurt by the accusation that, in their ignorance, they could be hurting other people.”

“So,” Moana continues her deadpan comedic act, “according to the ways of your people... you should only complain about people behind their backs, so as not to offend?”

“Yes, yes.” I try to talk in an upper-class Brit accent, it sounds dubious, “You see, darling, in polite society no one ever speaks the truth, and therefore...”

“You can’t handle the truth!” Henry interjects.

“Precisely.”

"Pip, pip."

"Of course we must be right," I continue the charade, "as the colonisers... because after all, it's the winners who write history."

"It's such a shame that you're kind of right." Moana is back to her normal voice and genuine intonation.

"Isn't it? People don't seem to see that colonisation is not just some slightly embarrassing thing that happened in the past – "but it wasn't out fault! We weren't even alive' – but that it's actually still happening all the time." I sigh.

"Hey! Not everyone has the privilege of your educational background, lady." Moana smiles at me.

"It's just so... tragic – and that privilege is invisible to the privileged makes it all the more problematic."

"Privilege is invisible to the privileged." Henry repeats and salutes the ocean.

"It's so easy to see when you're less privileged. It's easy to see unfairness when it affects you, and just as easy to dismiss it when we benefit from it – to rationalise the ways that we benefit from the oppression of other people – or to not see it at all."

"Well, that explains a thing or two about Isaac," Moana says.

"Yes. It's the kind of thing that he can't really see. He can't see through his own privilege."

"No one can," Henry says. "All we can ever do is try..."

"I have tried to explain to him," I say, "what it's like to be a woman, and to have your body in constant public speculation, as a sexual object – or a profoundly unsexual object, to be under consistent threat of sexual assault, to be expected to be sexy, and also innocent, not slutty, but motherly, not frumpy, but nurturing and kind and graceful – basically assumed to be a vessel – our purpose: to meet the needs of men and children."

"Or men who refuse to stop acting like Children!" Moana adds. "I don't like how being a woman is always defined in relation to men –

or how we are always talked about as victims either. It's not a bad thing to be a woman."

"No – this is subtle. It's underlying. That's how the patriarchy works." I raise my palms to the sky in exaggerated exasperation. I am performing a parody of the reality that is too heavy and hard to bear seriously. I look at my hands, surrounded in tiny strands of light, interconnected, our DNA defines us, our chromosomes correspond to our gender, or they don't, I can feel mine unravelling, just as time is unravelling, just as reality is, glorious entropy.

"And I bet Isaac explains that there are unrealistic expectations on men's bodies too, that they too are sexualised, and expected to have good pecs." Moana poses like a muscle man.

"You hit the nail on the head. That's exactly what he says!"

"And how do you challenge this?" Moana demands.

"I try to explain that it's different. Sure, men have to deal with some stupid shit as well – that's also part of the problem of patriarchy – we are all victims here. He doesn't get that argument at all."

"He doesn't believe in the patriarchy?" Moana feigns astonishment.

"Of course not. It's not measurable. He calls it a convenient fiction."

"Do you explain it's a useful construct to understand other things, including measurable things?" Henry asks, he's always keen to talk about the patriarchy. This detailed examination of our conversations is getting intense.

"Yes. Something like that. Anyway – where is Isaac?" He has been gone for a while now, or has it just been moments? I scan the beach but see no sign of any other beings.

"He will be fine." Moana repeats.

MOANA

I look up again to Ranginui, darkened in rest. The clouds roll over him slowly, quickly morphing into dolphins, flower bouquets, harakeke... kete and whariki and fate.

This stunning performance may always be here... if only we'd look for it.

I sing into the sea words that come from nowhere, in English, in Māori, she, the shimmering stunning sea, the names of gods and goddesses, Tangaroa, Hine Moana, Poseidon, Neptune.

The surface reflecting silver – an enormous moth's wing.

Goddess moth is guiding me on a journey into herself, into myself, marking out the old wounds and pain like polluted rivers. Colonisation trauma, the trauma of violence on my body, on the planet, on my ancestry, all echoes painfully.

Tobacco was a sacred herb, colonised to kill us. A wise spirit, a tool, used against us.

I cling to this destructive habit, perpetuating trauma in my body.

The smoking that is a temporary fix. The smoking that is holding the pain at bay. Distraction. Leaving black tar in my lungs.

I see it all spread out before me, fields of dreams and nightmares.

They came to María Sabina, the white men with their quest from enlightenment, they came for the mushrooms, the teonanácatl, the precious children of the gods, the medicine. They came for fun and they came with disrespect that brought the authorities down on the keepers of the medicine, and just like hundreds of years before when the Spanish came, the tourist colonisers brought destruction.

I'm lost in a sea of history. Aztec ruins. A voice breaks through.

"You shut me out," Henry murmurs. Barely audible over the waves, but he can't hold back the hurt behind his words. Ethel has wandered away. Henry and I are alone on the picnic blanket which is vanishing into the sand. "Or is it that you shut everyone out?"

It's true I've closed off like a dam – to protect myself – I need to be whole – how can I be whole... when there's so much more that I could be?

I am water – and all my desires all run off into water – all my desires get lost in this sea of emotion. We are all separate here. Disconnected. So why do I feel like I'm missing out? Because I know it could be more. So much more.

"It's not about you." I can't make it better. Only worse. I run my hands through the silky black sea of sand. We are slowly merging with the beach.

"Why is it..." Henry's voice is tender, aching. "that it can never be about me?"

"Oh Henry." I reach for him and he takes my fingertips, lightly. Our arms rock back and forth. "It's not your story."

"I know. I should know by now. You're not even into guys! You're not into me in that way. I just can't help the way I feel... I just want, more than anything, to be close to you."

"We are close. I love you"

"Closer." Henry says. It pains me to pull away, but I need to escape the nausea.

"You want to merge with me"

"I..." He looks downwards. "Yes"

"You want to surrender yourself..." I'm reading into Henry's emotions. Layers of rich feelings sweeping over just as the waves lap and overlap along the bay, rolling in, rolling through.

"Yes."

"Until you are nothing... with nothing... no more fears. No responsibility."

"I've never thought about it that way."

"But isn't it true?"

"Well..."

"Maybe it isn't really me you want. It's some kind of death wish." He lets go my grasp, stung.

"What the fuck? No. I don't want to die. I want to live... with you."

"You want me to take your pain away. The child in you wants me to be your mother."

"Thanks Dr Freud." He's irritated now, but probably because I'm right.

"I'm sorry. I'll stop," I say.

"Stop what?" Ethel asks, she has emerged from the darkness to our left.

"Where's the moon?" I ask her, childlike.

"Oh darling," she placates, "it will just be behind the clouds. Don't worry."

"There's nothing wrong with being childlike," I reflect out loud, but I'm really trying to talk to Henry, who has turned away. "We are all children still in some way."

"I have been thinking that. In some way..." Ethel's voice trails off. I watch the wind whip our thoughts down the beach before she finds the train of thought again. "It's like we are all the many echoes of ourselves..." she lies back against me, "dissolving into nothing, dissolving into our true selves..." Her head rests on my lap "A collection of memories that belong to former selves," I make agreeing noises, "never quite the same but always connected." I stroke her hair.

I close my eyes and the patterns track along with the sound of

Ethel's voice like the visualisations on a late '90s media player. "My visuals are so... digital looking." I'm not really complaining, but I am surprised. Henry laughs at me, and suddenly he's back, no longer mad at me for pushing him away, at least not for now.

"You thought they'd be more 'organic'."

"They usually are."

"Well, Moana," Henry teases, "what is the universe trying to teach you?"

"Obviously, we are a computer simulation. We are stuck in the Matrix." I'm practicing my sarcasm.

"Obviously."

"Yeah, that must be it."

"What must be it?"

A wave of fragmented feeling and wonder engulfs me. "Everything."

"Of course." She responds, looking around. "Where is Isaac?"

ISAAC

I can hear the others in the distance still. I haven't escaped far enough. Their shrieks of laughter echoes and blends into the sound of waves. The further away I get the further I want to go. I get to the other end of the beach and leverage myself between the giant boulders. Patterns are everywhere. Pesky fractals adorn the sand below, at intervals. The leaves of the forest above are a kaleidoscope of geometric variations.

I find the shelter of some bushes and unzip my fly. There's a thrilling sensation of freedom. I urinate into the dry sand, splashing an unintentional pattern that is brilliant in its symmetry. Oh sweet relief. A warm, wobbly, free feeling wells up as the pressure subsides. It is both startling and invigorating to be alone.

But here is the emptiness again.

All I have is ideas – logic – equations.

But nothing to grasp because there is no belief.

I cannot stomach it.

I cannot entertain the thought of God or afterlife or spiritual transcendence.

I'm not a fool.

But I am, I always have been. I played right along, right into her hands. I stayed behind in class. I waited for the room to clear.

SHE IS SITTING at her desk as the room clears. Looking down, but self-aware.

"What is it, Miss Price?"

"Call me Gina."

AT CATHOLIC SCHOOL they filled our brains with trivial mythology and baseless stories.

They tried to teach morality in a senseless fashion.

There was no questioning, only nauseating choir songs and too much incense.

We were taught to swallow up this bullshit whole like the communion wafers.

Nothing. Nothing.

Gina.

I followed her home.

How could I resist? The older woman, with her dark hair and long skirts. With her power.

Power corrupts, they say.

Just like Catholicism.

A self-serving hierarchical system.

Power structures and robes.

Iconographic stained glass and gilded towers.

It makes me feel ill, or is that the mushrooms?

I was taught to believe in such an illogical farce.

And yet here I am.

At the far end of the beach.

A free-thinking individual.

Something.

Something inside me made me question.

A spark.

Intelligence.

And I have it.

This is what sets me apart.

I won't swallow any of it.

I have no faith.

Faith is weakness.

Moana has it in bucket loads. Henry believes in reincarnation... even Ethel, so reasonable, has a whole hoard of spiritual notions she professes to be open-minded towards.

No.

No.

I can smell it again – the chalk dust of the classroom.

"There's something I want to discuss with you, Isaac."

"What is it?"

"Not here." She looks around.

She hands me a piece of paper.

"Here."

I read the address in messy cursive black ink.

I nod.

"After school. Don't be late."

What else was I supposed to do? Anyone would have gone along with it – it made sense at the time. Gina made me feel... different, special. It was a kind of spell.

No.

Anything immeasurable is merely a figment of the imagination.

At this point only I exist.

The others, the ocean, the sand... could well be figments.

It is a Cartesian epiphany without all that circular rubbish about clear and distinct ideas from God.

Cogito, ergo sum.

The waves breach their boundary and cross over onto my toes.

Normally I would step back, away, but the sensation is not unpleasant.

Suddenly I am very hot.

The sea is cooling.

I step towards it.

The clothes I wear are meaningless.

No barrier.

Irrelevant.

Soaked up to the ankles.

The knees.

It occurs to me that I am conducting a baptism of sorts.

A baptism of truth.

Religious experience.

Pure and unmarred by Catholicism or the new aged spirituality, or anything else at all.

I believe only in myself.

In *Self* I trust.

Here, I find it.

Stepping deeper.

Up to my thighs.

I'm outside the door, a plain oak door, nothing special, nothing sinister.

I knock three times.

She opens the door, wearing a dark blue silk robe, embroidered with flowers, peacocks, stars.

I can smell something burning, floral... incense, like the kind at Mass but different.

"Come in."

This is every boy's fantasy right? A hot teacher. Seduction. I went along with it, so willing. But there's something so wrong. Dread.

She leads me to the couch.

"Sit."

I obey.

She stands in front of me, her robe hanging loose. A gap reveals an inch of skin, a strip of breast, a dark patch between her legs.

I reach up.

"Wait."

I do as I'm told.

I MUST WASH it all away

Faith from hopelessness and desperation.

Faith in self.

A ferocious wave hits me and pulls me under.

My face scrapes against the sandy bottom.

I struggle for what seems like an eternity.

Powerless to these simple forces of nature.

Powerless because she took all my power away.

I have lost it again.

Helpless and pathetic life form.

It was always about power.

No breath.

Nothing.

HENRY

Here it comes.

Moana and Ethel have wandered down the beach together, Isaac is nowhere to be seen, and I'm still by the fire, letting its crackling heat tighten my skin.

Blissfully alone, and free.

The peak is coming; the waves roll in thick and fast. I have to move. But where? I don't feel pulled to go along with the others. No. This is my time. I have to act.

I grab my backpack. Everything I need (I have no idea what's in there anymore).

The taste of Moana's old trauma still lingers sadly in my throat but there is

no time like the present.

I've broken out of the ordinary, out of the familiar, I must make the most of this rare glimpse of the realms beyond my default brain.

Time to fly.

Everything is everything as I make my way up. Up. Up. Up. Climbing the rocky hill to the point above the waves. Climbing through the drudgery of my everyday life, the circles of my thoughts, shucking them off like the shells of wheat. Churning cream into buttery goodness. I must ascend above the fray, above the herd, above the mundane.

Would it feel like this, surreal and refreshing and somewhat wobbly, if I found myself in someone else's brain, or inside the perspective of another creature with a different receptivity to light or colour, a different nervous system?

I reach the top. Magnificent. So much horizon and I am the golden child of humanity, welcoming it home. The colours are surreal, when possibly there should be none. Colour blind people sometimes see colours for the first time on substances like this. I raise my arms in worship of nature. Creation burns through me. I am divine, we all are, we just keep forgetting. I breathe and the world breathes with me. The sea sparkles in the moonlight, sending electric patterns over the water. This is all meant to be. Destiny.

I see my role in this confused world. I am Mercury – the messenger – connector – magician. Nothing else in my life is working out as planned right now, but somehow all this failure is teaching me, leading me to where I need to be in the world. I don't have to be the best. It's such a relief. I just need to make peace with myself and play my role as best I can.

I've never felt so good, and I need this. I need to know it's possible to feel like this... to bring this experience back with me through my memory, to enhance my life because experience is all we ever have. Experience and love. Neither of which always work out the way we plan. I need to go deeper. I reach into my pocket for my stash of spare mushrooms and chew on a couple.

Acrid and leathery but so, so magnificent.

It's a minor tragedy that people on psychedelics have such meaningful experiences that are just dismissed as: "Bro, you were so fucked up."

Let's never do that, I make a pact with myself and my friends inside my head – let's never diminish each other's sense of meaning.

Tell that to Isaac.

Where am I going now? I need to explore the parts of myself that are holding me back. I need to go out of the safe zone. Then it hits me: the forest. The thought has just the right level of fear around it. The forest represents my unconscious mind, I decide. I need to explore.

I get to the edge of the path. If only it weren't so damn dark in there. I rummage in my backpack. I must have a light-making-device of some kind. I'm fumbling against something scratchy. Sequinned waistcoat. This is it: waistcoat time! I shrug it on and keep sifting through the bottom of my bag. Lollipop. Cigarettes. Water bottle (all useful). Phone (not useful). Ah – yes, I knew it. In the front pocket of my bag is a tiny torch that I've carried around at multiple festivals, I click it on, and thank the gods the batteries still work.

"Do you really believe in gods?" Isaac's voice in my head.

"As much as any other distinct possibility" I say aloud. "All we have is experience." The Isaac in my mind shakes his head but I wouldn't expect him to understand. He only accepts things that he already agrees with in principle.

The light of the torch reflects off the sequins. I am a human disco ball. I look around but the others are not close enough to witness my brilliance. Deeper into the forest I go. Every step makes a sound. A beat. The crickets chirp. The waves crash. Music. I find a small clearing and take off my backpack. Flinging the torch around my finger on its little rope I dance to the sounds of the forest and sea, to the beat of my own feet, my heart. I dance like I've never danced before. Immersing myself in the music, in the movement.

So this is my unconscious.

My unconscious is a solitary dance party in the forest. It is letting go, feeling the beat of my own body.

Makes sense.

I don't stop until I'm so hot the sweat starts to trickle from my forehead. I take a long slow drink from my water bottle.

Ah.

So refreshing.

What's next?

I make my way deeper into the forest. A figure looms ahead of me. My heart stops. Some kind of creature. Standing stock still in front of me, its gnarly arms reaching up. Wait. It's... "No, it can't be" I say to myself. "It's the old hammock!"

My uncle built this, it's close to the old path we used to take to the beach, before the flooding caused a slip which has long grown-over. I can't believe hammock is still here. Still sturdy, made of knotted heavy-duty fishing nets.

Of course I get in. This is just too perfect.

I settle in for the most delightful rest of my life.

Resting is really underrated.

When I completely let go of all my troubles, they drift away and I'm free.

Rocking with the trees in the breeze.

Glorious.

The temperature is perfect and the breeze is charming on my sweaty skin.

With my eyes closed I am inside a video game, shooting at the asteroids, shot out into space. Floating. Soaring.

What has my life has become?

A series of events randomly intersecting and the diverging again as quickly as they formed

Patterns emerging changing shifting

Merging with the scenery

Everything in my experience comes and goes

Detached. Beautiful. Frightening

And yet I know that I am safe.

Mysteries are being revealed to me, one by one, pulling back the layers of self.

As a child I saw so much more... that I'm now shut-off from.

The tragedy of growing up.
Self-protection.
My mother never gave me what I needed.
Moana never has.
Everything that is meaningful
And I wonder which still are
Some must be
Which are they?
My relationships?
My ambitions?
Something must have some deeper meaning
Or am I just talking to myself
Alone
Am I just experiencing?
Is it just human to create meaning?
The trees are beautiful
But surely they're always beautiful
Like the psychologists say, a child-like experience, free from the
heavy expectations of the adult brain. It's as if I'm experiencing every-
thing for the first time.
Awash with all the sensations
Taste
What was once a cigarette is now just my mouth
Disgusting.
The sounds
A plane in the distance?
Maybe
It comes
It goes
I just am
This being
This essence
In this life

Looking for deeper meaning
Enjoying
Letting go
Struggling
Letting go
And there's always this expansion and contraction
Spiralling in
Spiralling out
All these patterns are so simple
Yet so complex
I watch the symbolism
Every symbol of humanity flashes before my eyes
Every ethnicity
Too quickly
Every time period
I barely know
It's too quick
To know
Nothing can be grasped.

The hammock takes me on a journey through my life, from birth, though my early years, the loneliness, the isolation, peppered with happy summers here with my aunt and uncle before returning to my mother. She was a solo parent, working full time too busy to spend time with me or my sisters. Not making any friends at school, being teased for being weird, so alone, my golden retriever Jeffrey was my only companion and I cried myself to sleep the night he died. Then there was high school. Meeting Terrence. For the first time I made sense, everything made sense. He was everything, but he never knew. I never got the chance to tell him how I felt. Being part of his group of friends gave me confidence, and then he was gone. There was just me and Isaac for the rest of high school, brought closer by guilt and loss, Bill Hicks and our favourite movies, and endless debating. Uni was different. I went flatting. I made good friends. Elena and Tanya and

Ethel... and then there was Moana. Moana sent me spinning out of orbit, I lost all balance, all perspective. How is it that one person becomes everything? I know it's not healthy.

All the faces of the people in my life flash past me, they have all shaped me into who I have become and I start to wonder who I really am, until I remember that being shaped by the people around me is all part of the human experience.

I see lights in the distance, through the trees. It takes me a moment to realise they must be headlights on one of the winding coastal roads. I'm still here. Still resting in the hammock from my childhood.

This is the perfect time for it. The NOS is in my backpack, along with my cracker and balloons. I have everything I need.

I load the canister, screw it in gently, carefully attach the mouth of the balloon and then release the crisp gas into its temporary rubber bubble home.

The sound of the release is all part of the effect. Chh chhh chhh.

I pluck the cold balloon from the cracker, hold it to my mouth and inhale the sweet, cool, space air.

The sounds reverberate around me. Chh chh ch chh ch chh.

I'm high above, a million aspects of self, all condensed into being, a billion possible Henrys, I'm floating free. Ch chh chh. I continue to breathe in and out, to keep the gas circulating. I shrug off the baggage of the past. I don't have to be anything anyone thought – anything I used to think. This is a new moment. A new self. I reach peak relaxation before I let go.

The balloon fizzles to deflation in my fingertips, along with everything I no longer need. Phew. It's no wonder they give that stuff to birthing mothers. What bliss!

Everything is connected

A lot of these truisms...

Let go

Let go

Just be
Deep meditation
And I ask
From the kaleidoscope lotus prism
What is it that I need in this life, right now?
Right now
What are these energies in the universe?
Binaries?
Fractals?
Why do I need to ask?
Why do I need to ask when I am already whole?
When I truly feel whole then everything else falls away
And it's not just an endless charade
It's coming back together after all the fragments have been separated
And that's the journey of life, isn't it?
The universe experiencing itself subjectively
Bending backwards and staring at the stars
The kaleidoscope moving back and forth
Closer and more distant
And it's so fucking beautiful
And yet from my pinprick of consciousness
I want to be the centre of the universe
I am
And I want what I experience to be the most meaningful
And I want to express my meaning with everyone
And I just want to enjoy
And that is the ego I suppose
Ego is just personality, conscious mind
And there's the id – subconscious
Animal instincts
Getting me into dangerous circumstances
Getting me out of dangerous circumstances

Making life more of a soap opera drama comedy

Then there's the superego who's supposed to be telling me what I should and shouldn't be doing

What's appropriate and what's not

What IS appropriate?

I know what I've been taught

And I know to question

Because that's what I was taught

And what is it that's essentially me?

Just being

Just this energy

Just this essence

And if I can be unimpeded then let me

If I can be free then let me

If I can unlock any old stored up energy then let me

I can dance or not

I can sit or stand

I can enjoy the rhythms of life

I can enrich them

I can exploit them

I can exploit my body

And nourish it

And just learn all the while

And I can love and I can nurture

And I can hold people close

And I can feel the closest

Closest connections

It's time to go now – to the only place here that scares me more than the forest: to the cave.

PART XI

THIS IS WHERE EVERYTHING FALLS APART…

ETHEL

Moana takes my hand and pulls me along the beach. We dance like dervishes, kicking up the dry sand, sinking through the wet sand. We link arms and swing around in a circle. Centrifugal forces slide the beads of water that make up eighty percent of me out to the far edges of my being.

"Ahhhhhh.... Wow"

We collapse onto the sand and lie back looking at the stars, breathless.

"It's so wonderful how open you are when you're tripping," Moana says to me. I know. All my defences have fallen away, and I realise I don't need them, but I also know that they will come back again tomorrow. I will be insular again. Every peak experience makes me feel like I've come so far, but it's only a little step, a glimpse of how freedom feels. There's only so much I can take back with me into my every-day life.

"I'm going to miss you so much when you're in Melbourne." I can't believe my best friend is leaving the country.

"Eth, you are so special. I can't imagine life without you."

I smile, Moana is so nurturing, so caring. Her tone changes. "There's something..."

"What?"

"I went to the hospital, before your mum died."

"I know."

"You do?"

"Well, I figured. You were talking about Gretta and asking me if I wanted to visit her, then you went all funny for a few days." Moana nods. "She's toxic, I knew she would have that effect. Sorry you had to go through it."

Moana is silent for a while, looking down.

"That's not why I was weird for a few days."

"Oh?"

"She told us something."

"Us? Who did you go with?"

"Isaac." There's a little pang of betrayal that he didn't say anything, that two of the closest people to me went and did something like this without asking. Moana looks concerned.

"It's okay." It is okay. Nothing can really affect me in this state. I let it go right through me.

"Look," Moana takes my hand. We sit in the sand. With her free hand she reaches up to my temple. With my eyes closed I can see paisley, hieroglyphics, Arabic script that I cannot decipher. I'm staring into the collective unconsciousness. I feel her emotion, over-whelming love, pain, fear.

MOANA

T he moon
     folding and enfolding.
     Time and space
the secret lurks behind every fold

GRETTA'S BLOODSHOT BLUE EYES.
   She's tearing at her face
   "I need to see her."
   Desperation.
   "She doesn't want to come." We hold back.
   "I need to explain." She chokes on her own saliva.
   "Explain what?"
   "Everything."

I ASKED Ethel about her father when we were kids. "Gone" was all she
ever said. It's her mother I can't escape now...

· · ·

"Why did we even come here?" I ask Isaac as we free ourselves of the hospital, gasping the chilled autumn air.

Information is dangerous. It would have been better if we didn't go, if we didn't know.

"Would you have always wondered if we hadn't?"

I don't know the answer to that question.

"It would have been easier to bury Gretta, like the world already seemed bent on doing. It would have been safer for her to remain the enemy. But the truth will out."

"Whatever Isaac." I'm not in the mood. He doesn't even know Gretta or how awful she is. He doesn't know anything. Doesn't stop him from being the expert. I hate that he's right.

I breathe back to the present. My face is in the dry sand, the cool grains soothe my guilt, lament, my fingers rake waves through the top layer. I have become a human zen garden. Everything is spilling out of me, every last regret.

"I'm sorry," I say to Ethel when the call comes about her mother.

"It wasn't your fault." It is odd that we apologise at times like these. "And anyway, she was already dead to me."

It's a cold stone dropped down a stagnant well. This truth.

"You have to grieve, Eth. It's healthy."

"I've already done my grieving a long time ago." For the mother that she had or the one she didn't have — but deserved? Either way, I hope it's true. Isaac is right. Telling her can only make things worse. We can't take the risk; the truth could break her.

The waves build and build, rushing up my spine. Time folds and enfolds me. I breathe, release. I'm alone, in the moment, looking at the moon. The clouds whirl around her, transforming the light into a shimmering city in the sky, into a forest, a stream runs down over her then folds away like fabric, then chunks into blocks, like Escher's art.

"The moon is in Sagittarius," I recall from the moon calendar in my bathroom at home.

"What does that mean?" Ethel asks. She doesn't follow astrology, but she follows me, she is open minded. I look from Ethel's pale, round, moonlit face up to the sky, up at her, Te Marama.

"Sagittarius is expansion, nature, philosophy, exploring new ideas.... But the moon is only in a sign for a few days."

"It moves around the sun in less than a month," Ethel says.

"Yes." I close my eyes. The patterns become Celtic knot work, paisley, hieroglyphics. Sadness wells up inside me, leaking out of the childhood closet. So much pain and injustice, so much to let go of.

I feel the secret lurking under my skin, biding its time, waiting to get out. Up in the sky, the stars, the planets are twinkling down at us.

"Which one is Saturn?" Ethel asks.

"I can never tell. It's not that bright," I reply. I do know that Saturn is in Scorpio, delving deep, restructuring.

Saturn is time, is structure, the strict schoolteacher, the Devil, the old wise man. Saturn is discipline and hard lessons. It's the force that pries your hands off the bar and forces you to change. If you don't bend, Saturn will break you, but learn the lessons and you will come out super-charged, as Henry would say.

Scorpio is deep, dark, compelling, penetrating. Scorpio is life, death, sex, transformation, and power. It's the most cynical zodiac sign, and it doesn't take kindly to bullshit.

Scorpio brings up secrets.

Eyes closed. Breathe. Flashes of trees, skeleton leaves, skeletons, Ethel's mum's bloodshot eyes. Secrets don't die easily. They leap like wildfire, given the chance. Shifting the burden. I could see the weight lift from her and cling to me, heavy, like the One Ring, dragging me down. Saturn in Scorpio will not tolerate deception.

Intuition is guiding me here – to this point – this perfect point in time and space where she is open, where she is ready to know the truth and to heal.

I have to tell Ethel. If I don't do it now it will always be lurking in the back of my mind, scratching to get out. I reach towards her as waves of the past keep slipping washing over the present.

We walk out through the hospital's sliding doors, leaving behind that disinfectant smell. My head swims. What is the right thing to do? I can't agree with Isaac that there is no right thing, just more or less practical things. He has no empathy.

"Just wait until you leave the country," Isaac insists, as if in leaving the country I will become null and void, no longer relevant in Ethel's life. "You owe her that much." He twists the knife.

"What would you know?"

"She's your best friend."

There is no point even trying to explain things to Isaac. He doesn't have the capacity to understand. Ethel is closer than a sister, and that is why I have to tell her.

"Wouldn't you want to know?"

"Schrödinger's Cat," Isaac says, as though some dumb philosophical thought experiment explains everything. "To Ethel, the cat doesn't even exist, and if we open the box and show her it could go either way. If we don't say anything, it doesn't exist."

"You're not making any sense."

"Look, if Gretta didn't tell us, the information would have died with her. It wouldn't be reality because it wouldn't have been conceived of."

"It would still be real," I know it's pointless to argue but I can't help it, "we just wouldn't know about it."

"It wouldn't be anyone's reality."

"I would want to know."

"You would probably just consult your spirit guide and go on a vision quest." The patronising makes me sick. Any temporary closeness between Isaac and I has vanished.

EYES OPEN. I'm alone, but Isaac's words still echo in my head. I let them go. The only thing that exists is the moon, the waves, my breath. I delve deeper into my pain. It is always here with me, but little by little it unfolds. This is the gateway to the shadow. I plunge in because I know I can only heal through facing my own darkness.

I CAN TELL Ethel is thinking about her mother. Her closed-eye expression is concentrated, fluctuating.

"Do you have any good memories of her?"

"Some," she looks at me, "but they are swamped by all the bad stuff."

A moment passes, the silence is filled by crashing waves.

"She was sweet – sometimes." Ethel has never talked like this about Gretta before. Emotion pools inside me. Sadness. Empathy. She needs to understand why.

"Listen, Eth," A sense of urgency overtakes me and the conversation, "She said something – in the hospital – something scary – and part of me doesn't want to tell you because I want to protect you, but part of me thinks you might need to know – to heal."

"She lied a lot, you know." Ethel's voice is fast, tense, her body has stiffened like a possum caught in headlights, but I'm washed with relief – what if all this worry and suppression is over nothing? Then the moment flashes back: her eyes.

"I don't know..." But I feel like I do know.

"Tell me." Her tone is suddenly pleading.

"She said... your grandfath-"

"No."

It's all Ethel will say, over and over.

"No. No. No."

ETHEL

Moana inhales and my breath is ripped out of me. I know what she's going to say.

"No."

"Ethel?"

"No!" My voice is a petulant child's, someone far away, not my own. I'm not really here. Refusal. Denial.

"You know." Moana's voice is flat. She has me cornered. I can't breathe, or rather, my body is breathing too fast but there's not enough air in the world. No. No. No. Everything is chaos bar the one still voice in the back of my mind. Calm down.

Silence. Silence that extends infinitely towards the horizon, breaking off into shards of moonlight on the muted waves. The one thing I can't bear. Someone else knows. I've lost control.

I feel it start, the *unravelling*.

Moana is still behind me. I can't look at her, but I can feel her tears through the several metres of air and darkness between us.

"I'm sorry..." Moana says.

I hate apologies and she knows it, but what else is there to say? That voice again, competing with my anger and fear.

"It's not true." My denial fools no one, not even me.

"Ethel."

"She's a liar."

"She's dead now."

"Good riddance." With my eyes closed I watch flames burning me up from the inside. Agony. But over or underneath, somewhere in the background there is that calm clear voice as well. This is the right time. No.

"I know how you feel about her." Moana is using her most soothing voice, "I know you hate her, but..."

"What? It makes sense?"

Everything I was doing to hold it back slips from beneath my fingers. The door is flung open. A memory surfaces.

The crisp air, catching the bus, the nursing hospital's floral wallpaper and grey carpet, my anxiety building as I pinch my sixteen-year-old flesh, punishing myself for going at all. Helping Moana through her pain was what brought me here. Saying it over and over: you can't hide from this, you can't run from this.

Every word like a pill slipping slowly down my throat.

Ten years since I had seen her. Since I locked the door and thrown away the key.

You can never really escape childhood.

I jump every time a car door slams unexpectedly, my shoulders tighten at every raised voice, but confronting it might help.

I want to look my mother in the eye and show her I haven't crumbled; she hasn't broken me, despite years of trying. I want to scare her – not with violence, but with my strength. I'm doing well at school, top of the class in English and History, but I don't want her approval. I want to show her I'm better than her.

I know it's a mistake as soon as I get to the door.

My gut screams: run away!

Just as I turn to go a nurse walks past and ushers me in. "She's right here."

My stomach lurches.

She's in the bed, her head twisted to the left, away from the door, her grey-brown hair frizzy and bedraggled. The nurse looks apologetic. "We brush her hair every day, but she always fights and then ten minutes later she's back to this again."

I don't care about her hair and can't think of the right polite thing to say so I don't say anything. The nurse takes the barely-touched breakfast and leaves. Maybe I can get out now, before she sees me.

So this is what did this to you.

"Doesn't it, though?" Moana asks. "Doesn't it explain Gretta and the way she was?"

Looking at my mother, seeing everything spread out like that in its festering messy state, I could almost understand... but before I could feel sympathy the full force of what she was saying hit and the wall came down.

No.

"It's not – it's not something. It's..." words fail, everything is failing. I wish I could push the memory back behind the locked door at the back of the library. "I wish it didn't."

"I didn't know you knew." Moana's voice is sad, but I don't care.

"And you thought you'd tell me? Just drop it into conversation?" I look back at her, but her head is slumped into her hands. "I didn't – I mean... I was doing a good job of not knowing. I wish I didn't know."

"Me too." Moana is breaking into a million pieces. My best friend, my chosen sister, my real family. Betrayal? She would only tell me because she loves me. Because she hates secrets... because... I feel sick.

"Who else knows?"

Moana hesitates. "Just Isaac." Her voice is a whisper.

"Eugh," another blow to the abdomen. I lurch over. I want to vomit but nothing will come out. I want to purge this disgusting rot from my body, but I can't. It's in my DNA.

"We love you."

"How can you say that when I'm like this – this freak – this fucking revolting product of incest? It's disgusting." A wave of nausea comes up again. I struggle to breathe, and burp instead.

"No," she puts her hand on my shoulder. "Who cares - It just is."

I pull away.

More of the last time I ever saw my mother unwinds from its hiding place.

"ETHEL?" Her voice is high and scratchy. She hasn't turned her head. How does she know I'm here? It strikes me that maybe she doesn't know, maybe she's always saying things to no one, maybe she thinks I visit her all the time like a model daughter bearing no grudges.

"What?" My voice is surly, demanding.

She turns and squints at me. "You." Her voice is black, poisonous.

"Yes, me." Anger rises, followed by a wash of self-pity. I can't believe, after all this time, she could still be so evil.

"You should never have been born."

"Well that's hardly my fault, is it, Mum?"

Her posture shifts, deflates, her voice is childlike "No. It's just wrong." I almost pity her.

"What is?" I can't remove the venom from my own voice.

"You never knew. You should. It was him."

"Who? Granddad?" The only 'him' in my childhood, the only positive influence, the only kind person.

"Fuck." Mum spits at the sheets in front of her. "Fuck him."

I can't believe she would defile him like that.

"He didn't do anything wrong. It's you who's deranged. You messed everything up."

She glares at me and her mouth twists up at the corner into a mean smile. "I bet you don't know. I bet you don't."

"Know what?"

"You think he's all charm and grace, your granddad. You don't know anything." She spits again. "You don't know what he did to me. Over and over. Never would have stopped. You're lucky. You would have been next. Lucky. Lucky. Eat his dinner. Pick his mushrooms. Lucky for you."

I can feel my insides churning. No. no. no. The sensation of falling.

"I bet you don't know he's your father."

I DID KNOW.

At some point.

Before it all became too much.

It was festering there under the surface.

Moana sits with me.

She strokes the back of my hand as I fly through all the stuff.

It comes in waves.

Pain.

Tears.

Release.

All that old stuff coming to the surface.

A pus-filled boil that has been waiting to burst for too long.

I'm loosening.

I'm letting go of everything I have held for so many years.

Beautiful and terrible.

Everything is escaping out of my secret room.

I'm deflating.

All the poison is oozing out.

It had to come out eventually.
This was the right time.
I don't know who I am anymore.
I feel lighter
– unbearably light.

MOANA

I try to reach for her, I try to comfort her, but she has slipped away.

"No!" She screams at the sky. She drops like a brick to the ground and lies still in the sand. I wait. "What... the... fuck!" She laughs hysterically – it isn't happy laughter, it's insane. "Fucking bitch!" Ethel kicks the sand, pounds it with her fists. She is crying, sobbing, moaning. What have I done?

"She lied!" Ethel screams in my direction. "Crazy bitch!" I don't know if she means me or her mother.

"You can't believe anything she says." I've never seen Ethel like this, in twenty years of knowing each other, I've never heard her raise her voice... never.

I have been holding my breath until I realise silence has returned. I can only hear the waves. I listen. Waiting. I don't know for how long, but it feels like eternity.

"I knew." Her voice is unnervingly calm. Her demeanour has changed.

"What?"

"She told me when I was young – maybe four. She said, 'don't tell anyone'. She said no one would understand and bad people would come and take me away."

"Ethel..."

"I didn't tell you. I didn't tell anyone. I didn't even think about it. When he died, I cried about losing my father, my grandfather. I didn't really know there was anything wrong with that until I got older and learnt about incest. Oh God, Moana. I'm revolting, a disgusting freak, I shouldn't even exist."

"No." My voice is warm and firm. "You are who you are. You are one of the best people I've ever known." Everything I say sounds stupid.

"It's the worst thing to think about. I didn't want anyone to know."

"Only me and Isaac know."

"Isaac." There is pain in Ethel's tone.

"He didn't want me to tell you. He wanted to protect you. He loves you."

We sit in silence for what feels like eternity but is probably more like ten minutes. I can feel the emotional dust begin to settle. Calm.

Ethel sobs.

"We love you." My voice is as soft and warm as I can possibly make it.

"Even though..."

"Yes." I affirm. "You know I love you. Always. And Isaac does too. More than I give him credit for."

"Eugh, it's just so.. "

"There aren't any words."

"It's unbearable."

"Yes," I acknowledge, because sometimes feeling the bad stuff is the only way through.

"Do you know the story of Hine Ti Tama?" I ask Ethel.

"No." She stares blankly towards the horizon.

"She was... well.. she was the daughter of Hine Ahu One, and Tane Mahuta."

"The god of the forest?"

"Yes, Tane is the god of the forest and the god that separated Ranginui the sky father from Papatūānuku, the earth mother. He climbed through the heavens to retrieve the baskets of knowledge from Io the godhead. He created human beings too. He made Hine Ahu One from the clay, and breathed life into her."

"Why are you telling me all this? Why now?"

"Just bear with me. Hine Ti Tama was their daughter, and she was so stunning that Tane became her lover as well."

"I feel sick," Ethel says.

"So did she, when she found out that her lover was her father, she... well... she went into the underworld and became Hine Nui Te Po – the goddess of death."

"That..." Ethel says. She coughs, splutters then starts again. "That makes sense... It means... I don't know." Ethel throws herself down into the sand again.

"It explains... Gretta." My voice is barely a whisper. "In a way... her awfulness. Her descent into the underworld."

Ethel lets out a low sob.

"I didn't know." Ethel's voice chokes on her own tears. We are both hovering, floating, swimming in a river of her tears, in space, near but far away. "But I knew... at some point, I must have known." Her pitch rises. "I didn't know it was rape."

"You were too young to know." I brush my fingertips over the sand, through the flowering patterns of everything, my strokes ignite new patterns, interconnected with the universe. I hear myself sigh deeply. Ethel does too. I reach towards her again and she takes my hand. We breathe together. The same organism. In this moment.

"I guess... I didn't think about it."

"That's understandable," I say, "We all have shadows in our families, even the gods do. Gretta was carrying your family shadow, and now you are the only one left."

"She was so... awful. I hated her... so much."

"She was horrible, but she was so damaged."

"And he was so... kind."

"Yes."

"The only memories I have of him were good memories... and now..."

"I'm sorry." I am, but isn't it better that this comes out into the open, rather than festering in the dark? It's too early to tell.

"It's too much to process."

"Some things are."

"And the mushrooms."

"What?"

"That is the other thing I figured out." Ethel says, "The first time we were on this beach, we took the mushrooms and I thought about my grandfather dying from a heart attack - from poisonous mushrooms."

"That's right. I forgot that," I wonder how I could have forgotten.

"We always used to gather them," Ethel says, "he took me, he knew the mushrooms." She takes a sharp inhalation of breath. "I remember Gretta cutting them up, the funny smell. She yelled at me – sent me to bed without dinner."

More sobbing follows. Ethel looks as if she is trying to busy herself in the sand. I want to wrap her in my arms, to soothe her, comfort her, but I know better. I wait.

"She poisoned him, Moana." Ethel says, tears stream from her eyes. "It's like a tacky soap opera, I swear." She wipes her face dry and hiccups. "And the saddest part is I don't know if it was a whim that made her send me to bed. If she was planning to poison me or not."

"Maybe she wanted to save you," I say, "but even if she didn't, she was deranged. You can't take it personally."

"Take it personally? How the fuck can this not be personal?"

"Ethel."

"I need some time. Alone."

She pulls away leaving a painful wrenching sensation as she disappears into the shadows.

ISAAC

I have lost everything in this vile ocean.
   The moonlight sparkles patterns of mockery at me.
   Heartless nature.
I wrestle myself to the surface and back to dry land.
The others!
I can't hear them anymore.
They have all gone for a swim.
I can see them in my mind.
Moana has led them into the ocean.
That siren.
She has always wanted to take everything from me.
Like my mother.
She took everything away.
Made everything impossible.
I see her face.
Moana.
My mother.
Swimming before me.
Serene.

Laughing.

I want to take her.

Perverse desire.

Rage.

I want to kill her.

I've never met these awful parts of me before and now they have me hostage. Freezing.

I balance on the rocks and climb higher. I don't need the others. Certainly not Moana, whose chaos and delusion are grating on my nerves more than usual. Henry is not part of the equation. He is irrelevant for now. Every time I look at Ethel I see her weakness, and mine. She is perfect but broken. There is a complex puzzle here that I can't solve. She has always been an enigma and now I am closer than ever to uncovering why. Of course she can't know. She can never know. There has always been the problem of the paradox that lends itself to every kind of absolute thinking. Ethel is a paradox. In observing her we can't help but be drawn into the impossibility. Below that is something awful. I can feel it at the edge of my mind, clawing its way up.

They are all slipping away, more and more, as I climb higher, scrambling into the brush. The bracken scratches at my clothing. The sound of the waves and wind escalates. It's boring into my head. The gorse stings. I yelp, but no one is here to witness my weakness. I crawl under the canopy of manuka and the noise is muffled. Finally, I am in private. I can begin to recognise how wonderful I really am. I'm thinking in physics. Equations dance before my eyes before transforming into Arabic, into Thai. I don't even know these languages and yet everything must be connected. This is it. I'm touching God – but it is not the Christian God, it's the God of science. Not personified, but distributed throughout everything I breathe it in. Harmony. Everything finally makes sense. I am at home in my mind. Satisfaction. The world is rational. Logical. Made up of molecules, atoms, forces, and relativity. When I relax and allow myself to feel this moment in its fullness I am blissful, floating, connected somehow to everything like the mycelia in the earth, like the rays of light from the sun. Life is a series of astonishing chances. Of micro-organisms, or evolution.

Macro-orgasms.

I can feel them blooming all around me.

I laugh at the absurdity of it all. Lying damp in this forest, having the most profound experience of my life. My laughter spirals around me, into symbols and numbers. It goes on and on. I've never laughed this much before. Laughter is an orgasm for the whole body, for the mind. It's spectacular until it hurts my diaphragm. I relax again listening to the crickets who continue laughing all around me. The world is laughing, at me, with me, near me. Peculiar. There is elation to be found. I lie on the dry earth in a kind of revelry. Isn't is miraculous? Miraculous? Surely not.

Something is falling away underneath me, but the earth is still there, stable. I double check. No. The thing that is falling away is inside. The curtain of revelry in science is lifted to expose a gaping dark void, into the gap between what I am and what I want to be.

All this. Everything... is pointless. I roll onto my front and bury my face in the fallen aromatic leaves. No. No. No. I could be a great scientist, a great lawyer. I could write books. I could influence thought. These dreams console me for a moment before they're sucked in along with everything else that has ever been meaningful. My family, friends, Ethel. I am left with nothing. My body trembles. Just a body. Just particles. Nothing. The void closes in on me, sucking me, particle by particle, into emptiness. I groan, but no one will hear me. I could die here, and no one would find me. I could die, a second-rate bank teller on a bad trip. My profession is about to be obsolete and I haven't even worked my way up to being a mortgage broker yet. Mortgage means 'until the death'.

That's when it hits me. I am dying. This is it. A wave of anguish overcomes me. Regret for all the things I never did. A young life, wasted. *Don't be silly.* Ethel's voice in my head. *You'll be fine. Get up. Sort yourself out.* I try to push myself upright. My head strikes a low manuka branch and the ground comes up to hit me – my whole body – hard. I can't breathe. I close my eyes. Breathe. All I can see is neon lights. Colours that etch themselves into shapes. Flowers. Leaves. In kaleidoscope. Skulls. Skulls. Skulls. It's the day of the dead like Moana said. Rotting flesh. Faces. Skulls. A pirate flag complete with cross bones. This is really it. This is death, and I feel so unprepared. It's embarrassing. How inappropriate to be embarrassed. No one is here to see... and even when they do find me, I won't be here to know the difference. The void encroaches again. Pain. But pain is something. I have nothing to lose. I am nothing. Disintegrating. Integrating. My atoms were never really mine to begin with... are leaving me already... all the time. Leaving me and becoming part of other things. This is normal. Everything is normal. *Pull yourself together Isaac.* I'm not dying. I'm just metaphorically falling apart. I hate metaphors for their inaccuracy. Now I am one. Disgust. Choking. Breathe. I am all alone. A young boy again. My father has left for a conference in Sydney. My mother is out. The babysitter is watching television. I am struck by a sudden dread. There has been an accident. Everyone has died. I am empty.

JUST AS I'M DYING.

    Dread engulfs me.

    My heart slowing.

    The tree branch must have caused some kind of deep injury.

    Internal bleeding.

    Swelling on the brain.

    Panic.

    I can tell Moana.

    I have died and nothing happened.

That will show her that her delusional spiritual beliefs are rubbish...

only I won't be able to say anything.

I will be dead,

of course.

What a stupid, pointless, tragic waste of life.

Moana's face.

Back again, from the darkness.

She laughs at me.

Her eyes become gaping holes.

Flesh consumed by maggots.

Rotting into her skull.

I smell the decay.

I am lying in it.

Writhing.

Revulsion.

Retching.

Darkness.

Henry's face appears then becomes a cruel jackal.

It too, rots into the skull of Henry.

Then Ethel.

Her beautiful, delicate skin appears.

"Ethel," I say to her image.

"Everything is dying. Everyone..."

I feel her warmth. Calm. Cooling.

Her eyes shine.

As I look they darken and become blood-shot.

Her face becomes older.

Wrinkles appear.

Cracks in her façade.

Her mother's face.

I see into her skull

Her brain.

The veins.

The universe.

She laughs.

Insane.

We are all insane.

We are all dead.

Maybe we always have been.

Stuck in some Phillip K. Dick dark, repetitive fantasy.

Agony.

Heavy.

Everything aches.

Dark and revolting and ugly.

Remember, you're tripping dude. Henry's voice, inside my head.

Yes.

Mushrooms.

I should never have taken them.

I'm splitting open.

We are all doomed.

Why did we even think for a moment that this was a good idea?

Skulls.

More skulls.

I see God – repenting for his sin of creating this fucking mess

Exploding into dirt and fireworks

The devil

Burning up in his own flames

Darwin

Cross-dressing, growing spider legs, tap dancing

I'm in hell.

What else could it possibly be?

If only I could use this experience to gain some insight into life.

But what's the point?

We are all dying...

Now or in the future.

It's so pointless.
Even with all the great things humanity has accomplished…
We will all die, on this dying planet.
No one will even witness the tragedy.
Nothing will last.

HENRY

Down through the forest.

The plants around me morph into jungle vines, tropical flowers, alive and growing with me. Bright green and pink. Stained glass. They merge into mazes, labyrinths. I pause a moment and close my eyes. I'm high above, coming down to earth, through the trees, separating out before me like kale leaves. Landing on the forest path that I open my eyes to find before me again. Along the path we fly, my trusty waistcoat and I. Brilliant.

The forest opens up to the sky. The sound of gentle running water.

I find a stream and drink from it – so fresh and so clean – I follow it down to a still pool reflecting the moonlight – symbolising my own reflections – projections – the good and the bad.

I look across, over the landscape of my life. The earth mother's body is my body, we contain the story of my life, of our world, the parts that work and don't. I sense them inside, the old wounds. The mycelial medicine works through my nervous system, healing the wounds of my childhood, mother, father, relationships.

Life is such a struggle.

The struggle is part of the process, the medicine responds to me.

I always get the journey I need. Not the journey I want.

I set my trajectory: through the forest, along the beach, to the cave, my shadow.

The tensions I struggle with form the plot of my life.

I accept you, ever shifting tensions.

I'm on my way to explore the darkness inside myself.

I breathe in. I release, to life-force. Flow. Turn to embrace the current, the breeze, gently, warmly and shine, shine, shine, like the fucking brazen sun that I am, golden and hot.

Sirens in the distance.

The cavalry is coming, or was that just waves?

They can arrest me if they want, but I'm just practicing my religion out here – self-awareness through psychedelics – healing through connection – exploring inner space.

I'm accelerating to take-off – launching out of the forest, along the sand. Full steam ahead!

THIS IS JUST this moment

    This is every moment

    Struggling

    Enjoying

    Achieving

    But what am I achieving?

    Right now I'm a god, but in real life I'm just caring for people who are suffering in a broken system without a hope in sight.

    I'm coming in and out of this moment

    Which is being

    And If I can just centre in on this moment

    Really deep

    Really deep

    My ego is expanding and contracting rapidly. It's funny how

psychedelics can do this, expand the ego or make it disappear entirely... but taking that expansion to its ultimate infinite conclusion we become everything, merge with the all, and therefore are nothing. Like mycelium spreading out to cover the entire earth, losing ourselves in the experience, connecting and communicating. I can see it tracing its webby veins over everything – the sky, the trees, the forest, the sand, the sea.

The cave is something you wouldn't notice unless you knew where to look – hidden in the rocks, above the high tide mark. I'm coming in for landing. Engines blasting. Running so fast that everything spills out except myself. There's nothing left but space and sense and the sound of the surf and the sight of the stars as they shoot past me.

An arrow of void through space and time.

My breath is a waterfall

A firefall

A windfall

A landfall

All the elements fall into me: amazing!

A Void

Void

Avoid

And there it is – my demon: I avoid the real problem.

I see the familiar rocks that hide the entrance, and I'm ready to enter into it, to face my darkness.

My thoughts blur in and out of realisation.

The mirror of Erised.

The tension of opposites.

Delusion. Melting and melding. Infatuation. Creativity. Distance.

Triangulation – because what I really want is not what I think I want, and yet I can't seem to see through the delusions... to get to that philosopher's stone – just to find it – not to use it.

Self-knowledge and understanding. Self-awareness. I can see myself untangling tensions... because I want to do that.

I ENTER the cave with trepidation and more than a little glee, shining my trusty torch around. The cave is narrow to begin with and opens up to the size of a single bedroom with a low ceiling. Stooping, I see a familiar figure slumped at the back.

"Isaac?"

"Everything is pointless, Henry."

"Isaac, you do realise you're part of my shadow right now."

"Oh, is that so?"

"It might as well be," I assure him. "What are you doing here?"

"Contemplating the unbearable meaninglessness of life."

"That's clearly what my shadow would say." I tell him.

Isaac is the beautiful one, the chosen one, the golden boy, so handsome, so tall. He is the one I've compared myself to, the one to whom things come easily, and yet, is he happy?

"It's all pointless," he says, and part of me is pleased to see him so miserable.

"But, dude, we are meaning-making animals – we are the great creators of the narratives of our lives."

Isaac lifts his head up, looking rough, his lips in a distinct pout, "but I don't believe in meaning."

I laugh, "there you go, making meaning even in your denial of it – you can't help yourself."

"You drive me mad!" Isaac snaps. He's up and pushing past me, and back out of the cave. I sit down and click off my torch. I am alone in the dark. It is peaceful and familiar and not at all terrifying - as I imagined it would be in here. The darkness is a resting place.

Sometimes you have to go to hell and back and that is part of the journey – not just part of it – the essential struggle of it. Haven't you ever wondered why crap has to happen in every story? Because if we were all just rainbows and sunshine and fun times we'd get bored really quick. No. We're not here for ease. Without tension there would be nothing to hold us together. Without bones we would be jelly. We need this hard grinding reality as much as we need sunshine and joy and oxygen to breathe. Sweet, sweet oxygen. I'm breathing it now.

So, if I know this – that the struggle is needed – then I can rise, just a bit above it, see the forest for the leaves, ascend.

My past life as Sol comes back to me again.

"Now, go forward, to the last day of this life. What are you doing?"

"I am pacing back and forth."

"How are you feeling."

I grimace.

"Pain... I feel pain and fear."

"Why?"

"My wife... It's my fault."

My face contorts, under the emotional weight. I choke back the prick of tears.

"What has happened to your wife?"

"She has been killed... and Jed..." I look down over Uri/Terrence's body. Crumpled in the doorway of the house.

I can't stop the tears now.

"Jed is gone. They left a message. He has been... kidnapped."

"Why has this happened?"

"The neighbouring village wanted me to send a message. Their leader... wanted me to lie about what I saw."

"What did you see."

"The missing girls from our tribe. They stole them."

"And you said you would not lie."

"I ran away. I didn't take the usual path in case they saw me. I took a longer track. They got here first."

"What does the message say."

"That I must return to their village. I must not speak to anyone in our village… or they will kill Jed."

"What do you decide to do?"

"I have no choice. I'm scared. They will kill me. But I have to return or they will kill Jed."

"So you return."

"Yes. I plead with them to kill me, to spare Jed."

"Where are you?"

"In the house of the village leader."

"Who else is there?"

"Some of his thugs. Oh god. These are the people who killed Uri."

The tears start again.

"What do they say?"

"The leader is fair. He will kill me and spare Jed. I ask that Jed had a good home."

"This is fair?"

"A life for a life. He will honour our agreement. This is why I have come."

"They killed your wife. They stole those girls."

"It was my fault. This is a different matter. I wasn't there to protect her, or Jed. I have failed as a father and mate. I shouldn't have been such a coward. I should have faced my fate in this town the first time and not run away. I could have lied. I was afraid. I was selfish."

"What happens now?"

I watch my death… Sol's death… play out, in slow motion behind the leader's house. Their weapons are blunt and not as quick as I had hoped. I lie, bleeding into hard dusty ground. Agony… longing… darkness… light… release. It's over.

. . .

I HAVE BEEN SITTING in the silence of the cave for ever, with just the occasional sound of water droplets, against the soft white noise of the ocean outside.

Terrence. I was in love with Terrence. Why didn't I say anything before it was too late? Why do the only two soul mates I meet not love me back?

Another sound breaks through, footsteps. My heart pounds, who could it be? Should I call out and find out, or keep my location secret?

"No, no, no."

"Ethel?"

"Oh – Henry," Ethel says her voice heavy with emotion in a way that is unfamiliar to me. I flick my torch on, careful to keep it pointed down away from her eyes. I've never seen Ethel teary. She is normally so self-contained, so composed.

"Are you okay?"

"I suppose you know now as well," she says, "everyone knows."

"What?"

"I'm a child of incest," Ethel says.

"What?"

"Oh God, you didn't know!" she clutches her face, "and now I've fucking gone and told you!"

"Ethel?" I say, approaching her cautiously, "come here" I carefully pull her into a hug, making sure she is okay with it.

"Why? Why would you want to hug me when you know what I am?"

"I don't know what you're talking about, and I don't care. You're my friend."

Ethel sobs into my chest.

"It's been horrible. Henry, how does the best night of my life turn into the worst?"

"Is it really the worst?"

"I never wanted anyone to find out how wrong I am."

"What do you mean? What is this about incest?"

"It's... it's just that. Oh fuck. My grandfather was my father."

"Okay."

"Don't you want to get away from me now?"

"No," I say, "I'm just glad you're safe."

Ethel steps away and sits down on a boulder. She rests her head on her knees, cradling herself.

"Some parts were supressed I think, some memories," she says.

I nod.

"I don't understand how you can still want to be my friend when you know what I am."

"You're Ethel, and I love you."

"But how can you?"

"Ethel, listen to me, if it was me saying this stuff to you, how would you react? Or Isaac? Or Moana?"

"Isaac, Moana," Ethel convulses in emotion of some kind or another. "They knew, Henry, they found out about me, they went to see my mother behind my back and they didn't say anything."

"So that explains the heavy silences."

"Henry, they betrayed me."

"Ethel, they both love you, just like I do, for who you are. I'm sure everything they did was with you in mind- caring about you."

"I feel sick," Ethel says, "I have to get out of here."

"Do you want me to come with you?"

"No, leave me alone."

And with that, I am alone again.

So this is my shadow. Darkness and stillness. Seeing sides of my close friends that I've never seen before. Ethel was crying. *Crying.* I normally envy her being so self-contained. She said it was the best and worst night of her life. She talked about herself in an unfamiliar way, as if she were disgusting. Images flash before my eyes of how her pain, her shame, her fears all relate to me too; and the feeling that there was something wrong with me, growing up. The other kids jeering at me, Mother's disdain for my interruptions, all those hours spent alone in the painful tension of boredom.

Isaac was here too, the fallen golden child. Part of me loved seeing him like that. Part of me has always wanted to be him, to come from his family with so much more wealth than mine, to be so tall, so handsome, to not have to give a damn what other people think because I'm clearly at the top of the food chain. I see it now, how I've always resented him for this, and for his own lack of awareness, his flippantness, his arrogance.

All these things are part of me. The golden and the dark, the glorious and the hideous. We are all part of each other, part of humanity just as humanity in all its changing facets makes up the whole of us.

I recall that these caves have a history, sheltering the local people from attack. They are safe harbours.

There is safety in darkness.

In the unseen.

This is where parts of ourselves go, to hide, in the shadow, when they are threatened, disconnected.

"Ethel?"

I hear Moana's voice. Why is she always calling someone else? It's never me she wants. It was always Chelsea, with her golden curls. Beautiful, terrible Chelsea, who is also part of me. I see it now: my erratic self, the me that freaks out. The me that wants to drink the pain of existence away. The me with no control and no regard for others. The jealous me. The vengeful, violent me.

"Ethel, are you in there?"

It's really Moana's voice, and I am so happy to hear it, even if it's never me she wants.

"I'm in here," I call back.

"Henry? Where's Ethel?"

Moana's voice is closer this time, louder. It reverberates off the cave walls. I shine my torch up at the ceiling. It all feels so precarious now. So dangerous. Why am I in here?

"Not here," I call back, careful not to be too loud, not to upset these ancient stones from their resting place.

I move towards the entrance, towards Moana's voice, but somehow she has already disappeared.

PART XII

DESCENDING

ETHEL

I've escaped Henry and the cave. I just can't escape myself. I'm coming down now. Alone. Face in the cold damp sand. Body heavy. I could choke here. I could end. Kissing Lady Death. Cold. Grainy.

I dig my fingers in and scream. Muffled release. Into the depths of the earth. My breath warms the sugar-stone granules. Temporarily. My body is. Hot and cold. Wonderful. Awful. Ecstasy. Agony. My life is over. Over. Over. I am here for an eternity. Everything plays out behind closed eyes. Evolution unfolds. Psychedelic patterned colours.

I am in Sunday school:

"But how did Adam and Eve have all the people in the world?"

The teacher scrunches up her face. "That's for God to know."

And for me to find out. "Does that mean we're all made out of brothers and sisters having babies?"

"Ethel, you ask too many questions. It's important to have faith."

Faith. Faith. Faith.

. . .

Isaac has faith in the empirical world. Moana has faith in spirit. Henry has faith in action. I have faith in libraries, in stolen moments of solitude, in my friends. But right now all that is falling apart.

There's a tornado in the library and it's tearing everything up. Pages are flying. The books on meaning and trust and friendship and identity are all being torn apart. I'm slipping. Over the edge. Dying. Skulls. So many colourful skulls. Moving to the backing track of the sea. The wind. My heartbeat. Is it worse to die or to want to die? This is what dying feels like. Falling down an infinite whole of dark matter consciousness. Old dead memories. Rotting flesh. The soul from my body. Separating self from self.

I hit the ground. All these slabs of concrete come together: I'm not afraid of death. I'm afraid of a life that's worse than ending. My rot. Exposed. So that everyone can see how hideous and worse than worthless I am.

I'm afraid of going back to that dark hallway. I'm afraid of Gretta. Powerlessness. Pleading. Pain. But most of all: I'm afraid of becoming my mother.

I'm lying here as the ages seem to pass around me, over me.

So dramatic, a soft voice says in the back of my mind. *Henry didn't care.*

This is the worst thing that could have happened, so why does a part of my brain feel so free in this release? Henry always says psychedelics are healing. I need to surrender to the process. Maybe this is also the best thing that could have happened to me. A paradox. It's too much to bear. I burrow deeper into the sand.

Henry didn't care. He didn't flinch. He found out for the first time and accepted me, as I am, just like that. But Moana and Isaac, they kept this secret from me, for months. They must have been disgusted. They must have plotted to ditch me, to expose me, to destroy me.

Whatever they did was out of love.

Henry said that too. Am I just projecting my own pain and fear onto them? Probably. Isn't that all we ever do as human beings? Project our experience onto one another?

My grandfather. Another wave of nausea hits. I'm getting sick of this spiral. Grief to acceptance to revulsion, over and over and over again.

I have to do something different. I pick myself up. The breeze feels good against my skin. I wander peacefully along the beach. It feels like gliding. Everything I see is stunningly beautiful in the early morning light, coming slowly towards dawn.

This was the worst thing that could have happened. In a way it was, or maybe it was for the best, maybe there is liberation here, if I can find it through all the waves of trauma. *You get the trip you need,* Henry always says, *not necessarily the trip you want.*

I find my bag, my drink bottle. I guzzle what feels like an ocean of water. It's the best thing I've ever done.

That was so good.

I sit and look out to sea, wrapping the picnic blanket around me, letting the sand cascade in a mess over everything. I need something else. *Chocolate.* I dig in Moana's bag and find the packet. Chocolate is the perfect taste, the perfect texture. *Exactly what I need right now.*

MOANA

I navigate the thick gusting breeze, to the end of the beach. The wind has picked up. I follow the rocky edge of the bay upward, to dry sand, still carrying some warmth from the sun, somehow, that seemed like a lifetime ago. My feet sink in. Deep.

Everything has a time... right? I feel myself sinking. Blackness is seeping in, like ink in water. The precious clarity of the past sparkling hours is obliterated by this shadow. Doubt. Despair.

I kneel into the sand digging my hands in. Looking out at the surreal greyscale landscape all around. The flower patterns have turned unto skulls, overlaid over everything. I can't escape them, even with eyes closed. Everything is rotting. Decaying. Isaac has been missing for hours. In my waking nightmares he is dead. Fallen off a cliff into the ocean. His body smashed against the rocks. Too soon. Henry and Ethel too. I don't know where they are. Everyone I love, even Chelsea, they all could be gone, but then again, death is the only certainty of life. Behind my eyelids I see the water-colour blue-black. I'm swimming through the dark of Hades, the depths of Hine Nui Te Po – the necessity of death for life to exist

I can't be sunshine and sparkles all the time.

Letting go of toxic positivity.

My faith keeps me warm like a white blanket of light. I feel it wrapping around me in dark moments like this. Reassuring me that my nightmares are not real – and that even if they are, I will somehow get through it. It's okay. I need this because life without it is too painful, and my pain won't help anyone.

So selfish of me to tell Ethel – just because it got too heavy to carry that knowledge. What good have I done? I have lost her, lost her trust. It's too late to take it back.

I should feel cold, but I am warm. I burrow into the beach, wriggling my body deeper into a shallow grave. Giving up. Giving in. I curl into a ball. Child's pose. Arms at my sides. Forehead against cool, damp grains of disturbed sand.

Darkness.

I listen.

Silence in my mind.

Only the crashing of waves.

Everything is consciousness and consciousness is everything.

Letting go of everything else.

Letting this agony drain away into the earth.

I need to go through to get to the other side.

Give up all hope in order to find it again.

Die to the past to remain in the present.

Listen.

If I'm quiet enough I can hear it in the distance. In the background. Whisper of grace, like music. A symphony. Leading me on, into the darkness. I have been walking in the dark my whole life. Feeling out the safest path. Scared of every step. Looking out for the others. Distant lights that shine perspective over my journey. The terror rises again and I know I have no choice. I must die this inner death so as not to have to live out my subconscious fears in my outer life.

Stillness.

The calm before the storm.

It's the process of fighting its way out of the cocoon that pumps blood into the butterfly's wings.

Ethel is fighting now. But I have faith in her. She's stronger than anyone I know. She will emerge.

When you love someone you want the best for them. Always. You also want the best for yourself and it's hard to tell, sometimes when things get so tangled up.

It occurs to me that I'm still lying here. Paralysed in my own fear.

Coming down.

In the sand.

Sand is everywhere.

What was I thinking?

I am cocooned here.

Letting go. Healing. Growing into the next stage in my life cycle.

Metamorphosis.

The energy floods back into my fingertips, my toes, arms, legs. I kick and scratch at the eroding ground, fighting my way out of this cocoon.

I don't need to be safe anymore.

I need to breathe and stretch and... fly.

I lift myself up, out of my cocoon.

The remnants cascade around me.

Lighter, but wiser somehow.

I spread my arms wide. The symphony rises into thunderous volume in my ears.

I run, twirl, spin, to this music, soaring with the waves. The wind at my back.

I fly down the beach.

Dancing.

In my own world.

Soaring.

"Moana?"

The music stops, abruptly, at the sound of a word I barely recognise, but so familiar. My own name from a lifetime ago.

"Henry."

HENRY

We are at the far end of the bay, near the karaka tree. I look across, towards the fire. I see nothing in the early morning grayscale light. There may only be a few embers left. There may be nothing left.

Moana has melted into a puddle in the sand beside me.

"I'm learning about love."

She speaks from her trance.

"About how to be love... about how to send love... about how to fill myself up... overflowing with love." She yawns. "In the face of suffering... in the face of all these violent hideous things that make me want to shut down – to protect myself."

Miles away and ever present like the outer planets.

"Tell me about them – the outer planets."

We look up at the sky.

"The thing is..." Moana begins, "mostly they are so far away you can't see them without a telescope."

"I can see everything in the universe right now," I inform her.

"Well, Uranus is unpredictable."

"Hah – yours is!"

"Silly. Do you actually want to know about this?"

"Yes. Sorry. Tell me."

"It symbolises sudden changes" Moana says, her voice low, musical, lilting "challenges – electricity – technology - the unconventional."

"Sounds like a weird guy... I can relate... wait, isn't Mercury the technology God?"

"Uranus is like next-level Mercury. I mean, they didn't even discover Uranus until the dawn of the technological age."

"True – so doesn't that mean astrology was all wrong?" I ask.

Moana pulls away and looks me in the eye.

"No. Astrologers reckon that the outer planets were discovered in synchronicity with developments in human consciousness – a kind or evolution or something. Although, if you chart back before the planets were discovered you see the patterns were there all along – just like when you uncover a new level of self-awareness, and suddenly you can see all the way back through how your patterns manifested in the past that you didn't see before"

"Like Neptune?"

"Yes – Neptune is a difficult one."

"Again?"

"Oh – all the outer planets are challenging in different ways."

"What's wrong with Neptune?" I ask.

"Neptune is mystery – its hidden – it's like a spell, a drug, intoxicating... everything with Neptune is confusing and delusional, it's even hard to explain... well, even the way it was discovered was like that – someone discovered it by telescope and then it seemed to disappear again for decades and then wasn't rediscovered until after Uranus."

"And what does my Neptune sign say about me?" I move closer to her, willing the boundaries between us to disappear.

"It says something about all of our generation – Neptune is slow moving. It can spend about a decade or so in a sign, so Neptune was in Sagittarius in until the Mid-80s then it went into Capricorn."

"But what does that say about our generation?"

"Every sign Neptune goes into – it kind of magnifies and also dissolves the way society thinks about that subject."

"What is the subject of Sagittarius?

"Saggi is the philosopher centaur – it's about big ideas – nature – exploration – travel."

"Our generation is so into nature and travel."

"Exactly – you know, it's like that article you shared a while back – in the last few decades the whole construction of nature has changed – it used to be Man vs Wild – something to be conquered and tamed – now it's something we must protect, value, nurture. Our generation is coming of age and is still influenced by the sign we were born into... it's just like, the way Neptune in Virgo generation – your grand-ma's generation – the granola generation – got all obsessed with 'health food', which at the time was eating lots of low fat pasta."

"So delusional." I sigh.

"Yes," Moana says, "and then Baby Boomers – post-war babies born into Neptune in Libra... Libra is all about peace, love, harmony, and beauty."

"Flower children, eh? Sounds like the 60s more than the 40s."

"Because they came of age when – first of all, Neptune went into Scorpio which is ultra-cynical and relates to power and money and sex... so there was a big stir up challenging the old-fashioned ideas around this stuff in the 60s. Then Neptune went into Sag at the start of the 70s and suddenly there's the rise of the Guru – Eastern spiritu-ality enters the mainstream West."

"I can see it now... so what happened to the babies born in between?" I wonder.

"Neptune in Scorpio? – they became the cynical Gen Xers – they contributed to the rise of metal and goth music like The Cure – all that stuff, critical culture."

"We have a lot to thank them for."

"Yes we do," Moana agrees.

"And *now*?"

"Neptune went into Capricorn..."

"The goat... my mother is a Capricorn," I say.

"The goat climbing the hill, despite its fish tail – ambition, structure, progress, authority... so these kids a bit younger than us are deluded about that kind of thing."

"That – you can be whatever you want – follow your dreams stuff" I guess.

"Exactly – Neptune represents dreams as well."

"So that was the 80s and corporate takeover – that explains all the power dressing and shoulder pads." It's all making sense to me now.

"Hey – I never said it was pretty." Moana laughs.

"Are we still in that stage?"

"No – in the Mid 90s Neptune went into Aquarius -technology – networking – innovation – humanitarianism..."

"Oh – you mean like the rise of the internets?" the internets, our technological mycelia, spreading over the earth, connecting us all.

"See – I told you," Moana says, "– it's weirdly accurate."

"Or we are just good at making meaning out of this kind of thing?" I wonder.

"Well, that too... but it seems too much of a coincidence."

"Does that mean the kids these days are deluded about technology?"

"What do you think?" Moana asks me.

"Tech native babies... hmmm..."

"Well, the babies now were born with Neptune in Pisces."

"What does that mean?"

"Neptune is in Pisces, which is the sign of..."

"The fish"

"Yes, and the subconscious – emotion – dissolving boundaries. It's

Neptune's home sign, and in a way it represents parts of all the other signs combined."

"So it's dissolving itself." We are all dissolving. Right here. Right now.

"Yes, and all the other delusions built up over all the other cycles... the delusions about health from Neptune in Virgo, about peace from Libra... about nature, the economy, technology, all that stuff"

"It does sometimes feel that way – despite the insanity of international politics."

"Well, the fact that the insanity is becoming so clear..."

"Maybe to us, but not to the swing-voters."

"It's not simple."

"No."

"It's complicated."

"Yes."

Moana closes her eyes.

"I'm learning how to open... to universe... to allow... to find unconditional, beautiful love – to pour through me and everything around me – Henry – I was reborn."

"Reborn?"

"Yes, just a few minutes ago."

Her voice is deep. It reverberates and blends in with the sea.

"Moana, I explored my unconscious... I went to the cave. I was visited by the three ghosts of Christmas."

I'm not sure if Moana has heard me at all. "Lately I've been finding myself in these situations... with people who need love more than anything, in environments that need love... and instead of closing and resisting, I'm opening, and I'm allowing myself to be a beacon, to be a channel for that love. I'm expanding beyond this case of human skin and bone. I'm part of everything. The ocean. Stardust."

I remain silent because this isn't really a conversation. It's a narration of the film of Moana's life.

"And it ties into what I've been learning for a long time: acceptance, faith, letting go, allowing, trusting the universe... because I have to do that... I have to let go of my own protections – those that are painful for me anyway but are trying to protect me from pain – in order to allow that love to flow though."

She breathes deeply.

"And I wonder if my relationships... are just another way of learning love, but also of teaching... maybe I have lots and lots of contracts in this life... to give love, to awaken, to share... to learn with these people... who need it."

I wish, more than anything, that I could be one of those people.

"The thing is, Henry, – you and I and Ethel – we are soul mates."

"What?!" My heart is pounding in my chest – getting ready to leap into my throat.

"We are – only, soul mates aren't the sappy Hollywood story that everyone is told. It's not a romance thing."

"It's not?"

"No, silly. It's a learning thing."

"Soul-learning."

"Exactly. We are here, helping each other learn lessons – and sometimes they're really hard lessons to learn. You know? Soul mates teach us the hardest lessons."

The past-life regression drifts back into my mind. It all makes sense. That afternoon at the festival – everything.

For a moment we are little girls in the meadow again. Bliss.

I wonder how many lives it has been now. How much pain and suffering? How many times have I been rejected by the one I love so much? Soul mates teach us the hardest lessons.

I reach out to stroke her shoulder.

"What?" She asks.

"You never told me about Pluto."

"Pluto?"

"Yeah. You told me all about Neptune but not Pluto."

"Ohh... Pluto." Moana sighs, "Pluto takes the longest time to move through the signs. It's the Scorpio planet - power and deep transformation, sex, death, life, money... dark stuff." Moana scoops up a handful of iron sand and lets the black grains run through her fingers. "Pluto was in Scorpio in in the '80s – and Saturn too – there was lots of freaky stuff around sex and power. Hard learning."

I exhale. Everything is coming together... I'm seeing the patterns. Heavy and dense. Fabric of history. It's too much to bear, or is this just the trip?

"What's Pluto doing now?"

"In 2008 it went into Capricorn – you know – the sign that's all about structure and ambition – the sign that most represents the economy..."

"The economic crisis."

"Yep."

"Hah – it's uncanny. I can't believe the planets could be causing all this stuff here on earth though... it seems so unlikely."

"It's not a cause – effect thing, Henry. Its more... synchronicity. You know... these patterns in nature, these cycles..." She gestures at the water painted in moonlight, silver, dancing across the waves.

"Everything is so unlikely."

"Everything."

"And with all this knowledge shouldn't you be able to tell what happens next?"

"It's not a science... you know, these things have elements of chaos."

"Chaos theory – it's too complicated to predict."

"Exactly – you know the most useful thing I find about knowing all this is just understanding myself better and seeing the patterns in the lessons I'm learning in my life."

"Tell me how. Show me."

ISAAC

I stopped believing a long time ago in all that – in God – in the Devil.

I was in denial.

But here it is.

Here it has been, this whole time.

Cold, solid, reality.

"You're so deep in your own subjective ego, you think it's objective reality." Henry's voice says inside my head. I thought I had escaped him.

I escaped the cave, escaped the bank, escaped death, escaped the ocean. I am a maverick. A true genius. I can escape anything.

I find myself back across the beach by the fire as it dies down. No one is here.

Have they left me?

Ethel's bags are still here, she would not leave them.

I warm myself close to the embers, listening out for sounds of life.

Moana says 'reality' is just a word for things I believe in, and isn't that the truth?

I know it.

They are good and light, my friends. They have something I don't have.

A soul.

Maybe I was born without one.

I don't believe in souls, anyway.

I hear something. Moana's voice in the distance.

I must escape her too – her and Gina, and Terrence.

I scramble back up the other side of the hill, back into the forest.

My feet are bare, how long have they been this way, where are my shoes?

Isn't that convenient?

Isn't that just what he would think?

Through the forest.

Through the trees.

The anti-Christ.

The one who walks amongst us bringing only destruction…

Me.

Out towards the sound of crashing waves.

You might think I sound crazy.

Who would believe in this kind of thing?

But I know it – I know it like I know physics.

Now I see that all of it – 'reality' has all been a game.

Made up to fool us into submission – into playing along.

Out towards the cliffs.

There is no truth, no morality. Only power.

The ground beneath my feet crumbles.

Everything will destruct eventually.

Maybe I can fly, or maybe fall.

Either way, I will know.

It's Henry's voice in my head.

Stops me dead in my tracks.

That Bill Hicks reference.

Birds take off from the ground first.

PART XIII

SUNRISE

MOANA

The sky is painted in all the colours of autumn. It's the most beautiful thing I've seen since the stars last night, but I can't appreciate it. I'm dry inside. I search for my water bottle and find it tangled in a pile of our clothes. I scull. The cold liquid runs down my parched throat, euphoric and delicious, but nothing will quench my thirst.

My body is heavy. I am emptied out. My mind automatically reaches upward towards inspiration and connection but grasps thin air. There is nothing left to draw on. I don't know where the others have gone. I don't care, as long as they are safe. I have nothing left to give. I collapse on the blanket. Sand is everywhere. I try to brush it off, but what's the point? I can't escape everywhere.

I realise I have not had a smoke in hours. It makes me want one, so I pull out my tobacco and begin to roll.

I'm leaving in two weeks. I'm leaving everything. I can't even think about it properly, but right now, I'm glad to go. I kneel wide and melt into child's pose. My head sinks into the sand. My thighs are tight. I find centre and feel the pulse of my beating heart. I am alive.

I light the ciggie in my mouth but the smoke scorches my throat.

Poison. Toxic. I cough. I think back to the moth goddess, the journey, María Sabina, colonisation.

"I don't need this crap anymore," I say to no one in particular. "I quit."

Let Go. I lean into the stretch and for a moment nothing else exists.

Breathe. I am here. I press my palms down onto the flat sand and push my hips up into downward dog.

Release. I thought I was empty but the pain begins to pour out, thick and fast. Lava. Syrup. Spicy. Sour. Sweet. Agony.

Trauma has brought me my greatest gift: my spirituality – the perspective I need to navigate through this life, to care for myself, to seek constant renewal.

I moan softly, then more loudly. I don't care if anyone hears me. I need to let go… of my trauma, of Ethel's, of the secret that was so heavy to bear before and has now left everything lighter and painfully bright, as if its return to its rightful owner has righted some kind of cosmic imbalance.

Ethel was cut off, from us, and even from herself, for all those years.

Isolated.

Now, at least she can realise we love her anyway. I dig my toes into the sand and lean in, deeper. We love her. The barriers start to break down. I can feel it, inside myself. The dam is busting. It bursts. What was achingly dry is now flooded with pain and joy and tears. I let them flow down my face, solidifying as they drop into the sand. All of this… all of this is necessary – the pain and the joy. Everything is… everything. I collapse again.

I drink more water and this time the cool liquid is soothing but it's not quite enough. I stand and move towards the end of the cove.

I shed my clothes like old skin. Relieved the others are out of sight because there is less to think about now. There is only me and the ocean.

The icy cold tickle of my toes. Creeps up my legs as I embrace the feeling. Walking into cold water. Let my body adjust to this release, this change. I'm open to emotion... even if it's pain. I won't wallow, I can just step back to lighter ground, and enjoy this life whatever it is now. I embrace this feeling of everything upon everything, like walking into cold water. Let go of my security and just dive in. Enveloped in mercury, this silver-papered sea. Let go of everything, even my friends. I will meet them when I'm through the other side of this emotional flood, then we can be free.

HENRY

Sunrise is flaming all over the horizon and I'm rinsed as fuck.

We just lived through ten years' worth of experience in the last ten hours.

We untangled ourselves and expanded into the stars.

Consciousness is just a concentrated point of awareness in a sentient universe.

Ego comes through it, the 'I' in 'we'.

I close my eyes and see intricate circles, filled with more circles, they zoom out and become more simplified.

We are becoming more simplified versions of ourselves, for better or worse.

We became one with the universe of the life force or the collective unconscious... or whatever.

I know I've been through something big, something deep, heaven and hell.

I want it to mean something, but maybe it doesn't. I want to have broken down the barriers between me and Moana, but maybe all this passion has just burnt me out. My hope is lagging like a new video game on an old PC. There's nothing more I can do. I need to set myself free... I need tools, but all I have in my pocket is a receipt for beer, my cell phone and house keys. I flick the keys around and dislodge the collapsible pen I picked up as a free gift at a hardware store. Maybe this is exactly what I need to break the spell. I stretch the receipt over my cell phone and sit with my back pressed to a boulder. I keep my writing small so I can fit everything in – all the things that killed me, everything I did in vain, burning hot anger – six years of longing, and then it hits me: *I know you're not my mother, but this is a child's emotion – Freud would have a field day if he ever met me.* I'm projecting like crazy.

The hypnotherapist's voice comes back to me again.

"Now, go forward, to the last day of this life. What are you doing?"

"I am pacing back and forth."

"How are you feeling."

I grimace.

"Pain... I feel pain and fear."

"Why?"

"My wife... It's my fault."

My face contorts, under the emotional weight. I choke back the prick of tears.

"What has happened to your wife?" I look down over Uri/Terrence's body. Crumpled in the doorway of the house.

"She has been killed... and Jed..." Moana, my child.

I can't stop the tears now.

"Jed is gone. They left a message. He has been... kidnapped."

"Why has this happened?"

"The neighbouring village wanted me to send a message. Their leader... wanted me to lie about what I saw."

"What did you see."

"The missing girls from our tribe. They stole them."

"And you said you would not lie."

"I ran away. I didn't take the usual path in case they saw me. I took a longer track. They got here first."

"What does the message say?"

"That I must return to their village. I must not speak to anyone in our village... or they will kill Jed."

"What do you decide to do?"

"I have no choice. I'm scared. They will kill me. But I have to return, or they will kill Jed."

"So you return."

"Yes. I plead with them to kill me, to spare Jed."

"Where are you?"

"In the house of the village leader."

"Who else is there?"

"Some of his thugs. Oh god. These are the people who killed Uri."

The tears start again.

"What do they say?"

"The leader is fair. He will kill me and spare Jed. I ask that Jed had a good home."

"This is fair?"

"A life for a life. He will honour our agreement. This is why I have come."

"They killed your wife. They stole those girls."

"It was my fault. This is a different matter. I wasn't there to protect her, or Jed. I have failed as a father and husband. I shouldn't have been such a coward. I should have faced my fate in this town the first time and not run away. I could have lied. I was afraid. I was selfish."

"What happens now?"

I watch my death – Sol's death – play out, in slow motion behind the leader's house. Their weapons are blunt and not as quick as I had hoped. I lie, bleeding into hard dusty ground. Agony... longing... darkness... light... release. It's over.

"It's time to leave this life behind. You are being wrapped in a healing white light, relieving you of all the sadness and suffering Sol experienced."

I can still feel the cold tears, drying tight on my face. I know where I am, in my body, in the hypnotherapy office. But I'm also still somewhere else behind closed eyes.

"I'm going to count from one to three. When I get to three you will arrive at in a safe place in the spirit world.

One

Two

Three

You are in a circle surrounded in golden-white protective light

In front of you is a campfire

Now it is time to call on a guide to help you process the lessons of this life

Can you see your guide?"

"Yes"

I see a glowing figure advancing towards us.

"Is this someone you recognise?"

"Yes!"

It's Ethel! But it's also not – it's her soul… or higher self. She comes closer to me, beautiful, shifting between hundreds of familiar faces. Past incarnations we have shared. She is my guide. My teacher. My friend. We communicate without saying anything. Shared meaning.

"What is your guide's name?

"Eloah"

This just comes to me. Maybe it's Eth's soul name… or something.

"Was Eloah in Sol's life?"

"No. It was a life without her… so I could learn to guide myself. She was watching my progress."

"Okay… now call forth the important people in your life: your wife, your son."

I see their shapes emerging into the circle. Not just them as I knew them in my life as Sol, but as their true selves, young and old, not physical, not confined to bodies, more like expansive orbs of light.

"How do you feel?"

"I feel guilty. I failed them. I was a coward. I was selfish. Even before the thugs came, I was always away. I didn't protect them. They were lonely and scared. I never listened."

"Do you have anything to say to them?"

Anything to say? We don't talk exactly... the feelings just come out. I try to translate an infinitely complicated stream of meaning into the blunt tools of simple English.

"I'm so sorry..."

"How do they respond?"

"They forgive me."

"Now it is time to call in the people who killed you."

"No."

"How do you feel?"

"I'm so angry... hurt. They took everything from me."

"Tell them."

I turn towards their glowing red and white orbs in fury. The rage blasts towards them. They seem to tremble. Satisfying.

"How do they respond?"

"They... are only baby souls. They are sorry. They are learning about power and fear. They haven't developed compassion."

"Okay... now, you and Eloah can reflect on Sol's life.

What are your lessons from this life?"

I have no idea. I hover. Suspended in this place within a place within my mind. Ethel/Eloah is there. I can hear her without hearing her. We communicate telepathically — with feeling and understanding flowing between us like electricity. I feel the lessons... but how can I translate them into words? Nothing... It's so unclear.

"What were you trying to learn about?"

"The lessons were about... facing up... bravery... vulnerability, no judgement, pure acceptance..."

I am disappointed by these lessons. I want something profound. The hypnotherapist guides me back into the present. I am just Henry. A few minutes ago I was also Sol... living another insignificant life full of drudgery. I had gone into this hoping to be someone important, an emperor or a mystic, some kind of prophet. On the one hand, my ego expectations have let me down... but on the other hand, I feel a growing elation – post-emotional release. This was real.

MOANA HAS BEEN BEARING the brunt of all my unmet childhood needs. I have made her into my mother – I have expected everything from her. I have demanded. I have been ignorantly, thuggishly self-centred. This has never been about love – or rather, the love I felt is nothing to do with my needs. The love is eternal. It spans lives and crosses time and space. I close my eyes and see Moana, before Chelsea snatches her away again, the rage returns, just as it did when my sisters got all of our mother's attention. Burning, singeing me. Stop. Breathe.

This was never about Chelsea. This was never ever about Moana. This was always about me.

I relax again and I feel it.

The love is the background of everything. The connection is real. It's the romance narrative that is bullshit. My writing is tiny and messy but I'm coming up against one of those glaringly obvious truths and it's so, so necessary. I need to break out of this pathetic cycle of longing. No one can be my everything – the mother to my inner-child – the panacea for my issues. I need to meet my own needs. I need to figure out how.

Sorry, I scrawl at the end of the note... for being such a child.

ETHEL

The piece of driftwood is full of termites, but I pick it up anyway. It reminds me of me and fits perfectly into my palm. The others are in the distance. I need to be alone. Twenty-four hours ago...

I was brittle.

I was holding steady. I had everything under control.

I brush off the termite eggs and stroke the smooth wood all around. I was an old mansion full of borer, a disintegrating library of rotting books and repulsive secrets. I kept a nice veneer over top of everything, for years. Plastic-wrapped as though to keep the dust and grime off. Everyone thought I held back to protect myself from being sullied by the world. Too precious. Too distant.

I was holding together to keep myself from myself. Nothing to do with anyone else. I couldn't bear going anywhere near the sharp edge of shame, of how disgusting I was on the inside. Wrong. Rotten to the core of my DNA.

I trace the grooves made from burrowing termites. Nature ruining everything and as sick as I am – or felt I was – I'm part of this nature too... this strange twisted decaying world full of darkness and light; beauty and devastation; grace and repulsive evil.

I hold the stick up, with both hands, to the sunrise, and twist. I'm releasing... along with this dust and decay.

Everything I do not need from my life, mind, body.

It is a metaphor or something. Symbolic. Breaking apart to come back together. Fuck. I exhale and laughter erupts from somewhere inside, from a place of transcendence or mania or whatever. I'm double-handedly destroying my family legacy. All the hate and violence, disgust and abuse and care and trauma. All the sickness that resulted in the fuck-up that was my mother's life. Years of psychotherapy condensed into a few long hours. I throw the remaining crumbled driftwood at the rocks and double over from the force of hilarity, insanity, brilliant, sublime chaos.

Moana and Henry, this is how they find me: curled around myself in the sand, laughing and crying with joy. Release. Ecstasy. They wrap themselves around me gently, perfectly. We are all broken. We are all whole. The tears on my cheeks refresh my face in the sea breeze. The old me is gone and I am free.

ISAAC

Someone has turned the light on.

Eugh.

So bright.

I open my eyelids to golden, flaming orange. The sky is on fire.

I'm awake.

My tongue searches around my mouth. Gritty, salty sand.

I spit.

I'm alive.

I get up and brush myself off.

Too fast. The world is spinning. I'm down again.

The buzzing in my ears stops as if by switch.

I'm alive and all this was in my mind.

Of course, it was.

There was no physiological reason for me to die here under the
scrub.

"Isaac."

I hear my name being called in the distance.

So someone else is alive...

or is it seagulls?

... some kind of aural hallucination.
I don't know what to believe anymore.
They've lost me...
or it's the police, come to arrest us.
My legal career is over even before it started.
I never did finish that law degree.
I only regret it now that I can't have it.
I only regret this awful pointless life,
and all the things I've squandered,
now that I've lost everything.
I lie here.
Disintegrating atoms.
Flying like flocks of birds into the surrounding environs.
Wasting away.
Days must have passed since we drove out here.
Since we left sanity.
Weeks.
Decaying.
Rotting.
I feel the maggots already.
"Isaac!"
I dig my hands into the earth.
Then I feel it, at last.
Peace.
My heart is racing.
Slowing.
It will stop soon.
I accept my fate.
The abyss.
"Isaac."
An eternity has passed.
Weeks, months, years.
Stillness.

Just get up – slowly – this time.

I obey Ethel's voice in my head. Pushing myself upright.

I still have hands.

Muscles.

Everything is shifting.

My body is whole.

Why didn't I do this before?

I'm alive.

I'm functioning.

Breathing.

My clothing is even intact.

I prop myself into a sitting position.

Everything is normal. Strangely normal. Everything is fine. A sudden joy. "I'm ALIVE!" What a strange revelation. I pull myself up between the branches and skid down the hill towards the boulders. Faster than light, but, of course, that's ridiculous. My whole experience was ridiculous. Everything is ridiculous! "I'm ALIVE!"

"Well, that was interesting." I say to no one in particular.

Time to re-join the others.

I feel disembodies.

My legs bound across the boulders, the sand.

My body, springing behind, towards the blobby silhouettes at the other end of the beach that must be my friends. Dark shapes warp against duller surroundings. I'm ecstatic.

I make my way back along the sand in long strides.

It's Moana, come across first.

"We found you!" She smiles. Safety. Warmth. She is flowing, connected with everything. Her arms are outstretched. For the first time I actually want to hug her, rather than just performing perfunctory social obligations. I let myself be enveloped.

"ALIVE!" I continue as if there are no other words, and perhaps there aren't.

"Yes – you're alive!" she exclaims. "We found you."

Ethel looks as if she's making snow angels in the sand. She doesn't make eye contact when I try to wave. I want to wrap myself up and take refuge in her, but something holds me back. She giggles, absurdly.

Moana stares out to sea.

Something is different.

"Everything has changed."

"Isaac!" Henry jumps out from behind a tree.

"There you are?!"

"Here I am."

"Where have you been?"

"Having a psychological death experience, as you'd call it."

"Oh shit bro."

"Yes."

"Sounds like it's time for some NOS."

"NOS – oh yes!"

Henry produces the cracker and balloons. I retrieve the canisters. The others gather around for holy communion.

I stretch out a banana yellow balloon and wrap the mouth of it over the small bronze cylinder of metal we call a 'cracker', place a new canister firmly inside, and twist. The sound is like an enormous soft drink bottle opening. Chhhhhhhhhhhhh hhhh hhh.

"That sweet sound of freedom." Henry sighs. Hand on heart.

The balloon has inflated, full of the compressed gas from the canister. I carefully remove it from the cracker, twisting it to keep the gas in, and pass it to Henry, who takes it graciously and holds on patiently. I produce another for Ethel and for Moana and myself. Chhhhh hhh hh Chhh hhh hh Chhh hhhh.

The sound echoes out across the waves.

Now. We are all ready. Holding our full balloons, cold steam drifts easily off them, a silent cue to inhale.

The balloon untwists in my mouth and sweet cold gas rushes in.

Increased concentration, into a single point in time and space.

Freedom. Rushing of the world below in glimmers. Repeating patterns. A fractal of things within things within things. The sound of the waves imitates the sound of the NOS.

Chhhh Chhh Chhh chhh chhh.

Laughter. Blends in. Henry's. Mine. Moana's. Ethel's.

I release my grip and the balloon deflates into my hand.

I've found it – the answer to everything. And in the same moment it's slipping away, and it dawns on me: I don't know who I am.

Who am I? Just the pieces of experiential puzzle I have been subjected to? Just my parents and school and television and the internet and my friends?

I'm a collection of experiences. Each thought I have must surely come from somewhere else. There's nothing original about me. I'm a garbage bag of impressions.

"What's the point of anything?" I ask no one in particular.

"Just to be," says Moana.

"To do awesome stuff," says Henry.

"To answer that question," says Ethel.

"Wow," Henry adds. "That's meta."

"It most certainly is not!" I assure him.

PART XIV

THE WALK BACK UP

MOANA

Coming back together

We pick up the pieces of ourselves, our minds, our lives, scattered on the beach.

My body is dampening my clothes still. Wet hair drips water down my back. It is a strange mix of uncomfortable and delightful.

"*There* you are." Henry bounds towards me. "Oh and you're all delicious and wet. Did you have a nice swim?"

"It was divine."

"It's time to go back up to civilisation."

"Where is Ethel?"

"Voila," Henry gestures to the bounders and I recognise the shapes of Eth and Isaac cuddled up in their grey clothing. Camouflaged. I'm surprised they are sitting together at all. Ethel is doing that insular thing she often does. I can tell from her eyes. Maybe she's just grateful for Isaac's warmth. He is looking rough.

"It's time!" Henry commands. "Hasten!"

We gather our possessions and ourselves, thrown together into bags.

"Everything is a mess."

"it's okay."

"It's life." Life is a sea of possibilities. Catastrophes. Mess and calm.

Looking at the movement to planets helps me feel like there are patterns here. Deeper meaning. Purpose. It might all be rubbish. Like Henry says, we are good at making meaning up. Ultimately, I don't care either way, I just know I need a map in this chaos, and this is the closest thing I've ever found to staring into the face of God.

Packing up. Brushing sand off my things. Looking forward to a shower. Bracing myself against the disintegration of the old, the flood of hope and fear of the new.

I always want to feel better – get better – be better.

I need to accept decline and decay and entropy. Chaos.

Chaos is as necessary as order. As Henry says, psychedelics create temporary chaos in the neural networks of the brain, the potential to disrupt the ordinary, the default pathways, to make new connections, to go beyond our egos and connect with source and spirit and cosmos. This is why they are so useful, so effective in treating addiction, depression, grief, obsessive compulsive thinking, because they free us of our mental prisons, give us a glimpse of the great beyond, but going beyond the comfort of shallow waters is not always easy.

Hard stuff, dark stuff, it's all part of me and this world.

I look out at the patterned landscape of the beach, the ocean, the sky. As a child I could see the patterns over everything. I could see the magic of everything. Why did it stop? Growing up is tragic in this way. We congeal – harden into the default, the normal, we protect ourselves from change. Change is terrifying. And here I am preparing to move countries for some unknown reason. I don't know if anything is pulling me there, I just know I can't stay here.

I bury my head in my hands against a wave of anguish and tears.

It's okay not to feel good, I remind myself.

It's okay not to be okay.

It's fine to not be okay about not being okay.

I can go through the hard times. I can survive a lot. I hope Ethel can forgive me.

I remind myself that we are resilient, not by avoiding all suffering, but through experiencing it, and processing and living on.

Resilience is not about the fight. It is about the part that comes after.

The fight will happen, no matter what you do or don't do, no matter how you resist. This is not my fight anymore. I glance at Eth, still in her introverted world. Not responding to those around her, the way she did when she was upset as a child. *She will be fine.*

I look up at the forest, the hill looming above us. It's going to be a long walk back up. I scull some more water. Water is life. Too much water is death. We are on such a narrow edge in this existence. So unlikely. So challenging. I begin the trek.

Trauma can be inflicted in a matter of moments and in it your whole body screams out against it. It doesn't matter how strong you are. This is life happening to you. It's not your fault. Then there is space. Silence. The emptiness that comes after intensity. The shock that you still exist. That life continues. That is what resilience is for, and how resilience is built. It's in the learning how to pick yourself up when you're in pieces, when everything is broken, and putting yourself back together again. Slowly. Knowing you will never be the same and that those fracture lines will always show. Knowing that it can and will happen again, because now that you have been broken you have a kind of fragility that can be triggered at any moment by the most surprising things, but you also know you've been through it before and survived. You know how this works now. There is a kind of strength that scar tissue has that unharmed skin will never know. It's not pretty but it's beautiful. Like the forest ahead, dense and dark and thriving, as I walk, this strange creature, through worlds in which I will never totally belong.

HENRY

So heavy. The tiredness claws at my muscles, my skin, scratching its way into my pores. "Do we have to walk back up?" I ask the others. "Can you carry me?"

"No." The answer is unanimous.

"Traitors."

"You have legs. You know how to use them," Ethel says.

"They are only ornamental." I insist.

"You do have beautiful legs, Henry," Moana admits.

"Somebody save me from the indignity of being mediocre!" I cry.

All my whining is in vain. I have to face the harsh reality of the hill ahead.

The others are dawdling, still packing up. I have everything on me, my trusty backpack, my fabulous waistcoat – so perfect last night.

"Did I tell you guys I had a dance party in the forest?"

"Don't call them guys," Isaac interjects, "someone is bound to get offended."

"I like the term 'guys'," Ethel says, "I want it to be gender-neutral – you know, it comes from Guy Fawkes, right?"

"I didn't know that," Moana says.

"I like that," I say, "Each of us has the potential to take down the bureaucracy!"

"It's true," says Ethel, "But you were saying, Henry?"

"I had a dance party in the forest, which was my unconscious, with just my torch, my sequins," I gesture to my waistcoat, "and the brilliant music of nature."

"It was your unconscious?" Moana asks.

"Yes, I decided it was," I say, "and then – oh my God! I just remembered – I found my childhood hammock and had the most blissful meditation of my life."

"That sounds wonderful," Moana says, but her eyes are sad and heavy.

"And I decided the cave was my shadow," I continue, sensing that Moana does not want to talk about whatever is bothering her.

"Your shadow?" Ethel asks, "That's right."

"Yes – all three of you visited me in my shadow – you were all just like the ghosts of Christmas past, present, and future; or whatever." My friends all look mildly uncomfortable, remembering the night we have had. "It was epic."

I look at Ethel; her face is pale. My heart goes out to her and the shit she's been through. That's it though – that's what I'm here for: I'm here to care. It makes sense that I do care work for a living. I just wish it paid better and that my mother thought of it as a viable career pathway and not a waste of life.

It hits me.

"I think I've been depressed these past few months," I say, "maybe longer."

"I didn't realise," Moana says.

"I didn't even realise," I say, "I've been so caught up in the drudgery of everyday life." Maybe this trip, and my quest through the forest, to the cave, will help me the way the research shows psychedelics have helped others. Maybe depression isn't a chemical imbalance in the brain so much as it is a loss of meaning, a disconnection.

"We are each on our own hero's journey," I tell my friends.

"What are you on about?" Isaac says.

"Don't you see? We are what we make of it."

"A broken hero's journey," Ethel says, "based on our broken culture."

"That's right," I continue, "our broken myths, our Hollywood stories where everything clearly goes from struggle to victory,"

" – that's not how life works" Moana interjects.

"Exactly!" I say, "– we were all raised with the myth that we are supposed to rise to immense success, win the sports game, destroy the evil empire, be the celebrated chosen one. It's fucked."

"Whatever you say, man." Isaac sounds tired.

"Do we have any more NOS?" I ask him.

"Enough for two more each."

"Can we have one before the walk?"

"It does sound like an excellent idea."

We settle down again into the rocks, awaiting communion. Isaac performs the priestly functions of releasing the crisp gas into balloons and passes them around.

"Ready?"

"Okay"

ETHEL

We inhale. At first there is just the sweet taste of cold gas, the feel of balloon rubber, my mind clears. Bliss. ss. ss. The sounds around become more vivid, blending with the sounds of breathing in and out. I take in more oxygen and release my breath back into the balloon to continue the cycle of the gas, to keep circulating it longer than it takes the body to process it out. Everything is light and easy, floating, soaring. Everything is echoing in on itself.

Everything of everything of everything.

Breathing.

Releasing.

Freedom.

Laughter, and the farting sound of deflating balloons.

"Sweet, sweet salvation." Henry sighs.

"How are you feeling now?" Moana asks him. Her voice makes me wince slightly. There is still healing to do.

"I'm feeling like a million bucks. I'm ready to smash that hill." Henry jumps up and begins the charge. "Upwards... and onwards!"

For me, every step is a milestone. A great leap towards something new and unknown. One foot in front of the other on the loose gravel, on the decaying leaves, over the roots of trees much older than us.

"What was it..." Moana touches my shoulder, "That prompted your amazing laughter."

"I destroyed some termites." I say matter-of-factly.

"Poor termites," Moana sighs.

"Well, there weren't actually any termites." I feel like this conversation is redundant. Suddenly I'm exhausted. Heaviness folds over me.

"It's okay." Moana reassures me, stroking my shoulder. "Actually, I'm surprised you touched anything with anything to do with bugs. You hate creepy crawlies."

"I did... but in the scheme of things it seemed so trivial."

"You know, in some parts of the world termites make amazing mounds – so complex – that human architects are amazed by their design."

"Yeah. I read about that – and no one can explain why creatures with such tiny brains can come up with such intricate patterns."

"That's right. Even the queen of the termites – she has an even tinier brain – so it's a mystery."

"Nature is very mysterious," I agree. The termites that seem disgusting, that seem to bring nothing but destruction and decay, are part of delicate ecosystems, are carving out and creating complex and detailed patterns, are in some kind of harmony.

Moana grabs my hand and we walk together silently, climbing through the dense native forest full of deep dark life. I can hear the rustling of creeping insects, eating into dead wood, carving out their livelihoods. Burrowing like the secrets that have carved me into the shapes and patterns of my life. Breathing through. Intensity. Pain. Acceptance. New life.

ISAAC

The others have walked up ahead of us. I want to hurry up, to take the lead, because that is always my impulse: to win. But Ethel grabs my elbow.

"What?"

"I need to talk to you."

The dread sets in. "Why?"

"You know."

"Know what?"

"Moana told me." I look up ahead at the path through the trees. Moana's legs are disappearing behind fern fronds. *Get back here.* I scream in my head. *Get back and deal with this mess.* No. She will make things worse. I will fix this.

"I don't know what you're talking about."

"Isaac," Ethel's eyes are downcast, shamed or disappointed, or both.

"What did she tell you?" I struggle to keep the malice out of my voice. *That bitch. Ruining everything.*

"She told me what my mother said."

"No." I straighten up. "She misinterpreted. I was there. I heard what she really said. I know."

"Isaac."

"She was deranged. She was babbling about all kinds of things. Moana just got the wrong idea."

"Isaac."

"It's okay. Look, I'm sorry she had to go and tell you. I told her not to. It's not fair on you. Moana's just jealous of us – of us being so close – she's trying to mess everything up." Even I can tell my voice has become petulant. Sulky. I try to shake myself, to restore proper dignity. I keep talking, making excuses, making everything alright.

"Isaac!" I've never heard Ethel yell before. She doesn't raise her voice. Not her.

"What?" I grab hold of her forearms.

"I know."

"What?"

"I must have known, all along, in some way. I just never let myself think about it." Tears are streaming down Ethel's cheeks. It strikes me that I've never seen her cry before, and that was one thing I've always admired about her – her stoicism – now vanished forever. "You don't need to lie to protect me."

"Of course I do – that's what people do for someone they care about. That's what we all do."

"No." She looks down again. "Just please. Be honest with me."

"Okay." I sigh. "Yes. The hospital. Your mother. She said…"

"I know. You don't have to repeat it."

"So what do you want me to say?" My tone rises, bordering on hysterical. What does she want from me?

"Just please." She begs. "Always be honest with me."

I shrug. "Fine. I'll try."

"Tell me now."

"What?"

"How do you feel about me – knowing – knowing the horrible thing that you know."

I shrug again. What is she on about? Then it strikes me that some people might recoil against this knowledge, against Ethel herself – her very DNA.

"It's okay," she says. "I thought so."

"What did you think?"

"I knew it would change things – change the way you see me, the way you think about me – knowing there is something so wrong with me."

"Ethel."

"I can't do anything about it. I can't change things that were always out of my control."

"I know. Ethel?"

"What?"

"It doesn't change the way I feel about you."

"But you lied."

"To protect you."

We stand, silently for a moment, save for her sobs.

"I care about you – more than any other person I've ever known – I didn't want this to break you, to take away the only happy memories from your childhood, I wanted to – "

"To keep me wrapped in cotton wool. You didn't think I could handle it." She accuses.

"I didn't want you to have to handle it in the first place – what good would it do?"

"It's not – it's not your choice." Her voice is quivering. "You don't get to decide this stuff about me. Don't you think I can handle myself, after all I've been through?"

"I – I honestly don't know."

"Well..."

"There's a lot I don't know about you. Moana knows because she was there, but I don't know and maybe I never will. You never talk about anything. I'm always in the dark.

"Wouldn't you rather not know? It's not good stuff, Isaac. It's years and years of abuse. Why would you want to hear about that?"

"I want to know you."

"You want to dissect me because you don't understand me." There it is, the razor in her voice again. Cutting me.

"I want to understand."

"Pulling things apart won't help you understand me, Isaac. You could dissect me into atoms and all you'd have is a pile of dust – none of which was ever alive."

"I don't want to dissect you. Just – just trust me – show me. Explain what it is that goes on inside your head when you go quiet and shut out the world."

Ethel's shoulders sag. I can tell she's given up the fight. Her anger has dissipated.

"Okay." She concedes. "But please stop being an asshole."

PART XV

BACK AT THE BACH

MOANA

My body is too warm again and I yearn for the ocean. We are out of the forest, nearing the top of the hill.

"Almost at the bach," Henry reassures me, catching a glimpse of my tired face.

"Always almost, because we are obsessed with destinations," I respond.

"And sick of the cliché that life is a journey," Henry adds.

"Even though it's true," I continue.

We open the dusty French doors on the back porch of the bach and step into a different kind of reality. I head straight for the bathroom.

I close the bathroom door

I'm sealed inside this white room

Built for letting go

Discretely

In front of me is a mirror

My camera still hangs around my neck from the walk back up.

I take a picture of the mirror that is mostly flash

Blinding

Brilliant
Accurate
It's all just about trying to capture
Isn't it?
The camera
How can you photograph things you can only see with your mind?
When you stare at yourself in the mirror
And your deepest fears expose themselves
You become an Alex Grey artwork
Veins, behind flesh
Blood vessels, tissue, teeth, organs
This skull, with live eyes
Living, beating, breathing
Everything at once
I can see into my brain,
Neurons firing
And beyond?
Space and stars.
And you see yourself
In all your infinite glory and ugliness and all your beauty and majesty
You youth and your age
And every incarnation
Flashes before your eyes
If only you could capture that
If only it wasn't so terrifying to talk to yourself in the mirror
And see a different face talking back
That old face with one eye
This young face
All the different faces in between
All the different strains you could possibly have
Oh me

Humanity
Oh you
The Virgin the Mother the Crone
Everything in between
The Victim cries in the corner of my psyche
The Saboteur in the other corner, sits in the dark, watching
The Predator is always right behind me
A shiver runs down my spine.
All these archetypes
All these parts of me... of everyone
Jung was right, and I can see it for myself
Venus – my voluptuous gorgeous goddess self
Mars – my inner-warrior, in Scorpio
Neptune – my rising planet, dissolving, illusion, this powerful
oceanic spell.
Reflected through my eyes
Mercury is so much like Henry
Saturn looks like Isaac with all his limitations... but also like Ethel
if it was in Virgo
They are all part of me
Oh wow
The Mirror – I see through myself, through my skin to my veins,
my skull. Beautiful and horrific as life and death. Every layer.
I accept this
I love you
Even if I don't know what love is right now
I am you
And it's okay to be you
It's okay
It's okay
It's okay
It's always okay to be you
It's always okay

And you are always loved
My child of the universe
And I close my eyes and see
The watermark of myself
I'm always loved
Mother
Child
And yes it is hard
Love is hard
A struggle
And how can we help you to deal with this struggle when it's so
hard?
And how can you let go when it's all so much?
This skin
This thin burnt membrane with swirling ropes beneath
It's all so much
In this white bathroom
The fan blurs in the background and I am here, myself
With whatever mask I'm wearing at the moment.

"Did you have a profound bathroom experience?" Henry asks.

"Fuck yes." How did he know?

"Life is full of profound bathroom experiences," Henry crows.

"Life is economics." Isaac tries to correct us, but I can tell his heart's not in it.

"It must be nice," I muse, "to belong to an ideology that tells such a simple story about the world."

"Like astrology?" Isaac digs.

"Astrology is complex."

"So is economics."

"Right wing economics isn't." Henry backs me up. "It tries to sound like it's very intricate and specialist, but it's basically a web of convenient lies – modelling systems that ignore complex 'externali-ties' and how damn messy everything is."

"People should just look after themselves," Isaac continues to parrot. Some things never change.

"See, that's exactly the problem. It's a simple story. It's a fiction. We are all interdependent, and not everyone in society can do all the things that other people can do." Henry continues. "The myth of the individual..."

"If Isaac wants to keep telling himself neoliberal fairy tales there's nothing we can do to stop him," Ethel interjects.

"It is a benefit of privilege," I insist.

"Yeah... whatever."

"I'm insulted." Isaac crosses his arms.

"It's about time." I punch him gently in the shoulder. "Maybe there is hope for you yet."

"Hope for what?"

"Empathy? Compassion? Seeing different perspectives?"

"Don't count on it."

"What I've never quite worked out is how much of your stories are just designed to be antagonistic and attention seeking."

"Excuse me?"

"You love arguing. I bet if you were surrounded by Tories you would take a Marxist or Keynesian approach."

"You're onto me," Isaac winks, and for a moment I don't hate him or even find him irritating. He is mostly air – all logic and jousting and dancing around. Henry is fire, fighting the good fight, burning with playful passion. I am water; deep, emotional and spiritual. Ethel is earthy, solid, stable... but what happens when the earth caves in. I reach out for her, but see she is deep in thought. I don't want to interrupt.

ETHEL

rriving back in civilisation is a strange mix of jarring and comforting. Moana has nestled into the window seat.

Henry has opened a packet of salt and vinegar kettle chips. I reach in towards the acidic smell.

"Breakfast chips?" He offers them around.

"They are the most delicious thing I've ever tasted," I decide.

"Oh – but so dry!" says Moana.

Isaac is at the fridge already. He produces a bottle of iced peach tea.

"The perfect combination of refreshing, tannins, and not-too-sweet."

"Speak for yourself." Henry manages to sound offended over everything.

"Not you, darling." Moana teases. "You're always too sweet."

"You know what we really need right now?"

"Sleep?"

"No. Cheese." Henry speaks the truth. We rummage for camembert, pickled red peppers, capers, and grainy crackers.

"Yum!"

"Tell me this wasn't the best idea ever."

"It must be pretty close."

"Cheese is perfect," I state.

"You are perfect, Eth." Henry leans forward and wraps me into an enthusiastic hug. I am warm and loved. Hot tears spring up, releasing more of the poisons and toxins of my past. Cleansing. My fears of being shunned, of being rejected and shamed by those closest to me, are evaporating into the cool morning.

"Thank you." I am connected – this is my chosen family.

Out behind the house is an old magnolia tree not yet in bloom. I walk up to it and wrap my arms around it's fine, silvery trunk. Magnolia tree worship. Belonging. Listening. Breath, releasing sight of old shackled mind. Clearing way for new life to sprout

HENRY

It is a whole different world. The beach. The bach. The psychic doors closing behind us, leaving our old experiences behind. New doors open to fresh possibilities. I crack open a crisp apple cider, cold from the fridge and scan my aunt's record collection. We need something warm, chill, nostalgic, connected. I pull out a Sam Cooke record and set the needle down gently.

"If you ever... change your mind," I croon along, "about leavin' – leavin' me behind." Moana joins in, her rich, deep voice washes over me. She walks over and reaches for my hand.

"Good choice," She cocks her head towards the record player. We are swaying. Slow dancing.

"Bring it all home to me." Our voices rise, dramatically. I swoop into ill-suited air guitar. Moana cracks up laughing. Ethel and Isaac smile at us from the kitchen.

Something has changed. I can tell that much. I don't know what it is, but hey, change is life – life is change, right?

Moana knows I have let her go. I can tell from the lack of tension. She's not holding back anymore. My desire, my desperate need for her is no longer standing in the way of our friendship.

It's better this way. I realised it on the beach, and it flashes again now, sparking memories. Childhood longing. Never being alone with my mother. Always sent off to my room for making too much noise, too much fuss, too much mess. Lonely. Disconnected. I go out to the deck for a smoke and Ethel follows me.

"You okay?" We ask each other, simultaneously.

"Hah." Ethel almost laughs, she smiles through her eyes.

"Snap." I say. Force of habit from childhood. There it is – childhood again.

"Do you think we ever outgrow our childhood habits?" I ask Ethel. She stiffens for a moment, then relaxes again, realising I'm not asking about her.

"I'm sorry." I should know better than to mention childhood when hers was so hard. The ghosts of the past gather around us like shadows, Ethel's mother, Terrence, Chelsea, even though presumably she's still alive somewhere. They are all part of us somehow.

"No – it's okay. I'm just – processing. I'll tell you about it when I've figured it out a bit more – promise."

"Okay." I smile at her.

"But I do want to thank you Henry. Your acceptance... your friendship means a lot to me."

We look across the balcony, out to sea. We are silent for a moment, in the way that only good friends can be.

"your childhood" Ethel says, picking up the strand of my thoughts from earlier " yeah – I get it. Your mother was too busy to spend time with you. Neglect." She knows me well. Too well.

I sigh. "It's just so... Freudian, or something."

"Yeah?"

"This insane, all encompassing, attachment I've had to Moana all these years."

"Mummy issues."

"It sounds so pathetic."

"It's more normal than you'd think." She's trying to reassure me.

"So now it's pathetic and unoriginal."

"I'm afraid so." Ethel doesn't pander to my self-pity.

"So what do I do about it?"

"Well, think about it in terms of human needs maybe – we all have these needs – to be loved and nurtured and accepted. Moana represented that for you, but partly because she was always unattainable… and you kept hoping, that if you were good enough it wouldn't matter – that you could break the spell and be the prince…

"Or princess" I interject.

"Or whatever – that you could live happily ever after."

"It's a broken romance narrative. I get it."

"Exactly."

"So how can I fix it?" I ask Ethel, "Oh wise one, knower of all things."

"Maybe you need to learn to mother yourself – you know – meet your own needs for nurture, so you can feel like a more whole and complete person, so you're not looking for someone else – outside you – to complete you."

"Hmmm." She has a point.

Ethel shivers. "I'm going back in." She says, "oh, and Henry?"

"What?"

"Nice waistcoat."

I smile and she leaves me – just like everyone else. I close my eyes, exhaling the smoke from my cigarette, and picture the child me. About six years old. Lonely. Longing. Yearning for a mother. Maybe I can nurture this little guy myself. I imagine the kind of mother he might want – like my mother, only not like my mother at all. My mother was always so tired, so shut off. This mother is warmer, kinder, gentler. She overflows with love. I will her to go over to the six-year-old me, to wrap her arms around him. To tell him things will be okay. The patterns play against my eyelids.

Sparks.

Flames.

Fireworks.

Something falls into place inside me. Maybe not forever, but for now, I am complete.

ISAAC

They are all asleep. Moana, tucked herself away on the window seat, as if she can't quite bear to be further from nature. Henry, on the couch. He just sat down for a minute. Lay down to rest his eyes, still listening to that infernal racket on the record player. Ethel's tucked up in bed. I was there a moment ago but couldn't sleep.

Too many thoughts.

And that flicker again. Something is not quite right.

I knew it on the beach. When I wandered away from the others.

I knew it with my head in the sand and dirt.

There is something more to this.

I need to get out of here. I need to be free.

I let myself out of the ranch slider and break into a run.

Towards the forest. I see her, all the way down, out of the corner of my eye.

I can't escape her.

GINA STANDING OVER THE BED.

Gina with her hands on my fly, on me, pulling me in.
Gina with her hands on my throat.
Terrence at the door.
No.

DOWN THE PATH.

Through the trees.

Out into the open.

My heart is racing.

I have been through so much tonight.

And for what?

I'm flying across the sand towards the sea.

Like the wind.

The wind can escape everything.

My bare feet break through the small waves, crashing against the bay.

No. Bigger. Deeper.

I scamper across the rocks, the boulders, towards the open ocean.

"Moana means ocean," she once told me, not long after we met.

That girl drives me crazy... and now I see it – there is the resemblance again.

She seems so benign.

So frothy, so bubbly, so little substance.

Dangerous.

The rocks are slippery with green moss and seaweed.

I steady myself.

Arms out.

Balancing.

Carrying myself out.

Closer. Closer.

Here it comes. A wave. Big enough to sweep me in.

I dive.

I'm under.

She can't follow me here.

This is it. This is what I needed. Not the fake death experience of earlier, when I was just a moron lying in the dirt. No.

I splutter. Salt water claws at my throat.

Here comes another wave.

I feel it. The world goes upside down. Something hard smacks against my shoulder. Smashed against the rocks.

That's when it kicks in. The survival instinct I've been looking for all my life.

Adrenalin.

Fighting for my life.

Wrestling the ocean.

Foam. Bubbles. Everywhere.

Rage.

Vengeance.

Moana.

I hate her. More than anything.

Another wave comes, and with it a current, pulling me from underneath. I can't seem to raise my arms. My body is limp. I feel myself, being dragged out to sea. And wasn't this what I wanted all along? My death wish? What was I thinking? What about Ethel?

It's all over.

My eyes open. Stinging salt. The agony of water in my lungs.

For a moment I think I can see her, in the distance, long black hair.

Something is shimmering above the water.

A mermaid. A figure. Not her.

Moana.

She drags me out, against her naked flesh.

What kind of magic is this?

"What the fuck, Isaac?"

I can't talk. Coughing up salt water. Heinous pain.

"What were you thinking? You know it's not safe to swim here."

"You..." I look at her. "You're naked."

"I swim naked." She says. Not a hint of self-consciousness.

"You saved me."

"Of course I bloody did. You idiot." Her anger is infectious.

"You!" *You're just like her*, I think, but no, that's not it. There's something else I didn't have the chance to talk about before. A bone to pick. "You told Ethel!"

"So? She deserved to know the truth, and anyway, she already knew."

"You could have ruined everything." She raises her chin and smiles; I catch a flash again. *Gina.* "Bitch." I can tell the word has stung her. She recoils and I catch my breath. I'm teetering on the edge. Everything is slipping away. I'm losing ground.

"You're crying." Moana sounds confused.

"It's not you – It's her." Everything is spewing out of me. Poison. Pus. Logic. Rationality. Reality. Until there's nothing left. No solid ground. "She won't leave me alone."

"Who?" Moana sounds surprised. Obviously. Obviously. She doesn't know.

"Gina – you – there's something about you that's just like her."

"I don't have any idea what you're talking about, Isaac." Of course she doesn't. I catch my breath. Gazing at my hands.

"Oh God. How do I explain?" I put my head into my hands, how do I even explain it to myself? "Do you remember how we told you about Terrence?"

"Who?"

"Our friend who died."

"Oh, I guess."

"Well, there's more..." and the whole story spills out of my mouth – Gina, the seduction. Terrence confiding in me that he was in love with her. Terrence walking in on us, together, in bed. "It was all my fault." I concede. "You were right about me. There's something deeply wrong with me."

"But you were only a child," she exclaims, through my shame and guilt. "She took advantage of you, Isaac. It's – It was rape." And I can see from her face that there's more going on beneath the surface, a deep well. Empathy. I can't stand it.

"No. You don't get it. I saw it – the pain in his face – and I laughed. I had won. I had triumphed over my friend." I put my hands over my face. "Everyone will hate me when they find out what I'm really like, what I'm capable of."

"What are you talking about?"

"Ethel will leave me."

"I never could see why she was with you in the first place." Moana has said that before, but this time it cuts deep. More tears, out of nowhere. Emotions I didn't remember I had.

"It's true. You're right. I'm worthless." I always thought I was the one who saw through Moana, now I can see it was the other way around.

"No. I mean, I never saw it before, I never saw any depth in you – just this pompous exterior – just this arrogance. I didn't realise you were even... human."

We sit in silence. It doesn't matter that she's naked, just wrapping her hoodie around her shoulders, shivering against the wind. It doesn't matter that I'm fully clothed, drenched, alive.

"You're not that bad." Moana says, finally. "I just wish you'd realise it and stop overcompensating - stop projecting all your petty shit onto everyone else. You know, it's fine to disagree with other people and to have your own opinions, but you don't have to be such an..."

"Asshole?"

Moana breathes deeply. We are finally having the conversation we never had the chance to have before, or maybe it is the same conversation we always have but this time it is striking a chord I haven't felt until now.

The chord cascades into a sudden onslaught of feeling, the dam breaks and before I realise it, I'm crying. Tears are streaming down my cheeks for the first time since childhood. I'm sobbing, beating my fist against the boulders like a child. I've lost all semblance of dignity and I don't care. Moana is right. Gina took advantage of me. There was a power imbalance. It ruined us, Terrence and I. She stole something from us that we may never be able to retrieve. I just wish I knew what it was. I should feel embarrassed at this outburst, this tantrum, but I don't. Moana sits silently by my side, her gaze is firmly down towards her hands until my sobbing subsides.

She looks up at me, and the absurdity of the situation strikes her – strikes us both at the same time. The laugher takes over and possesses us both. Doubled over in the sand. Naked. Convulsions of my diaphragm unearth dirt and disgust in the folds of self revealing an even less bearable truth: I'm not so bad. Moana sighs. Everything changes again. Brightens.